Twice Upon a Time

JENNIFER WAGNER

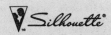

INTIMATE MOMENTS™

Published by Silhouette Books

America's Publisher of Contemporary Romance

For my grandmother, Clare R. McEneany,
who touched many lives and left them better for it.
Our family thrives on your legacy of love,
support and infinite writer's imagination.

We love you, Mema. This one's for you.

 SILHOUETTE BOOKS

ISBN 0-373-27162-X

TWICE UPON A TIME

Copyright © 2001 by Jennifer L. Wagner

This edition published by arrangement with Harlequin Books S.A.

® and TM are trademarks of Harlequin Books S.A., used under license.
Trademarks indicated with ® are registered in the United States Patent
and Trademark Office, the Canadian Trade Marks Office and in other
countries.

Visit Silhouette at www.eHarlequin.com

Printed in U.S.A.

Prologue

" "The Lord is my shepherd..." "

The priest's rich, monotone voice carried to the small crowd through the cacophony of rain pounding against the canvas tent.

An American flag embraced the shiny black coffin. Its red, white and blue colors stood out starkly among the mourners, giving it a clashingly festive look.

" 'I shall not want...' "

Rico lay in that box. That long, cold box.

A tremor shook Anna, an effort to keep from throwing open the casket and dragging his lifeless body away to a warm, safe place. Rico shouldn't be dead.

Not big, strong, invincible Rico.

" 'Even though I walk through the dark valley...' "

Grief began to burn off the numbness in her body, burn off her last desperate hope. Hope of the media's error, hope that Rico hadn't been shot to death in some godforsaken country. A country the government wouldn't name. Not even now.

" 'I fear no evil for you are at my side...' "

"He died for his country." Anna heard his mother, Lina, sob. "At least we can console ourselves with that."

Console ourselves? Anna raged silently. *Console* ourselves with the knowledge that Rico died fighting a silent war no one could win. Fighting a never-ending drug war controlled by power and greed. A war whose "generals" were only replaced by other, more greedy animals. She should feel *comforted* by this?

"'Only goodness and kindness shall follow me...'"

Anna felt a wild scream move through her chest, into her throat. She pressed her lips together, shuddering in an attempt to keep her grief caged. Her chest heaved with her erratic breaths, her body fighting to keep up with the violent emotions clawing her heart.

"'All the days of my life...'"

Her last memory of him flashed in her mind, still painfully vivid after three years. Face taut with anger, golden eyes flaming with rage, his soft voice whipped across her sensitive feelings.

"You love me?" he'd whispered. "How well did you *love* the others, Bella? How well did I teach you?" he'd drawled maliciously.

She never saw him alive again.

"'And I shall dwell in the house of the Lord...'"

Anna's blood raced through her icy veins, the effort to still the quaking, almost snapping bones.

He'd died hating her, never knowing the truth. Maybe she should have tried once more to reach him and convince him of her innocence, convince him there'd been no one but him. But she'd been too full of hurt, too full of righteous virtue and naive pride.

Now it was too late.

"'For years to come.'"

The storm unleashed its full fury, lifting the tent that covered them, sending it tumbling across the cemetery until it snagged itself on one of the hundreds of white tombstones.

The priest tripped over his religious prayers, racing the storm. From the trumpet came the mourning cry of "Taps." Men in uniform folded the flag in brisk, emotionless movements, creating a snug, perfect triangle before handing it to Rico's sobbing mother. Anna stared at the heartbroken woman, thinking of all the things Lina hadn't known until today. All of the things that could have changed her life.

The small crowd dispersed, running through giant mud puddles to their cars, leaving Anna and Lina standing rigidly by the casket. Anna hesitantly laid her hand on the cold, smooth surface. Her strength nearly gone, she barely kept from lying across the top. Water ran in rivers down her face, mingling with the endless tears. She didn't want to leave him here alone, but she couldn't watch them lower him into the ground.

"I'll always love you, Rico Carella," Anna forced out of her tear-clogged throat. "I hope you know that."

Her shaking hand caressed the cold, slick casket one final time.

Finally she wrenched away and turned to Lina. Each step away from Rico became body blows that echoed the emptiness of her soul.

Frigid, sinister eyes watched Anna and the older woman stumble from the casket and climb into a car. An evil slash of teeth revealed victory and a promise.

A promise that it wasn't over.

It had only just begun.

Chapter 1

Anna arched and rolled her neck in an unsuccessful attempt to loosen tight muscles. With a sigh she checked her watch, amazed at how quickly the hours passed.

A tired groan escaped, but she grinned at the mountain of finished boards. High-pitched giggles floated up the stairs to her workroom, making her smile. She silently thanked Lina for the umpteenth time since Rico's funeral almost two years before. Without her diligent care of the kids, her work would never be completed on time. The twins were at an age when naps were rare and play was constant.

Heading downstairs, she stopped at the foyer mirror and gathered her thick, untamable hair into a ponytail. Tilting her head, she studied the pink tinges on her cheekbones and nose, a result of playing at the park the day before. With a wry grimace, she figured she looked like a cheerleader instead of a twenty-seven-year-old mother of two.

"Mom!" yelled a miniature tornado. Rebecca rounded the corner, her acute hearing picking up sounds of Anna.

"Hi, honey. What did you do this afternoon?" Hefting her

daughter on a hip, she made her way to the bright kitchen, listening to Rebecca recounting her day.

Lina stood at the island in the center of the sunny lakefront room. She stopped cutting vegetables to admire her grandson's drawing of the sailboats skating on the sky-blue water.

"Hello, you two," Anna said.

Lina looked up, smiling widely. Anna studied her, noting the map of lines and wrinkles aging her far beyond her fifty-two years.

Coming from Puerto Rico with Rico's father at nineteen, Lina had been pregnant when he'd died months later. She'd then struggled to raise her twin sons while learning a new language and way of life. Anna always remembered her as smiling yet quiet, with a sadness she couldn't completely hide.

Forgiveness had been easy for Anna to give after seeing Lina's complete devastation at the funeral. Inviting her to move to Idaho with her and the children had been an impulse, but one she'd never regretted. Lina's dark eyes, once shadowed with the torment of losing so much, now glowed with peace, contentment and love.

They were a family.

"What is that glorious smell?" she asked with a cheeky grin, sneaking a carrot off the butcher block and popping it in her mouth.

"What does it smell yike?" her son drawled, rolling his hazel eyes at his mother.

Anna's face froze for an instant as her son imitated the father he'd never known. Her daughter wiggled down her leg as a warm hand covered hers on the butcher block.

"Every day he grows more like Rico," Lina murmured. "It's a painful blessing."

Anna nodded. "I know."

Taking a deep breath, she turned to the refrigerator and found the door handle amidst her children's artwork and alphabet magnets. Bantering with them, she poured their drinks into cups, snapped on lids and carried them to the table.

Dinner was a boisterous affair, the children each vying for adult attention. Vivacious, happy children, Anna thanked God every day for them and the joy they brought her. Now, with Lina, another adult shared in the crazy, unpredictable lives of twins. It was enough, but sometimes she felt pangs, wanting to share the twins' escapades with their—

Shaking her head, she banished thoughts of Rico. Deep down she still found it impossible to believe he was dead. The feeling that she'd *know,* she'd *feel* the severing of the bond between them tormented her. She'd gone to his funeral to convince her mind, at least, that he was gone, but her heart refused to listen. Maybe it never would.

No, she reminded herself, she felt the bond because she hadn't seen him for years. Pain twisted sharply through the holes in her heart. At the end he'd died hating her, thinking she'd betrayed him in the worst way possible.

Any connection she felt was only in her mind.

"Mom! Someone's here!" yelled Rebecca. It seemed as if the twins were determined not to learn volume control. Everything was yelled, screamed or screeched.

"Rebecca, lower your voice. I'm right here."

A big sigh blew inky black curls off her child's forehead.

"I said," she drew out slowly, as if her mother was deaf and needed to lip-read. "Someone's here."

Anna glanced at Lina, both successful now at hiding grins to keep from encouraging the twins in their cute, although borderline fresh, behavior. Not even questioning the hearing of her four-and-a-half-year-old, Anna pushed back her chair and walked to the kitchen door. Looking past her driveway to the bed and breakfast across the street, she was taken aback to see a dark-blue Jeep Cherokee pull into the driveway.

"Lina, did Jim and Emily get back from their daughter's?"

Permed salt-and-pepper curls quivered with a negative shake. "No, they won't be home for another month. Why?"

"Someone just pulled into their driveway."

Lina got up to take a look. This prompted the twins to scamper down from their chairs, not wanting to miss a thing.

The four of them stood there, crowded behind the screen door watching as a large man stepped slowly out of the truck. Standing very still, he looked around the front yard before turning in a circle. The sun bounced off his aviator sunglasses, and a shiver trickled down Anna's spine. Even though the shadow of the porch and doorway hid them, she had the eerie feeling his eyes connected with hers.

"That must be Jim's nephew. Emily said he might take care of their house, but she wasn't sure last time I talked with her." Lina frowned. "I think his name is 'Cage.' Or some other silly name."

Cage?

"Mom," her son whispered behind a small hand, obviously able to control his voice volume when it suited him. "He's as big as Off'cer 'Luso."

"Yes, he is." Gosh, we're nosy, she thought with a laugh. She picked this town for its family-type atmosphere, but since nothing different ever happened, a new neighbor became a major event. "Okay, time to finish dinner, guys."

She herded the twins back to the table and settled them. Sitting down and picking up her fork, she listened to them compare the man to one of their cartoon heroes.

"Lina?" The woman still stood by the door, an unnatural stillness surrounding her.

"It's nothing," she replied softly with shadowed eyes. "I thought he looked familiar for a moment."

Anna turned back to her children. Every time Lina saw a tall, dark man, he reminded her of her son. Anna couldn't blame her, she'd felt the twinge herself.

He wandered around his borrowed home, basking in the kind of silence not found in a busy hospital. Three stories, it towered higher than the one across the street. There were eight bedrooms with little rooms attached, four connected by bathrooms. All decorated in soothing colors and comfortable furniture. No two alike. The downstairs was all windows and space, light and sound bouncing off the hardwood floors.

The scent of leather drew him to the den. Enormous hunter-green leather couches cornered one end of the room, flanking the windows yawning from the floor to the tip of the twelve-foot ceiling. He already knew he'd spend most of his time there. Not only for the view of Lake Coeur d'Alene and mountains beyond, but he could also see the entire front and right side of Annabella's house. Toys littered the porch and made the steps an obstacle course.

Toys belonging to the two small children.

He was going to put himself through daily hell just to make sure his family remained safe. Also, he conceded, he was there for himself.

He needed the sight of them the way the earth needed the sun.

Even though he was assured agents had been in place since the staged funeral, he wasn't taking any chances. They'd lied already by not telling him about his children and Anna months ago. And for all their contacts and information, they didn't know the identity of the mysterious hacker who tried to access his sealed files three days ago. It could have been an accident. But when his mother's and then Annabella's names were run through the banks, there was no doubt someone was interested in a dead man.

Picking up a barbell, he vented his frustration with rapid biceps curls, wishing he could storm across the street, reveal his identity and demand answers. But the less they knew, the safer they'd be. Which was why he'd hide behind his new face and keep the truth hidden until he dealt with the danger.

Fragmented thoughts pummeled him. Before he could come up with an answer for one, another question would hammer away. He put down the weight and strode to the window, ignoring the twinges in his legs. Another question, one that had haunted him for weeks, stopped him dead. Had Anna known she was pregnant the night he ended it? Damn it! Why hadn't he just forgiven her five years ago?

Because it had been easier to walk away.

Self-disgust churned through him. Even before his capture and twenty months of surgeries and rehabilitation, he'd not only reevaluated his life, but relived that night over and over. When anger and pain dulled, he easily remembered the fine trembling of her body, the stunned disbelief that darkened her eyes to deep black as he coldly told her it was over.

He could still hear the desperation in her voice as she pleaded and argued with him, telling him of her love, her dreams—their dreams. And he could hear his own voice, ugly with anger as he insulted her.

God, he'd been stupid. Stupid, macho, taking the easiest way out. The list was endless. But he'd been furious and filled with a pain close to the agony he'd felt at his brother Rafe's death. Betrayed by one of the two people he'd had left. Betrayed by the woman he wanted to spend his life with.

Years cushioning the pain, he could see how young they'd been…especially Annabella. Her childhood had been much worse than his, but somehow she'd kept her innocence. She'd believed in fairy tales and heroes and love. And he'd been hers.

That's why her cheating had destroyed him. He'd come to believe he was everything to her and never questioned her loyalty to him and their relationship. Never suspected she'd been seeing other men.

But his mama never lied.

Figuring he had no reason to stay, he jumped at the opportunity to become part of a special recon unit. His commendations while in the infantry proved he had the discipline and intelligence, and to be included among the best was too strong a pull to turn down. He'd used all of the fire and strength that burned in him for the good of his country. He'd never intended to just drift through life like so many of his peers, never changing or experiencing. He wanted to see the world, make a difference, live out his dreams.

Scoffing at his own naive intentions, Rico leaned against the frame of the open sliding glass door. His arms stretched above him, he curved forward, feeling his muscles stretch with newfound strength. If only emotions were as easy to heal as the body.

Because now he lived in a hell of his own making. If he hadn't reenlisted, if he'd forgiven Annabella, he wouldn't have been in that jungle, wouldn't have been captured and wouldn't have made enemies who threatened his own blood.

He'd still be Rico Carella.

Anna's pencil flew over the paper. Spiky hair, big, golden eyes and freckles across a little nose completed the gamin face. Two big dimples framed a tiny grin and a wealth of little-boy mischief. The body quickly followed, not as short and plump as before, but stretching up into a sturdy frame.

Next, the girl. Long, corkscrew curls, enormous dark eyes, same freckle pattern and nose, and a grin different only in its feminine curve. Her children and yet not. They were actually Ronnie and Roxie, the leading characters in her best-selling syndicated cartoon strip, Double Trouble. What started as a monthly strip in a parent's magazine was now featured in daily newspapers across the country.

Double Trouble began with depictions of Ronnie and Roxie in the womb. Two babies holding conversations and discussing the world they could hear, breathe and taste. Most of the cartoons were funny and appealed to women carrying children: the daily ''boxing'' matches to see which of mom's organs could be pushed farther out of the way or to see how many times they could make her go to the bathroom. Others dealt with the serious aspects of pregnancy, such as the twins coughing because the womb filled with secondhand smoke.

All in all it was fast becoming one of the most popular cartoons in the country. Double Trouble gave her a chance to share the magical world of twins and motherhood with millions of people, while supporting her family in comfort. She'd been lucky in many ways.

"Anna!" hollered Lina.

Anna's head snapped up. A note of panic threaded the yell.

Hurtling down the two flights of stairs from her attic office, the first things she saw were blue and red lights discoing off her living room walls. Outside, Pete, aka Off'cer 'Luso, was getting out of his car.

She flew out to the porch as he opened the back door, reached in and lifted out her children one after the other, setting their feet on the ground. Arms held straight out in front of them, but bent with their hands pointing up, they looked like mummies that had run into a wall.

They were in handcuffs. But obviously Pete couldn't find any small enough so they had to hold their forearms up to keep the cuffs at their elbows.

Calming herself, helped by the amused glint in Pete's eyes and the ridiculous sight her kids presented, she managed to walk slowly down the porch steps.

"Ms. Ramsey, we seem to have a problem on our hands," his deep voice boomed, only the women able to detect its underlying humor. "I had to arrest your children. First, because they disobeyed their grandmother and climbed over the backyard fence."

Out of the corner of her eye, Anna could see Lina's horrified expression.

"Second, because they decided to 'get the mail with pictures like the grown-ups do.' Seems they needed more for their 'art,' so they decided to take their neighbors'."

Anna looked down at the hanging heads, then back up to the bundle of junk mail in Pete's hand. "Well, Officer, are you going to take them to the slammer?"

Drooping heads whipped up, eyes about to pop from their heads.

"After all, stealing mail is a federal no-no, right, Officer Joncaluso?"

"Umm, yes, Ms. Ramsey. This means they broke the president's law, not just mine."

Tears welled up and spilled out of four eyes. Anna kept her face serious, though it took effort. "Officer, is there anything we could do to keep them out of jail? After all, this is the first time—" she tipped two small chins "—and definitely the last time they'll break any laws. Do you think I could help them return the mail?"

Pete crossed his massive arms across his chest, and Anna feared for the straining material. "I think that'll be fine with my chief."

Anna stared at her children until Rebecca understood the look.

"We're sorry, Off'cer 'Luso." Her brother gave a small nod, all eyes and trembling lower lip.

Anna opened her mouth to correct the name, but Pete had obviously taken as much as he could before falling on the ground laughing. Bad enough he looked guilty and on the verge of apologizing to them.

"Go sit on the porch while I talk to Officer Joncaluso," she said instead, arching a look at the equally amused Lina, who ushered them onto the porch swing and then disappeared inside.

Anna and Pete turned to face the lane with huge grins on their faces. "I know I should be upset at my juvenile delinquents, but—" She coughed, trying to camouflage the laughter bubbling out of her.

"Anna, it was the damnedest thing. I'm driving up the lane and there they are at the house next door, pulling everything out of the mailbox. Their arms were full and they were dropping the pieces they didn't want on the ground. I guess the bills weren't colorful enough for them." He cleared his throat, fighting his laughter as much as she. "Smart kids. Wish I could throw away the bills."

"I want to know how they got out of the yard without Lina noticing," she said, peering around him to the four-foot wooden fence.

"I asked that, too. Seems they pulled over their slide and helped each other somehow. They're lucky they didn't get hurt. That's the only reason for the handcuffs and thirty-foot car ride. We may think this area's safe, but you never know. I want them to think twice before doing something like that again."

Anna sobered with the thought and the fear of what might have happened had Pete not found them. "They're so quick!"

"And smart, too," he added.

"Well, thanks for teaching them a lesson. I'll make sure they return all the mail," she said, smiling up at the large, gentle man. Although, everyone was large in her eyes since she stood only two inches over five feet.

He smiled back. "They'll remember this." He paused and his smile died. "I hope I wasn't too rough on them. They looked so upset. What if they have nightmares?"

"Oh, no. They'll be fine."

"Listen, why don't you bring them by the station next week? I don't want them thinking police are people to be afraid of," he said. "I'll even treat to lunch."

Startled, Anna searched the face above her. Pete had asked her out before, after finding out she was a widow. She'd started the story when she was pregnant, not only to protect her children from labels, but to fend off advances. Her heart was closed to all other men, and with Rico's death she'd felt like a widow in many ways even though they hadn't married.

"Pete, that's not necessary—"

He cut off her words. "I know it's not, but I'd feel better. As for lunch, I know it's not necessary, but I'd like to."

There was no way she could refuse without hurting his feelings, something she loathed doing to anyone. Especially a man as nice as Pete.

She smiled. "We'd love to have a tour and lunch with you."

He blinked in surprise before grinning. "Great! Why don't you give me a call next week and we'll pick a day?"

She nodded and he handed her the rest of the mail before getting back in his car. With a sigh she watched him go, wishing she was attracted to him. He was a kind, good-looking man, but she felt nothing more than friendship for him. Maybe she wasn't giving him enough of a chance, but the thought of loving and making love with him or anyone else seemed wrong.

"Mom?" called a wobbly little-boy voice.

Anna looked to the house and saw the children huddled together on the swing, their skinny legs swinging and trailing loose shoelaces back and forth. "Let's have a talk, you two."

The three of them cuddled on the large, wooden porch swing. "Are you going to tell me why you stole everyone's mail?"

Her son sniffed. "We only wanted the stuff with colors. We need more for our pictures."

Understanding dawned. Her children were currently using their inherited artistic abilities to paste pieces of junk mail together. Personally she thought their collages were genius material, but she just might be a little prejudiced. "How would you feel if someone took all of your colorful mail?"

Rebecca looked at her gravely. "Sad."

"That's right, you would. Now I know you're both sorry and I think it will help if we bring back everyone's mail and tell them that." She pulled their heads onto her chest. "Okay?"

"Okay," they chorused in soggy voices.

They climbed down and Anna began flipping through the mail, realizing they'd only gotten to three mailboxes before Pete found them. Dana's, the Hendersons' and their new neighbor of two days.

Oh, great. What a way to make an impression, she thought wryly.

"Let's go, guys."

Rico wasn't sure which upset him more…the cop handcuffing and scaring the hell out of his kids or his first look at Annabella. When she smiled, his guts twisted into knots. He had no rights to her, but the thought of her with another man shook something in him, bringing back the endless nights after his mother's admission. Telling himself it was the shock of seeing her, he strode away from the window and up to his room.

"Thank you, Dana. They've promised me this will never happen again."

The twins nodded and Dana Solomon did her best to hide her mirth. "I'm glad to hear that. You know," she said, bending at the waist, her hair sliding in a smooth black waterfall over one shoulder. "I usually throw all the colorful mail away. How about I give you the pieces I don't want and you can make me some pretty pictures?"

Rebecca's mouth formed a small *o*. "Really, Aunt Dana?"

Dana was around the house so much, it seemed silly to have the children call her Miss Solomon.

"Really," she promised, brushing her hand against Rebecca's hair.

"Cool," Rafe whispered, obviously impressed.

Dana followed them back down to the lane, and the twins walked over to their neighbor's driveway.

"Anna, can't you give me some warning before you do that? I could hardly keep a straight face," she chuckled.

"There wasn't time. Besides, by making a big deal about this, I hope to keep from showing up at your door in twelve or so years because they've stolen your car," Anna responded dryly.

Dana gave up and laughed heartily for a few minutes while Anna kept a sharp, albeit amused, eye on her kids.

"I want an autographed copy of the strip you do for this," she said, merriment tearing her cerulean eyes.

"I'll do better. I'll draw you your own."

"Oh, great!" She looked at the last two envelopes. "Are those for the new guy? G. Moran, huh? I saw him yesterday. Talk about a hunk of man!"

"You make him sound like a slab of meat."

Dana sighed impatiently. "You know what I mean!"

"Uh-oh. Dana's got her prowl look on."

"Hey, just because I date," she shot back. "Some of us aren't letting one bad relationship keep us from fishing."

"Fishing? That's when you use a pole, not a net!"

Dana burst out laughing. "Whatever. I can see you're not ready for reality. Let me know when the strip is done, and we'll get together for coffee."

"You bring the cheesecake this time."

With a groan and a pat on her slim hip, Dana gave a thumbs-up and returned to her small, red cottage.

"He's gonna yell," whispered her son.

"He might," Anna answered, although she hoped he didn't. She would have to come back later and do her own yelling at the poor, defenseless man. "But I don't think so."

"He's just so-o-o big," Rebecca said, walking slower and slower up the front walk.

Anna reached Mr. G. Moran's front door, trying to guess his first name. Greg? No. Gary? She pushed the bell. Grant? No, too stuffy.

The door swung open so suddenly the kids took two steps back and bumped into her legs. Her mouth went dry, her knees weak. And it wasn't from fear.

He was *beautiful!* Black, wet hair tumbled around his head and down his neck, resting on his shoulders. Thin, black brows arched over liquid brown eyes. His nose was long and aquiline and she immediately thought Native American blood, especially with the amazing cheekbones. His mouth. Oh, my…his mouth. Thin upper lip and full bottom one with a slight scar slicing through both on the right side. Must have been the women fighting over him, she thought, only half in jest.

Her fingers itched as her mind pictured sketching him in charcoal. Yes, definitely charcoal, she mused. His striking bone structure would look magnificent! Her artistic eye scanned downward, noting the three-inch-long scar running horizontally on his neck, ending at his esophagus. What had happened to him?

His red T-shirt clung to wet patches on his chest and stomach, outlining amazing abdominal muscles. Clay. She would try emulating him in clay. Molding his chest, stomach, hips…

She heard him make a noise.

Or maybe she did.

"Ah, yes, hi. My name's Anna Ramsey and these are my children." She was furious at herself for ogling him. She could only hope he didn't notice and assume she was a frustrated widow.

"They, uhhh, borrowed your mail." With her other neighbors Anna told it like it was, but she found herself reluctant to tell this unsmiling stranger. Plus, she couldn't string two words together, much less tell a story intelligently. Her composure was shot.

"I see," he replied slowly, his voice gravelly yet smooth. James Earl Jones with a slight unidentifiable accent. A ball of heat unfurled in her stomach.

Holy Hannah, what was happening to her? She'd analyzed her single status not thirty minutes ago when talking to Pete, and now she was reacting like a teenager on hormonal overload.

And the familiar negative reaction wasn't there.

"Here it is, only these two letters." She wanted to grab the kids and run to her house, put distance between herself and this disturbing man. "Kids, don't you have something you wanted to say?"

Both stared up at the man, then glanced at each other, communicating in the silent way of twins.

Rebecca, of course, spoke for them. "We're sorry!" she yelled, her head tipping all the way back. "We...didn't mean...to make...you sad," she continued, even louder this time.

"Rebecca, don't yell," Anna admonished, heat filling her face. The situation grew more embarrassing by the moment. Rebecca's yell shook windows.

"Mom," she threw over her shoulder in a normal level. "If I don't yell, then how's he gonna hear me up there?"

Anna quickly looked at Mr. G. Moran's face. A quirk lifted the right corner of his mouth and softened the chiseled planes of his face. He bent down at the knees, resting one on the ground as he reached her eye level.

"This better?"

He sounded as if he had a sore throat, but Anna found herself soothed rather than flinching in compassion.

"My name's Gage. What's yours?" he asked, putting out a hand to Rebecca.

"Rebecca," she replied, placing her small hand in his.

Anna saw his apprehension and looked over Rebecca's shoulder to see what caused it. Biting back the gasp surging to her lips, she couldn't hide her shudder.

Pink scars crisscrossed his hand, ending at knuckles and fingers that had been broken, in several places if she was correct. She felt his pain so clearly, along with the desire to lay her hand across his and take it away somehow.

Then Rebecca bent her head and she placed a smacking kiss on the back of his hand, where the scars were mostly thin, white lines.

"There, all better," she said in a sweet, singsong soprano. "You just need a Snoopy sticker now."

Anna watched him as closely as he watched Rebecca. Poised, she was ready to jump in if he so much as looked at her daughter wrong and bruised her generous spirit.

Instead, she felt her throat tighten at the surprise followed by tenderness in his velvet eyes. He cleared his throat loudly. Anna realized his reaction was genuine and wondered if he'd had any experience at all with little people. He stared at Rebecca with incredible wonder, almost as if he'd never seen a child before.

"A Snoopy sticker?" he asked.

Anna leaned forward, over her son's head. "A Band-Aid."

His lips quirked again. "You're right, Rebecca. I think a Snoopy sticker will help."

Rico's chest tightened as his daughter beamed at him. Two huge dimples appeared in her chubby, pink cheeks. He stared at them for a second, recognizing another problem he hadn't foreseen.

His child had his dimples. He hadn't smiled in a long time and definitely not in a mirror, so had no idea if his were still there.

He turned his attention to the young boy standing so still in front of Annabella. His breath caught at his first true look at his son. He hid it by changing position, switching to his left knee.

Sticking out his mangled hand, he hoped his son would have the same reaction to his scars as his daughter. *Son. Daughter.* He kept savoring the words, their echoes whispering through him.

Childish expression hesitant, the boy extended his hand, and Rico was touching his son. Breathing slow and deep, he squeezed gently and examined the face before him. The child had his golden-hazel eyes, but with the same young/old wisdom he remembered in sixteen-year-old Annabella's.

"Hi. I'm Gage."

"I yike your voice," his son told him with a small smile.

Rico's eyes narrowed, a splinter of memory flashing through him. "Thanks. I like yours, too. What's your name?"

His son's head cocked to one side as if still hearing Rico's words. He smiled fully this time and, as he answered, Rico remembered where he'd seen that smile before.

"I'm Rafe."

Annabella had named his son after Rafael, Rico's own dead twin.

Chapter 2

Alarmed by the pain in Gage's eyes, Anna spoke in a rush. "Well, Mr. Moran, I'm sorry we bothered you. I don't want you to think these things happen all the time. Usually you won't even know we're here." She could see a scar running down the left side of his hairline. From the looks of it and the one on his throat and those on his hands, his accident must have been horrific. His legs could also be hurt, she realized. His look of agony must be from his awkward kneeling. Her heart warmed. How nice of him, to suffer for her children just to make them more comfortable.

"Gage." Wincing as he pushed himself up, he repeated, "Call me Gage."

"And call me Anna," she said. A shadow passed swiftly over his eyes. The poor man was in a lot of pain. She took his hand quickly in her own, wanting to take her currently obedient children and leave this man in peace.

Heat. Her first impression as his hand swallowed hers. The man gave off tremendous heat.

They looked at each other, the moment stretching, shimmering between them.

Rico soaked up her familiar features. The triangular-shaped face and big, black-lashed eyes gave her the fragile appearance of a doe. Her full, pink lips were made for his.

Her hair was shorter now, its waves reaching just past her shoulders instead of to her waist. He'd always loved her hair, its colors endlessly fascinating. He'd seen a picture of a New England autumn and immediately thought of Annabella's hair, the vivid autumn colors the only comparison he could find to explain it. From brown to red to gold, each color described her. The brown her serious side, the gold her sunny outlook on life and the red, well, the red could only be seen when the light reached in. The red was her passion. Her passion for life, children, animals, anything in need of protecting, and at one time, for him.

He never counted on this, never counted on one touch, one look, rekindling the desire they'd shared so long ago.

Annabella yanked her hand from his, doe eyes blinking with desire and panic. The desire he understood, the panic, he did not.

"We're going to be late for dinner if we don't get home." Reaching down and taking a hand in each of hers, she led the children away. "It was nice meeting you," she said over a shoulder, halfway to her house.

He stood there and watched his family leave, part of him feeling disappointed she hadn't recognized him. Even knowing it was virtually impossible for her to find any resemblance, especially with his eyes hidden by dark-brown lenses, and knowing it was imperative that she not suspect his existence, still…

He found himself in a big chair on the porch, watching the sun slide gently down into its mountain bed. Beyond Annabella's house, Lake Coeur d'Alene looked dark and cold without the sunlight dancing over it.

He knew exactly how it felt.

* * *

"Anna, I don't know if I'll ever forgive myself," Lina choked out, loading the dishwater in a frenzy of movements.

"Lina," Anna said, putting down the leftovers and wrapping her arms around her friend and second mother. "Please stop blaming yourself! You take wonderful care of the twins, and I couldn't raise them without you. It could've happened just as easily if I'd been with them."

Lina swiped tears from her eyes and glanced to the den where the children sat building a castle out of blocks. "When I think of what could have happened—"

"Don't torture yourself! Nothing happened to them. They're safe, and I don't think they'll try climbing over the fence again."

Lina kissed her cheek. "I love you, Anna." She paused. "I've made so many mistakes with my life, and to endanger my grandchildren just to answer the phone—"

"First of all," Anna interrupted, "I've already decided to keep my bedroom cordless with me when I'm in the office, and I'm going to get another one for the kitchen." She smiled. "I can't believe I hadn't thought of it before now, especially with all the time we spend outdoors."

Some of the tension eased from the older woman's face, but Anna knew something still bothered her.

"What is it? What's wrong?"

Bustling around the kitchen, Lina avoided her gaze. "I keep thinking about Rico."

Anna felt her face freeze and forced herself to relax the muscles. "What about him?"

"Oh, I know you say you understand and forgive me for lying to him, for breaking the two of you up, but I'll never, never forgive myself," her voice cracking. "If I hadn't lied to him, maybe he would have come home instead of reenlisting and joining that group of trained killers. I only meant for him to think you'd been going out on a few innocent dates. I wanted him to see how young you both were, not that you'd—'' She gestured with one hand, clearly too embarrassed to say ''slept around'' as Rico had assumed.

''If I had only sent your letter or known about your pregnancy, maybe he'd be here right now, loving and taking care of you and his children!''

Anna sighed and rubbed her temples, not wanting to discuss the past again, but knowing Lina's troubled heart needed easing. ''More ifs and maybes, Lina. *He* chose not to believe me, *he* made the choice to join the platoon. You did what you thought was right for your son. I understand you wanted to protect him and get him out of poverty. I'm not saying you were right,'' she said quickly, ''but your motives were.''

Anna pulled out a wooden chair for Lina and sank into the one across from it. ''If you hadn't lied to Rico, then he could still be dead,'' she said intensely. ''He could have followed the same path Rafael did years ago and died just the same.'' She saw her flinch and explained, ''Rico wanted to succeed in life, Lina. And, yes, he was willing to work for it, unlike Rafael, who wanted it the easy way. But poverty and violence work on people's minds in funny ways.'' She stared into the flower centerpiece, seeing her past clearly. ''You either grow stronger or weaker from it. Rico grew stronger, joining the army to get out and learn the skills he'd need to support himself and the family he wanted. But Rafael grew weaker, dealing drugs because of the immediate and high profits. What he hadn't counted on were the risks Rico constantly warned him of.''

Anna shrugged, wrung out from the day and from rehashing the past. ''Maybe Rico would have chosen the same path, although I doubt it. Maybe he would have gotten caught in gang gunfire or hit by a car or fallen in the shower.'' She took Lina's hands in her own. ''All maybes. We'll never know. But you have to learn from it and let it go.''

Tears rolled down Lina's cheeks. ''I don't deserve you,'' she whispered, pressing a finger against Anna's lips to stop the denial.

The women smiled, one young and insightful, the other older and uncertain, both bound by loss.

Anna squeezed her hand. "Why don't I give the twins their bath and settle them down, then you and I can watch a movie?"

"*Bueno.* I'll make popcorn."

"Yum," she said with a wicked grin, then called her kids. "Rebecca, Rafe, put your toys away. It's bath time."

A mad scramble of sounds floated from the den, and two little dynamos ran into the kitchen. Anna took them upstairs and, while they played in the bubbles, she talked to them about how badly they'd scared their grandma. When they padded down to say good-night to Lina, she heard them apologize and give loud kisses.

Finally they trudged up to their room, and she read them a story as they settled into their beds. When it was finished, she bent and kissed each of them, tucking their light summer blankets over them.

"Mom," Rafe said, "Yuv you."

"I love you, too, munchkin," she replied, stressing the *l*.

Rafe smiled impishly. "L-l-l-love you." When he concentrated, he caught most of the *l*s, but still slipped sometimes.

When she shut the light off, hundreds of glowing green stars and moons came to life, blanketing the walls. She'd arranged clusters of the stars in constellations, even created the twins' birth sign, Pisces. Two big fish swam in a large circle, representing the pulls and pushes of life.

After the movie Anna tried to sleep. Even though she was exhausted, thoughts of Rico crowded her mind, refusing to give her rest. Eventually she climbed out of her four-poster bed, grabbed a shoe box out of the back of her closet and sat in her window seat overlooking the lake. Lifting the lid, she was assailed by memories. The scent of her first present from Rico, a bottle of perfume she'd wanted but couldn't afford, wafted into her room. She'd put it in the box, unable to wear it and wrap herself in the past every day but unable to throw it away.

Carefully leafing through the pile of letters, cards and other mementos, she didn't read them, just looked at Rico's familiar handwriting. And underneath them all were the pictures.

One was taken at a small boardwalk booth and showed four small shots of them crammed in, smiling, laughing and kissing. An ache filled her heart as she traced his beloved features in the next photo, a shot of just his face: laughing golden eyes, surrounded by thick, dark lashes; his Spanish/Italian heritage evident in his dark skin tone, strong nose and thick, black eyebrows. His black hair was buzzed, its length no more than an inch, and his smile revealed a chipped front tooth from a street brawl. But it was the gentleness in it that Anna hugged to her heart. The big dimples he'd handed down to his children were there, giving his face a boyish appearance.

He'd worked out constantly, at first to protect himself and Rafael and later, her. His presence alone would cause many troublemakers to back down, his six-foot, four-inch linebacker build enough to convince others not to start a fight.

She chuckled at the next picture of them standing side by side, her petite frame making them look like Mutt and Jeff. He always made her feel so secure in his arms, safe from her alcoholic mother, safe from the poverty and crime-ridden streets where they lived. She'd loved him from the first time she saw him, ten years ago at the tender age of sixteen when she and her mother had moved in next door. He was twenty-two, tough and gruff, not wanting a young girl following him around. But they'd been drawn to each other and had become unlikely friends. She the young girl, he large and mean, softening only with his mother, brother and her.

The last picture was the day he joined the army, a week after her eighteenth birthday. He'd buried his brother two weeks before and told her that joining was an opportunity for him to get college money and see the world. She remembered trying to be nonchalant and grown-up, but failing miserably and crying. All she could think of was that someone else she loved was leaving her. He'd hugged her and she finally blurted out her feelings. He'd grabbed her, roughly tender, and kissed her breathless. For the four years he was enlisted, they exchanged letters and phone calls and were inseparable during his rare weekend visits and his two-week leaves.

Sadness clogged her throat, and she leaned her head against the window, staring unseeingly into the dark night. She'd been so happy then, working while finishing up at the community college on scholarship, studying her art and planning for the time she'd become Rico's wife. On his last visit home before being discharged, she'd waited for him by her living room window, her mom already passed out upstairs. Rico had taken his mom to dinner, and she anxiously waited to see him again, wanting to touch him, feel his body against hers. They'd made love for the first time two months before, on his last visit home. They'd wanted to wait to be married, his mother's Catholic influence and their environment persuading them not to risk pregnancy. But the passion and urgency had been too hard to fight, and the risk seemed small. After all, if the protection didn't work, they'd be getting married, anyway, as soon as they could get the license.

A harsh laugh escaped her. How stupid she'd been! How in love. She threw the box onto the floor and sat up, resting her head onto her raised knee. The position made it easy for her to see Rico's picture lying on the floor where it had fallen. Oh, Rico, why? Why couldn't you have just believed in me? Again hearing Lina's words, ''I never meant for him to think it was more than a few innocent dates.'' She wondered which had hurt more—that he hadn't trusted her or that he believed her capable of something so horrible. He knew her! He knew how important honesty was to her.

Anna remembered his tight face when he'd gotten out of the car, Lina glancing her way as she disappeared inside. The fight that followed was explosive.

''My mother told me, Annabella! She told me about the

other guys!'' He paced her small TV room in four heavy strides.

''Rico, it's—''

''I never thought you'd cheat on me, Bella. Never. Dammit, I trusted you!''

''Rico, listen to me! I love you!'' Her heart breaking, she tried to reach the cold stranger whose fists repeatedly clenched, arms lifting jerkily then falling as if unsure whether or not to hit the wall. ''I don't even talk to other guys. How could you think this?''

''Are you calling my mom a liar?''

Her mind raced with confusion at the thought of his mother, whom she loved as her own, telling him such lies. ''I don't know. I just know the truth. I have never, ever cheated on you. You've got to believe me!''

He stood rigidly, his back to her. He can't even look at me, she thought, pain lancing through her. ''Rico, I love you,'' she stressed, sincerity ringing in her words.

''You love me? How well did you love the others, Bella? How well did I teach you?'' he drawled silkily. His endearment of her name became something dirty, and he sounded exactly like the young boys who used Rico's absence to yell explicit suggestions at her.

Anna shook her head fiercely to dislodge the past. She fled downstairs and outside, gulping in cool, clean air. Gripping the wooden porch rail, she fought to put the memories back behind the locked door of her mind where they belonged. She rarely allowed herself to remember, knowing it wouldn't erase the bitterness from her heart, wouldn't help her raise her kids if she was an emotional wreck.

Under control again, she fell into a porch chair, staring at the moonlit lake and listening to the crickets' nighttime symphony. Tilting her head back, she studied the sky, its stars royally displayed on a cobalt backdrop.

Was Gage looking at the stars? As quickly as the thought popped into her head, she denied wanting to know the answer.

She admitted after silent seconds that he was the reason she'd put herself through the walk down memory lane. His effect on her bothered her in ways she didn't want to examine, his touch alone calling up an immediate heated response, a reaction she didn't realize her body could still have.

Her best bet was to avoid him. After all, her response could have been an extension of her scare with the twins. Yes, that was it. Her emotions were already charged, and she reacted like any artist would to such a beautiful sight.

Relieved, she walked back inside, shutting and locking the sliding glass door. But it was a long time before she fell asleep.

Dawn exploded the next morning, staining the dark sky in streaks as red as blood. Rico leaned his forearms against the porch railing, carefully cradling a mug of steaming coffee in his towel-protected hands as he enjoyed the cool, woodsy air. Absolute tranquillity sank into him, soothing a mind that had survived another endless night of broken sleep. Although the nightmares visited him less and less frequently, his shrink had warned him it could take years before they stopped completely.

He studied Annabella's house and imagined the kids cuddled in bed. Did they have separate rooms or did they sleep in bunk beds? Did his mom still sleep with the radio on now that she no longer needed to drown out fighting neighbors and wailing sirens? Did she still take her blood pressure medicine before bed or was that under control? Did she have any other health problems? Any stemming from his ''death?'' Was she happy?

He stretched up, watching the sky turn shades lighter as the sun rose. Annabella. He'd only seen her sleeping once. The night he'd rented a hotel room and they'd first made love, telling their moms they were staying with a friend of his in Orlando. She'd curled trustingly against his side, her arm across his chest, silky leg thrown over his. He'd lain awake for hours staring at her face and wondering what he'd done in his life to deserve her. She'd supported him and believed in him like no one except his mom and brother. She'd held him and cried with him over Rafael's death. She gave so much of herself, not only to him, to everyone, and he often wondered if she would run out of love, selfishly wanting every bit for himself.

He'd never known another woman who could make him ache and laugh at the same time. Making love to her had been the most incredible experience of his life. One he'd tried to find with others. After her betrayal, he'd set out to replace Annabella as quickly as she'd replaced him.

He hadn't been successful.

He pushed off the railing and went into the house, up to the small room off his bedroom. He flipped switches, and machines hummed and clicked to life. Michael hadn't faxed him yet, but would soon. Checking his watch, he figured his partner had probably just gotten up, having adjusted easily to non-military hours.

Dropping into his plush black chair, Rico typed a few letters on his computer and called up files. He might have left the army with scars, but he'd also taken a vast amount of computer and security knowledge. With Michael's help he'd put it to use.

"You want to do what?" Anna asked, looking across the table at Rebecca.

"I wanna bring Gage a sticker." Her daughter shoveled another mouthful of soggy Cheerios into her mouth.

Rafe looked at his sister, his brow knitting for a moment before he smiled. "Me, too!"

With a sigh Anna bit into her toast and looked at Lina. Just before the kids came down she'd told her about Gage's scars, and they'd speculated on their cause.

"Honey, I'm sure Mr. Moran has enough Band-Aids in his house."

"Not Snoopy ones!" Rebecca insisted, her face screwing up for either a tantrum or a cry.

Rafe spooned more Cheerios into his mouth, his gaze ping-ponging back and forth between his mother and sister.

"Rebecca's right," Lina said casually. "I'm sure Mr. Moran could use some Snoopy Band-Aids."

Anna shot her a quizzical look, not sure why Lina was backing her granddaughter.

"Okay. When you two are done and dressed, we'll take a walk over." Besides, how long could it take? The twins could give him a Band-Aid and they'd leave. She could handle five minutes in the man's company.

"Yeah!" Rebecca shouted. They finished breakfast in record time and ran upstairs to change out of their pajamas.

Anna trudged up the stairs after ten minutes to see how they were doing. What patterns would they mix today? She cringed, remembering a particular day of blue plaid and black polka dots.

"Rafe, put this on!"

"I am!"

Anna peeked around the corner and watched her children trying to dress themselves and each other. The artist in her sighed in relief. They'd picked one of her favorite matching outfits. Light blue overalls were shorts on Rafe and a skirt on Rebecca. Underneath they wore white T-shirts, Rebecca's having light-blue flowers bordering the collar.

"Well, don't you two look great!"

Proud grins dimpled their faces.

Anna leaned down, lending a hand with the tucking in of shirts and clasping of suspenders. "You guys brush your teeth? Didn't think so." She swatted bottoms. "Scoot."

When they were finished, Anna brushed Rafe's honey-colored hair and French-braided Rebecca's black curls, leaving a thick rope swinging against her back. "Run downstairs and I'll be there as soon as I get dressed."

Anna had learned early on to shower before the twins awak-

ened, leaving only dressing and hair for afterward. She pulled
on a coral bodysuit and shoved her legs into a broken-in pair
of jeans, then slipped her feet into sandals. Usually she didn't
bother with makeup, but decided today that maybe a little
mascara wouldn't hurt. Not that it had anything to do with
Gage, she told herself quickly as she brushed color across her
cheeks. Taking hair from either side of her head, she pulled it
up and secured it with a clip, letting the natural curls and
waves settle around her shoulders.

Oh, who was she kidding! She slapped her comb onto her
dresser and glared at her reflection. She was trying to look
good for Gage. Stop being ridiculous, Anna, the man won't
notice you. He's too gorgeous and could have his pick of
stunning women. Besides, she lectured reasonably, she wasn't
interested in getting involved with anyone, much less someone
who wouldn't want a ready-made family.

Chanting this like a mantra, she jogged down the stairs to
join her impatient little people. Rebecca grasped an entire box
of Snoopy Band-Aids and Rafe cradled a plate wrapped in tin
foil.

"What's that, Rafe?"

"Grandma's brow-knees."

"Wow! Isn't that nice of her?" She hoped she put enough
enthusiasm into her response. Could Lina's neighborly gift be
more than it seemed?

"Grandma said Gage is a battler and probably can't cook,"
Rebecca piped in.

"That's *bachelor,* sweetie. It means he isn't married, and
we don't know if he has a wife or not. Also, Mr. Moran is an
adult, so you shouldn't call him by his first name. It isn't
polite."

"Lina," she called. "We're going over to Gage's."

"All right!"

Walking across the lane to Gage's house, Anna hoped he
was awake. It was only a little past 10:00 a.m. and most people
slept in on the weekends. A luxury she missed!

Rebecca rang the doorbell, and Anna shifted on her feet, squelching the fluttery nervousness in her stomach. Breakfast didn't agree with her, she thought.

The door swung open and Gage stood there with surprise and, it looked like, pleasure in his eyes before becoming devoid of all expression.

"Hi," he said in that bone-melting voice. "What's all this?"

Anna found her voice and a smile. "This is the neighborhood welcoming committee."

"Come on in," he said, his eyes flitting over the three of them.

He stepped back into the empty foyer and leaned against the open door. He wore an indigo knit pullover that stretched across his chest, and his jeans clung to his legs. Her glance strayed down, taking in his bare feet and was unwittingly aroused by the sight. Feet, she thought incredulously. She was excited by his feet! Rolling her eyes at her strange reactions to this man, she ushered her children inside and followed him into the den.

"Please, sit down. Can I get you and the kids something to drink?"

"No, thanks, we're fine," she answered in a breezy attempt at casualness.

He sauntered over and sat on the opposite couch.

"Go ahead, Rebecca," Anna said softly, urging her daughter to give him the Band-Aids.

Instead, Rebecca looked at Gage with a frown crunching her eyebrows into a vee and pursing her tiny lips.

"Are you a battler, Mr. Moron?"

Weren't these embarrassing out-of-the-mouths-of-babes comments supposed to get easier to handle and less mortifying as they got older? Gage looked as if he'd been hit in the forehead with a two-by-four.

"Rebecca," she began with a parental sigh. "His name is Mr. *Moran*, not 'moron' and asking if he's a bachelor isn't polite.'' She smiled at Gage but had a feeling the smile looked as strained as it felt.

Rico found it difficult to keep from laughing when he heard Annabella's explanation. His daughter looked so serious. Who wanted to know if he was married? Annabella?

"Anna, it's okay," he chuckled, not worrying about his dimples after checking in the mirror. They weren't as deep as they'd once been, and with his teeth capped, his whole smile looked different.

Annabella looked relieved when he laughed, and he wanted badly to tell her how much he enjoyed their daughter. "Yes, Rebecca, I am a bachelor. I don't have a—" the next words rang wrong "—a wife...or kids."

Rico was treated to Rebecca's beaming smile once again. He vowed to somehow make sure it stayed there.

"Mr. Mo-*ran*," she said haltingly, glancing at both adults and getting nods at her correct pronunciation. "These are for you."

Overwhelming love rose up when he saw the box of Band-Aids. For several seconds he stared down at it, trying to control his emotions.

"Thank you, Rebecca. Thank you very much," he whispered, trying to get a handle on the emotions surging through him.

Rebecca, having been raised around affectionate adults, didn't hesitate to throw herself into Gage's arms. She was confident she would be caught.

Rico's eyes closed as he hugged his daughter for the first time. This little child is mine, he thought, the idea still so new and fresh. Mine and Annabella's.

Rebecca wiggled out of the embrace like a puppy held too long. "Okay, Rafe, your turn!" She hopped from foot to foot with the excitement over giving presents.

Rafe levered himself off the couch with his legs, the brownies still held securely in his arms. He walked over to Gage and placed the plate in his hands.

"These are from my grandma 'cause you can't cook," he said quietly, his eyes waiting for Gage's reaction.

He chuckled. "What is it?" Not really caring as long as he could talk to his son. He saw pieces of himself and Annabella in each of the children, but all of his brother's goodness shone in little Rafe.

"Brow-knees," he replied, pronouncing each syllable so carefully, it came out as two different words.

"Really?" Rico asked in disbelief, peeling off the shiny foil even as he asked. His mom's double-chocolate, chocolate-chip, marshmallow brownies? Oh, God, he was in heaven!

A grin transformed Gage's face, his joy unchecked for a moment. Anna sat stunned, her breath lodged in her chest. The beauty of Gage's face in repose made you appreciate God's talents as a sculptor, but when he smiled, you saw the angels' involvement. He was, beyond a shadow of a doubt, the most beautiful man she'd ever seen, despite the few visible scars. Raw masculinity wrapped in gentleness with a dash of danger and mystery thrown in.

It was a breathtaking combination.

Then he turned from the children and pinned her with those fluid brown eyes. With an expression that reminded her of Rafe's little-boy charm, he held out a brownie to her. Only his eyes held a decidedly grown-male glint, daring her to play. "Want one?"

Her heart shifted, and in a timeless second of perfect clarity, she knew nothing would ever be the same.

Rico waited for any sign of recognition, but instead saw a woman's admiration and something totally mysterious. She wanted him. He knew that as surely as he breathed. The electricity between them was there, subdued by the children, but there just the same. If they were alone he'd have a hard time not touching her.

With difficulty he refocused on his children. "Thank you, Rafe. Please tell your grandma for me that these are really cool!"

Without realizing it, Rico hit on Rafe's favorite word and won his son's approval.

Both males looked at each other before Rafe slowly took a step forward. How different they are, Rico thought curiously. He opened his arms and experienced again the miraculous feeling of holding his child in his arms. Rafe's arms wrapped trustingly around his neck, and when Rico went to let go of him, Rafe maneuvered himself so that he was sitting on Rico's right leg.

Rico saw the withdrawal on Anna's face and wondered at the cause. Didn't she like him touching the children? His parental side could understand her concern in this day and age, but his ego rebelled at the thought.

"Okay, kids," she said, rising to her feet. "It's time to go."

"Oh, Mommm!"

She stood firm, and he released his son. He didn't want to push and invite them to stay when he didn't have a reason to. The fact he'd seen them twice now was too good to ruin.

He walked them out the front door, the kids yelling goodbye before tearing toward the lane, halting there to wait for their mother.

"Anna," he said, stopping her with a hand on her arm, "thanks for bringing them over and for the presents," he told her, not knowing how or what to say to her, but not wanting her to leave yet.

"The kids wanted to bring them over," she told him, keeping one eye on the kids.

An awkward silence stretched between them.

"Listen…"

"Well…"

Both spoke at once and relieved laughter followed.

"You first," he said, smiling down at her.

Ignoring what his closeness was doing to her senses, she began, "Mr. Moran…" At his look she changed to, "Gage, I realize a 'bachelor' isn't used to kids. Thanks for being so nice to them."

"You have beautiful children. They take after their mother."

Anna was shocked, wondering if the mascara and blush had that much of an effect on him. Long-ingrained instincts kicked in even as she backed away from the approval in his eyes. She gestured with her left hand. "Well, thank you. Their father helped."

"You're married?"

Seeing the absolute shock on Gage's face banished all Anna's thoughts except why it was there.

"Gage," she said earnestly, laying her hand on his arm. "What's wrong?"

Rico looked at her slim hand, resting so lightly on his forearm. Here he was acting like a crazy man, and she was concerned for him. He smiled inwardly. Still wanting to help and protect everyone, Annabella. Even strangers.

"Nothing's wrong. I was surprised at you being married. I didn't see your husband the week I've been here, just the four of you." His excuse rang lame even to his ears, and he could see she wasn't buying it.

"Oh. Well, the truth is, I'm a widow."

Relief swept through Rico leaving him a little light-headed. A widow.

"The children's father died?"

Her face closed and she turned her face away. "Yes."

The ring was either a protection for her or it meant she still loved Rico. Could she love him, the new man, the way she'd loved him before? Damn, even he was confused!

"I'm sorry for your loss, Anna," he said in a hushed voice.

"I've got to go," she said hurriedly, the aura of intensity that surrounded him beginning to envelop her, its warmth giving her a disturbing sense of peace.

He nodded. "Bye, Anna."

She stared for a second longer, feeling herself pulled to him and fighting it for all it was worth. Last night she cried for Rico, and now she fought the urge to stay with this stranger.

She jogged down to the lane and grasped a small hand in each of hers and didn't look back when the door slammed behind her.

For the next three days Anna did everything she could to avoid seeing and thinking of Gage. Rico was a constant in her mind and she held on to the good memories, holding them close.

This was the first time in years she'd allowed herself to remember everything, every detail her mind had retained of their time together. Once she opened the floodgate, though, it was impossible to close. The memories haunted her, chasing her to her office where she worked long into the night. She wasn't sleeping, she wasn't eating and she wasn't any closer to the answers her heart was asking.

And this desire she felt for Gage, it was as strong as the magnetic pull she'd once felt with Rico. Was her desire truly for him, or was her body responding to something similar in Gage, responding to the memory of a passion that had burned so brightly?

The sleepless nights had produced weeks of work, even enabling her to finish the strip portraying the twins' stolen-mail adventure. She drew up the extra copy for Dana, scrawling Solomon across the mailbox, and decided to personalize two more, for the Hendersons and for Gage. Mounting them carefully on blue posterboard, she gave them to Lina, who said she'd be more than happy to take them around with the kids.

Anna took this opportunity to commute into Spokane to drop off her work at the newspaper and pick up her check, instead of waiting for it to be mailed. As usual, the amount of money she made doing what she loved made pride surge through her. She'd worked hard to get out of poverty, with her cousin, Brooke, and Aunt Clare giving her a place to live and helping hands for a few months before she'd saved enough money to get an apartment. She'd be forever grateful to her aunt for not hesitating to offer her estranged niece a home and for giving everything her mother, Clare's much younger sister, had been too selfish to provide. As soon as she found out about Anna's pregnancy, her mother had packed her own meager belongings and left with a man she'd met in a bar, telling Anna she was trash, just like her father.

She winced a bit, recalling her mother's harsh words, but shrugged it off. Her mother, her father, Rico. They'd all left her. But they'd taught her a very important lesson. When it came down to it, you could only count on yourself.

Glancing at her watch, and seeing it was only noon, she picked up some flowers and dropped by Aunt Clare's to visit and catch up. Retired, her aunt spent much of her busy time volunteering at the local hospital and bragging about her niece "the successful cartoonist." She never knew that Anna had paid off the mortgage on Clare's home. Since her aunt would never have willingly allowed her to repay her, Anna and Brooke had come up with an idea and told her the bank made an error and she'd been overpaying her mortgage for years. It was the very least Anna felt she could do.

She called Brooke at work from her aunt's and the two women met at an Italian restaurant in the city. She was waiting, sipping a Coke, when her cousin arrived.

As usual, Brooke was impeccably dressed, so stunning that even women turned their heads as she walked by. Tall and willowy, her fiery hair confined in a French twist, green eyes expertly enhanced, Brooke's looks were model beautiful. But few people failed to look beyond the beauty to the shrewd intelligence in her eyes, a failure she took advantage of in the courtroom.

The women hugged and exchanged small talk before settling into their chairs. After they ordered, Brooke pinned her with an attorney glare and said, "All right, give. What's going on in that complex brain of yours?"

Anna attempted to look surprised at the question, but since Brooke knew her so well, it was a waste of time.

"Is it my godchildren? Are they giving you the fits?"

Anna shook her head, and Brooke tapped her straw against her glass, waiting for Anna to speak.

"Is it Lina? Is she okay?"

"Oh, yes! She's fine," Anna said, knowing she should just spill it out. "Oh, Brooke. I don't know what to do."

Brooke looked alarmed, and Anna knew it was because of the dismay she couldn't completely hide. Brooke could probably count on one hand how many times she'd seen her upset enough to cry, and one of those times had been during labor.

"I have a new neighbor," she finally said.

Brooke inclined her head, urging her to explain.

Anna took a deep breath. "He's…beautiful."

A huge smile spread across her cousin's face. "You noticed a man! Holy cow, it's a miracle!"

"Stop teasing. This isn't funny."

"I can see that," she countered in amused concern. "Although I'm quite thrilled. You know I've been waiting for this to happen. I was afraid you were going to expect Rico's ghost to keep you warm until you were ninety."

Anna shot her an exasperated look. "I don't want to be with anyone else, and I know I'll never feel that kind of love again. Besides, I don't want to risk the hurt. I have my children, Lina, a great job. They're enough. Why is that so hard for you to understand?"

Brooke took a sip of her drink, a frown creasing her otherwise smooth forehead. "I guess because I've never experienced the kind of love you felt for Rico. When you talk about him, it's like you were never whole unless you were with him. I've never cared for anyone that way, even the ones who stuck around." Her eyes widened and she said hurriedly, "Oh, Anna, I'm sorry. I didn't mean it that way."

"I know you didn't. The truth hurts, right?" Ignoring the regret on her cousin's face, she propped her chin in her hand and squinted across the table. "You've never experienced love," she said, beginning a never-ending contention between the two, "because you run when a man gets too close." She continued when she saw Brooke's mouth open to object. "And I'm not talking physically, I mean emotionally."

"Back to you, cousin. I can see that psychological white coat of yours being slipped on, and I don't need more analyzing of my love life. I know you don't approve," she said mockingly. "Anyway, we're not here to talk about me. We need to discuss this new neighbor. What's his name?"

"Gage Moran."

"What does he do?"

Anna frowned. "I have no idea. He doesn't seem to keep normal working hours so maybe he's taking the summer off."

"What does he look like?"

"He's beautiful, despite the scars. Absolute, unbelievable male beauty."

Brooke started choking on her iced tea. "Anna, you're in love with this guy!"

"I am not!" she refuted hotly.

"Well, you're at least halfway there. I've never seen you look so dreamy, not even when I introduced you to those Chippendale dancers. And they were gorgeous! For crying out loud, you shook their hands and smiled politely." She tipped her head to one side. "Or maybe you're just in lust."

"Oh, Brooke," she said in disgust.

"What's wrong with that? There's no rule saying you can't enjoy men. I'm not saying get married or anything. Why can't you have an affair with him? He's attracted to you, right?"

Anna recalled the blaze of emotion in his eyes. "You could say that."

"What's stopping you then?"

Anna just looked at her.

Brooke sighed. "He's dead, Anna. Rico's dead."

She turned her head and looked out the window, watching the people and cars hurry back and forth. Life never stopped, even if you felt as though it did.

"Not in my heart, Brooke. He's never seemed more alive than he does right now."

Chapter 3

Anna drove home, replaying the conversation in her mind. Brooke's advice to have an affair didn't turn her off as much as she let on, but she didn't think she could just make love with Gage and then casually return to her own bed. Also, making love while Lina and the kids were in the house was out of the question. And although she didn't want to incur Lina's disapproval of her, she realized this was her life and she couldn't keep living it to everyone else's expectations.

That was one of her biggest regrets about Rico's death. Yes, they'd been very close, but there were so many parts of her he never knew, things she hadn't shared with him because she'd been busy being the girl he loved. It hadn't been intentional, but after Rico left for the army, all of their conversations centered around his life on base and the things he dreamed of doing with his life afterward. He'd included her in those dreams automatically and he'd been so excited that she never wanted to interrupt and tell him her dreams of writing and illustrating her own children's book or traveling to exotic places. Granted, she'd wanted nothing more than to become his wife and have his children, but she wanted to try other things, too. Things she'd try now that her work was successful and she had a substantial weekly paycheck to support her family. A paycheck she'd earned all by herself, without a husband or a father for her kids. I wonder, she mused for yet another time, what Rico would think about me now? He'd always viewed her as fragile. A wry chuckle burst from her as a realization hit her.

"He never really knew me at all." The sound of her voice in the confines of the car shocked her as much as the words. But in a weird way the person who had known her better than anyone had never really *seen* her.

Then another disturbing thought—where would she be now if he'd believed she'd been faithful? In Miami, fighting to raise the kids in a tiny apartment and dodging gang drive-bys on the way to the supermarket? Would she have created her comic strip Double Trouble or would she have been too busy being his wife, as she'd been so consumed being his girlfriend? Would they have been happy? Or would he have walked away later on or shown his mistrust in other ways?

She raised a hand to rub her temple, her questions bringing up disturbing realizations. She drove down the lane and into her driveway. Getting out, she didn't hear giggles or voices from the backyard and there wasn't anyone inside. She stood in her kitchen, trying to figure out where they all could be. Then she glanced across to Gage's house. Lina and the children must be delivering the cartoons.

Well, I'll just wait awhile before looking for them, she thought on her way to get the aspirin. But before she could completely close her mind to her introspection, a tiny voice whispered, *What would Gage think about your wanting to write a book?*

Rico sat in a large leather chair, Rebecca and Rafe each perched on an arm. His mother sat on the couch across from him, bursting with pride as she answered his questions about Annabella.

"So Double Trouble is syndicated."

"*Sí,* and it has been for two years. The strip started in *Parents* magazine and was picked up by a Spokane newspaper. It became popular with their readers very quickly and was syndicated shortly afterward."

He stared down at the blue posterboard in his hands, holding the answer to one of the more persistent questions plaguing him of late. Now he knew how she was supporting the family. He shook his head, amazed at her talent, never having realized the range of it. The doodles she made on napkins or people she'd drawn in letters hadn't given him a clue.

He easily recognized his children as the strip's characters and, seeing her humorous way of portraying the 'mail adventure' as his mama called it, he could easily understand why parents loved it. Even people without children could enjoy it, relating it to their own childhood mishaps.

"That's me," Rafe said, pointing to the little boy.

"He looks just like you," Rico said with a smile.

Rafe smiled back and leaned against Rico, eliciting a raised brow from Lina.

"Did she start Double Trouble when they were babies?" he asked her.

Lina beamed with pride. "Actually she started it when they were in her—" she glanced at the children "—her stomach."

Both twins nodded. They'd heard this before.

"Really?"

"*Sí,* she did strips portraying what they may have been thinking and had them talk about what was going on 'on the outside.' She drew funny ones about them kicking her and the twins keeping score, knowing exactly how uncomfortable they were making her. She also did serious ones, showing the twins listening to their mother's voice as she read to them or talked to them."

"So she basically kept a chronological record of their lives," he murmured.

Lina smiled and nodded. "You could experience the twins' whole lives through the cartoon strip."

Rico was unaware of how contemplative his expression was or that Lina noticed.

"Mr. Moran," she began.

"Please, call me…Gage," he said, stumbling over giving his mother a different name than the one she'd chosen over thirty years before.

"How did you get those scars?" That was his mother. Outspoken and blunt, she'd learned long before to throw tact and subtlety to the wind for the answers she wanted.

"An accident, Lina. A very unfortunate accident."

She examined him as if trying to decide something. "Would you like to have dinner with us tonight?"

He was startled until he noticed the gleam in her eyes. Was his mom matchmaking? "I'd love to," he accepted, grinning at the cheers from his children.

"There you are!" Anna said, bending to give her children hugs and kisses. "Did you finish giving out the cartoons?"

"Yes!" and "Yup!" they yelled.

"Dana was thrilled with hers and said she's holding you to your coffee date. The Hendersons immediately put their cartoon up on the wall, and Gage had a lot to say about your talent." Lina paused. "So I invited him to dinner so he could tell you himself."

"You did *what?*" Anna exclaimed.

"I invited him over to dinner," Lina answered calmly.

Anna breathed deeply, scrambling to find a legitimate reason why she couldn't be at dinner in her own house.

"Anna," Lina reproved, "he's living in that big house, all alone, and from the looks of his kitchen, he's not a cook. He probably hasn't had a decent home-cooked meal in years!"

This was a cardinal sin in Lina's book. Anna rolled her neck. There was no way out of this.

"When will he be here?"

Lina's wink ruined her serious expression. "You have an hour to do your hair."

"Lina!"

"Don't Lina me, child! I've seen the look on your face when the twins mention him." She walked over and grasped Anna's upper arms. "Honey, I've been doing a lot of thinking. You're still very young, and you can't keep comparing all men to Rico." Despite the younger woman's shocked and immediate denial she continued, "I think I've been doing you a grave injustice. I haven't meant to, but I may have given you the impression you shouldn't be with anyone but my son." She pulled her into a hug. "It's sin enough I kept you two apart. I would never keep you from living the rest of your life, sweetheart."

She struggled against the swell of love Lina's words conjured up and hugged her hard. "I love you, *Madre*," she whispered.

"And I love you, *hija*."

"This does not mean," Anna began, pulling away with a sniff, "I'm going to get involved with Gage. But I've been doing a lot of thinking myself these past days."

"*Bueno*," Lina whispered. "Rico loved you very much, *hija*, but not always very well. It's your turn."

Anna smiled, although she could feel it waver. "Can I help you with dinner?"

"No, we're having spaghetti and meatballs. I have some of my sauce in the refrigerator and some leftover meatballs in the freezer. You go change."

"Okay. Anyone want to come upstairs with me?" she asked the twins, who were parked in front of the television.

"Me!" yelled Rafe, running to join her.

"Rebecca, why don't you help me make garlic bread," Lina

said, drawing the little girl away from the television. Both women tried to limit their hours of TV viewing.

Anna jogged up the stairs after her son, tickling him as he scrambled up ahead of her.

"Can Mr. Moh-wan help me with my puzzle?" Rafe asked as he climbed onto her bed.

"Mo*ran,* honey," she said, correcting his *r.* "I'm not sure he'll have the time." Seeing his crestfallen expression, she added, "We'll ask him after dinner."

"Cool!"

She opened her closet doors, surveying its contents while Rafe played with a couple of plastic action figures he'd left in her room. What was she going to wear?

With Lina's approval on top of her own shaky decision to start living her life, she turned to the closet with a lighter heart. Taking out dark-blue jeans, she paired them with a silk blouse and applied a minimum of makeup, not wanting to look too obvious and give him the idea this wasn't a normal dinner. Her hair she took down from its customary clip and bent over, attacking it with the hair dryer. Rafe helped, pumping hairspray where she directed until she stood back up and her hair settled in a cloud of curls and waves over her shoulders. Not bad, she thought critically. Slipping on gold hoop earrings, she posed in front of the mirror.

"How do I look?"

Her son tilted his head to one side then back to the other. "Cool."

Anna laughed. Didn't get much better than that.

It's like I'm going on my first date, Rico thought, irritated and amused at his own feelings. Carrying a bottle of wine and three bouquets of colorful flowers, he knocked on Annabella's front door.

She answered, a hesitant smile curving her rosy lips. She wore a gold shirt, its dull sheen sliding across her chest and molding to the full slopes of her breasts. Jeans clung to her small waist and long thighs, dragging up memories of her legs tangled with his.

His throat went dry.

He shot his gaze back to hers, hoping his arousal wasn't written on his face. The flowers did their job and provided a shield for the area that couldn't disguise his need.

One look into her eyes told him she hadn't misinterpreted anything. Midnight dark, they hypnotized him, reminding him of so many other times.

How could he hide this need for her when just looking at her made him tremble? He ducked his head and strove for control.

He'd have to tell her, but not tonight. As soon as he knew there was no chance of danger.

Why did he look away? The heat in his eyes had been so intense, so arousing, and she couldn't help her body's instinctive sway toward him.

"Hello, Anna," he said politely.

Humiliation flooded her, stinging her face. Had her own desire blinded her, made her see things he didn't feel? Had the connection she felt when their eyes met been a complete illusion?

She wanted nothing more than to run up the stairs and disappear until he left. My God, what did she expect! To be swept up in a passionate kiss?

"Hello, Gage. Please come in." She stepped back and closed the door behind him, using the precious seconds to mask her seething emotions. Never, she vowed, would he know how close she came to making a fool of herself.

Her children saved her when they bounded in, no longer restrained by Lina.

"Mr. Moran, Mr. Moran," they yelled, ignoring Lina's shushes.

"Hi, guys. Rebecca," he said, handing her a miniature bouquet of wildflowers, "These are for you."

Her eyes round as saucers, Rebecca regally took the flowers from him, showing an inherent grace that would flourish in her maturity. "Thank you," she said, her voice muffled by the flowers pressed to her face.

"Lina," he said, handing her a bouquet of purple lilies, pleased by the enjoyment evident in her soft thank you.

"And Anna." Did his voice deepen on the last word? She focused on the bouquet of tiger lilies, carnations and pink roses she'd taken automatically.

"Thank you very much. They're beautiful." Did she sound like a woman who received flowers all the time? Or was it obvious that her last bouquet had come from Lina at the birth of the twins?

"Well," Lina said in a cheerful voice. "Let's all go inside and get some drinks. Gage, Rafe will put your jacket in the living room."

Rico handed it over before following them into the kitchen.

"Oh, Rafe," he said when the boy came in. "I almost forgot. I have something for you."

Anna had her wits about her enough to be proud that her son hadn't pointed out he hadn't received anything.

"If you look in the right jacket pocket, you'll find it."

Rafe beamed and took off with Rebecca on his heels.

"Please have a seat. Can I get you a drink?" Lina offered, indicating one of the kitchen chairs. Anna turned and started arranging flowers in vases, trying to appear cool and confident. She vaguely registered the conversation behind her and jumped when Rafe yelled, "Oh, wow! Cool!"

His feet pounded into the room. "Mom! Mom! Look!"

She had to face her son and swiveled with her head bent, avoiding Gage's gaze.

"It's a yo-yo, the kind that will glow just like my stars!" Rafe's chubby hands cradled his new toy protectively, and Anna's heart dropped. In her mind's eye she heard Rico's voice.

I want my son to have everything I didn't. Two parents, a safe neighborhood and a yo-yo instead of a gun to play with.

"This is a great yo-yo," she enthused, hoping her son didn't notice the weakness of the reply. Was her mind so full of Rico that a coincidence made her paranoid? After all, there wasn't any reasonable explanation for the pull she felt to him or the yo-yo.

"Hey, Mom, can we show Mr. Moran our room and stars?" Rebecca asked.

Anna wanted to yell yes! Anything to get him out of the room for a few minutes so she could calm this paranoia. "It's not quite dark enough for your stars, honey, unless you close the blinds tight."

"We will," Rafe said.

The twins looked at Rico, who in turn looked at Annabella.

"I can't wait to see your room," he finally said, taking a small hand into each of his and letting them guide him out of the kitchen.

Lina went to Anna's side immediately. "Are you okay? You look like you saw a ghost!"

"Lina, I don't know what's going on." She explained about the yo-yo and the pull she felt for Gage. "I mean, it's got to be a crazy coincidence, but it's so eerie. It's like he walked through my memories and is playing them out."

"Okay, Anna, look at me." She waited for Anna's attention. "Now, I admit I had a strange feeling at Gage's house before, but it's nothing I can put my finger on." She wrapped her plump arm around Anna's waist. "What I think is that Gage is the first man we've spent time with in a while. He's stirring up emotions and memories, that's all."

Anna sighed. "I guess so." She hugged her. "Can you please go upstairs with them? I'll watch the spaghetti."

"Sure," Lina murmured.

Anna didn't want to think Gage would hurt her children in any way, but she wasn't letting a virtual stranger in her children's bedroom by himself. She took the time alone to run cold water over her wrists and have a few gulps of wine from her glass. She had to get ahold of herself!

Rico leaned against the wall of his children's room, taking in all the toys and colors. Their beds flanked opposite walls, and the whole room was decorated with Walt Disney characters. Their bedspreads, pillowcases, the two lamps and pictures on the walls depicted Mickey, Minnie, Goofy and Donald Duck, plus some he didn't recognize. Rafe's closet door, as his son showed him, was painted a bright red, while Rebecca had picked blue for hers.

"Now watch this, Mr. Moh-wan," Rafe said, missing the *r* sound completely, Rico noted with an inward grin.

The blinds closed, the room was plunged into complete darkness. There were green stars everywhere! The ceiling looked like a miniature outer space and there were even some stuck to the lamps. On the door she'd arranged the stars in an arrow, as if to point out direction to a sleepy child. During the day the glowing stars were unnoticeable, but now they turned a child's room into a universe of possibilities.

She's done so much for them! He was glad for the dark to hide his painful wave of emotion. Everything he'd ever dreamed of for his children was in this room.

There was a tap on the door before Lina's head popped in.

"Well?" she asked Rico.

"It's fantastic," he replied.

All three smiled. It hurt his heart to look at them. They were his family and he'd never felt more alone.

Would Annabella accept him, scars and all, and forgive him for all the hurt he caused her? Or would he lose them for good when she found out the truth?

Dinner turned out to be a bittersweet affair for Rico. He was a stranger with his own family and he didn't like it.

Not one bit.

"So, Gage, what do you do?" Lina asked, twirling the spaghetti around her fork.

"Right now I'm a computer analyst for a firm owned by a longtime friend. It enables me to do a lot by modem and work from home." Seeing only Anna understood, he was glad he left out *security* from his job description and explained modems and how they worked.

The Rico part of him felt a full measure of satisfaction at the impressed lift of brows Annabella tried quickly to hide. He'd found his niche in computers, understanding them more than the complexities of human emotions, although he was working on that.

Rico heard all about his kids' favorite animals, toys and television shows and even learned about his mother's life. She attended the local church and was very involved in all of its functions. Other than that, she seemed to care for Annabella and the twins with a zealous determination. It wasn't surprising, he thought. She's lost so much, yet less than she knows.

"Can we go play?" Rebecca asked.

Anna nodded and the two were in the den in no time. Conversation resumed, again with little contributed by Anna, other than small smiles and nods.

Suddenly Rafe's high-pitched voice shouted, "I shot you! You're suppose ta fall, Becca."

Anna's reaction was so extreme Rico stopped talking. Her head whipped around, eyes growing wide in her pale face. She shoved back her chair and stood, spine rigid, and stormed into the den. Rico looked at his mother, and they stood at the same time, following her.

"Rafe, how many times have I told you that I don't like you playing these games?" She bent, pulling Rebecca up from her death pose. "Even pretending to shoot your sister isn't funny!"

The twins stared up at her in mute apology.

"Give me the stick," she demanded, holding out her hand for the "gun."

"But, Mom," Rebecca whined.

"No buts, Rebecca. I've told you over and over that guns, even play ones, aren't a game. Shooting someone is serious! And they don't just fall down and get back up like they do in cartoons."

"It's just pretend, Mom," Rafe said quietly.

Anna drew in a deep breath, obviously calming herself. "I know it is, sweetie, but some things you shouldn't pretend about. There's no reason to play a game that needs one of you to be hurt or pretend to be dead."

As he watched Annabella hug the twins and set up a board game for them to play, Rico saw the scars she carried from her childhood. Even though she'd argued about him using guns in the army, he never realized how deeply she despised them.

Yet another contention between them. A gun threatened her idea of safety; he didn't feel safe without one.

All too soon for him, the twins tired and Rico got to see the other side of their personalities. The cranky, obstinate sides.

"No," Rebecca pouted, her right index finger further twisting a black curl, a gesture he remembered making himself at her age.

"Yeah," Rafe said belligerently, obviously not liking the idea of bed any more than his sister.

"How about a story," Anna asked gently, cuddling Rafe to her side, his head nestled on her shoulder.

Rico clenched his teeth, frozen by the picture they presented. Light bounced off their hair, blending blond highlights and blurring them together like a large halo.

He'd missed so much.

"Only if Gage reads it," Rebecca said, coming to stand next to Rico, her small hand diminished even further by lying on his forearm.

Annabella opened her mouth to deny them.

Rico interrupted her.

"I'd love to read you a story," he said soothingly, running his fingers through his daughter's silky curls before he could stop himself.

The frowns became smiles, and Lina started collecting their dirty dishes. "I'll clean up while you two read to them. Come here, *angeles,* give your grandmama a hug and kiss."

She called Rafe and him angels, too, Rico remembered.

Each twin pulled on an adult. All he could think of as he rose from his chair was how this should be a normal family evening, reading a bedtime story to their kids.

Both children began pulling off clothes as soon as they walked into the room. He was surprised at how neat they were, putting their shoes next to their closets and throwing their clothes in a big, green hamper in the corner of the room.

Annabella must have noticed his surprise, because she commented, "I wanted to start them on this as soon as possible. Plus," she added with a brief grin, "picking up after these two little tornadoes would be too time consuming."

Rico grinned back, and for precious seconds he felt the special closeness they shared all those years before. Then her smile slipped, and the tension returned.

The twins scrambled into pajamas with a little help, then into their beds, pulling the covers way up to their chins.

"All right, rascals, which story?" Annabella asked them and then added after their answer, "Your favorite, huh?"

They both nodded.

Anna picked up a book and looked at Rico. She was waiting for him to back out, he thought. He stuck out a hand and then smirked at the title. "Guess I should have known from the decor," he said, and quirked a brow at her.

She looked away and hurriedly crawled onto Rebecca's bed, lying behind her and propping her head up on a hand.

He threw himself into the story, reading to his children the way he wished his father had read to him. It wasn't long before they nodded off, giving in to the sandman's inevitable victory. He sat there, his forearms on his bent knees, and drank in the sight of his slumbering children. Never before had he understood the meaning of hope until he'd looked into his children's eyes.

They *were* hope. Hope for a future without drug wars or color wars, hope for a time of peace.

For him and the rest of the world.

He blinked hard and caught Anna watching him.

"You should have children, Gage," she said, a maternal glow in her eyes. "You'd be a wonderful father. Now, we've got to get out of here or they'll be up and ready to play after their ten-minute catnaps!" She carefully moved off the bed, tucked in covers, gave kisses and walked to the door.

They returned downstairs, and Lina finished the last dish as they walked into the kitchen.

"I have some coffee ready if you'd like to have some out on the porch." Lina bustled around, pulling out mugs, milk and sugar. "I'm going to take mine to my room and watch that new miniseries."

"Oh…thank you." Rico could hear the edge in Annabella's voice. She didn't want to be alone with him.

"Lina, thank you for a wonderful dinner. I haven't eaten so well in…" His voice trailed off as the truth of his statement hit him. "In many, many years."

"You're very welcome, Gage," she said, patting him on the arm and disappearing into her downstairs room.

"Well…um…I guess we should do as she says." A weak smile accompanied the strain in Anna's words.

"Anna, I don't have to stay for coffee," he said. "I know you weren't aware that I was coming for dinner, and maybe you have work to do or want to put your feet up."

Her hair trailed over her shoulder as she looked up at him. "No, I'm sorry. I don't mean to be a bad hostess." She turned and filled their coffee cups, adding milk to hers before handing him his mug.

"Here you go. Let's sit out on the deck." She led the way

through the sliding glass doors, not noticing his silence. "Do you sit out on your deck at night?"

"Uh, yes, yes, I do," he muttered, leaning his hips against the railing next to her. "How did you know I take my coffee black?"

She spun fast, the moonlight filtering through the strands, bouncing off the lighter ones as they fell over one shoulder. "Excuse me?"

"You gave me my coffee black automatically. How did you know?" He didn't know why he was pursuing this. After all, she didn't do it because she remembered "Rico" drank it that way.

Her eyes grew wide and her mouth opened and closed a few times. "I...I don't know. I wasn't thinking, I guess," she managed, her voice barely audible.

"Hey, it's okay, I was just curious."

She visibly relaxed when he let her off the hook.

There they stood, watching the moonlight slither across the still water, winding to the shore. Their shoulders were only inches apart and his body was responding to her closeness. He breathed deeply, his nostrils flaring to take in the lavender scent slowly enveloping him. He wanted to touch her, slide his fingers through her hair, feel her skin.

"You know, when Lina and I found this house, I was so happy." Annabella's voice was like a bucket of cold water. "The kids and I had been living in an apartment in Spokane, and there wasn't a lot of room for them to run and play."

She took a sip of coffee, heat lancing through him as her pink tongue slid over her lips, catching the last drops. He breathed deeply and concentrated on her words.

"I grew up in Miami." She didn't look at him, her eyes unfocused on the lake. "There was no grass or trees and certainly no lake. I wanted more for them, and I know their father would have wanted the same."

His desire melted away, replaced with self-disgust.

"Anna..."

"No, I'm sorry, Gage." She faced him fully, and he could see her clearly in the white-blue light. "I shouldn't be talking about Rico with you."

She shouldn't? "Why not?"

She made a move to turn away and he touched her shoulder, his hand curving around it. "Anna, tell me why not?"

"It doesn't seem right."

Her eyes implored his for understanding, but he wanted to make sure he understood her.

"Why? Do you feel like you're betraying him somehow?" Frustrated satisfaction had him gritting his teeth. She obviously still felt strongly about him, but he couldn't tell the truth. He couldn't be sure it was safe yet.

"No, not exactly. It seems…inappropriate for me to talk about him right now."

"Why? Because we're all alone, surrounded by moonlight? Because you also feel this attraction between us? The attraction we've both felt since the moment we saw each other?" He reached out and touched her cheek with a trembling finger.

Her dark eyes widened and her pink lips parted on her rushing breath. God, she's so beautiful!

"I'm going to kiss you, Anna," he said quietly, waiting to see her reaction. Her gaze slid from his eyes to his mouth, giving him his answer.

He pulled her closer, their bodies barely brushing, sliding his hands down her upper arms, the silk of her blouse heated from her skin and his hands. The material provided a barrier that only heightened his senses.

"Last chance. Last chance to tell me you don't want this," he murmured roughly, inches from her lips. "Don't want to taste me…"

She moved toward him, erasing all space from between their bodies.

"I can't tell you that," she whispered, and lifted her mouth to his, giving him breath even as she stole it back.

Chapter 4

Anna felt her body come into contact with Gage's in slow degrees, chest cushioned against his ribs, hips cradled against upper thighs. The heat flowed from him into her, sending shivers through her as her cool limbs warmed. His hands slid farther down, fingers inching to her inner arms and wrists until they brushed against her trembling palms, awakening nerve endings she hadn't known existed. His strong fingers traced each finger, then slipped between hers. Seconds passed as their fingers slowly joined and their palms pressed together, linked as tightly as the hearts now beating together in heavy cadence.

Anna felt a wonder at the rightness of the dual embraces and couldn't hold back the surprised cry that erupted as he rubbed the sides of his fingers along the sides of hers, sending streaks of fire to the pit of her stomach. Desire coiled there and ringed outward in pulses, heating guarded places that had been cold far too long.

She blinked, focusing on his tightly drawn face, marveling at the hunger burning in his eyes. She caught her breath, anticipation filling her as his head lowered to hers, not sure if she could take more than the maelstrom of feelings already churning inside. Her heavy lids closed and she breathed deeply, his scent mixing with the woodsy, night air around her.

His lips, heavenly soft, brushed her forehead, right temple, warming her skin with his breaths. He took his time, grazing her cheekbone, the slope of her nose, chin and traced her jaw-line back up to the other temple. Her breath shattered at his tender assault, needing more even as she trembled from her already overloaded senses.

His hands released hers and he looked deeply into her eyes. He pulled her impossibly closer with a light pressure against the small of her back, then ran his thumbs along the hollow of her cheeks, his hands resting against her neck. He shook his head and she could hear as much as feel the breath shudder through his body.

At that moment she would have given anything to know what he was thinking.

Lowering his head, he touched his lips lightly to hers once…twice, before changing the angle and brushing again and again until she lost count and patience with the endless teasing. She needed to fill the clamoring need within her, and slid her hands up his muscled back to his wide shoulders, pulling him down closer and arching into him. The emptiness in her was nothing compared to the need for a deeper kiss, a harder kiss that would quench her desire to know his taste. He remained unmoving, and she wasn't aware of the frustrated cry torn from her throat.

Rico almost lost control hearing her need for him. Never had he thought they could ignite a desire more consuming than before. All the time he'd been a prisoner, he'd refused to let them drive her image from his mind, and during his long re-covery he'd dreamed of holding her again, loving her again. She was even sweeter than his dreams and memories com-bined.

He didn't know how much more he could take, and they'd only just begun.

Still the delicate, skimming kisses continued until Anna wanted to scream at him to kiss her, *really* kiss her, but she couldn't find the breath or the will to break even their smallest contact to speak. They were balancing on the edge of fire, and Anna wanted nothing more than to be burned by him.

Finally she heard him groan and felt his teeth close on her bottom lip, the caress making her release her breath on a soundless moan.

His tongue touched the seam of her sensitive lips. She parted them eagerly, like an arid desert during its first rain, and felt his mouth fuse completely with hers, the heat and taste of him buckling her knees. He caught her up against him, lifted her high and set her on the porch railing with him as an anchor between her legs. Seeking his mouth once more, she lost herself in the velvet warmth as ribbons of flame twisted through her.

His hand caught up the hair at the back of her head and held her willingly captive, and Anna's only thought was that she didn't want this to end. This learning of tastes and textures tangled together. This intimate game of penetration and retreat in which there were no losers.

Timeless kisses later Anna found other curiosities needed satisfying. Her newly sensitized fingers discovered his collarbone, the points and dips a provocative playground. Feeling Gage's shiver, Anna's sense of feminine power surged forward. Her fingertips abraded the slight stubble on his neck and jaw, and she withdrew from the kiss, wanting to see him in a way she'd craved from the moment she'd first seen him. She "saw" him with an artist's knowing fingers, measuring him and finding him everything she imagined.

Rico could see a desire matching his own in her brilliantly dark eyes and swollen, moist mouth. Her fingertips against his skin were bad enough on his control, but combined with the seductive look in her eyes, it was all he could do not to throw her onto a lounge chair and give in to the throbbing need in his body.

"Oh, Anna," he growled and encouraged all at once.

An almost reverent look mixed with the desire in her eyes as she studied his face. She touched him in much the same way his mouth had touched her, light, grazing touches across his brow and cheeks that excited as much as they soothed. She unraveled him entirely, though when she cradled his face between her hands and leaned to press a kiss on the scar slicing through his lips, he stiffened, feeling the flick of her tongue, and he struggled with the tender desire threatening to consume him.

This was no girl in his arms. This was a woman. A woman who would command her own passion and his. Another wave of excitement hit him, and his hands dropped to her upper thighs, digging into the jean-clad flesh. Her back arched, and he raked his short nails up and down the long limbs. He repeated the caress from knee to the crease of jean against her upper thigh, not sure who he tormented more.

Coherent thought fled when her body molded to his, a surprising, feminine strength holding him securely. But deep down, under the layers of hot need lay a bed of guilt, one he'd made a long time ago, and he couldn't let this go on. He was deceiving her as surely as he was loving her, and it was going to be hard enough for her to understand.

Anna felt his withdrawal before his lips left her own. And even as she mourned the loss, the rational part of her awakened, making her realize where they were and the intimate position they were locked in. She concentrated on untangling her limbs from his, accepting his hands on her hips to help her off the railing. She wondered where the flood of embarrassment and humiliation was, but only felt regret that the kisses ended.

"I think I should go," he said, his voice huskier than usual, a slight question woven among the words.

She hesitated, not wanting to break this new intangible bond between them, but knowing instinctively that although physically she was ready to make love with him, emotionally she was still fighting ghosts. She didn't want to make a decision that would haunt them both later on. With relieved regret, she nodded stiffly and walked inside, shutting the glass doors between them.

Smoke curled lazily from the cigarette, a gray cloud briefly blocking the view of the houses, but in no way interfering with the clicking efficiency of a calculating mind.

Gage Moran. No physical resemblance to Rico Carella beyond height and hair color. The check revealed a man with a clean record, far removed from any association with the military, two Ivy League college degrees and enough inherited money in the bank to explain his lack of work.

But masks came in all shapes and sizes.

He could be an agent. Sent to keep an eye on Carella's family. So far there had been no indication Carella wasn't dead.

Maybe the bastard really was six feet under.

Unfortunately, the revenge would be less sweet, the reason behind its delay. Either way the decision had been made.

Tomorrow Carella's children would be taken in place of the lives Carella had cost the Balangerio family.

The Balangerio name would live on.

An eye for an eye.

Rico wandered through his house, using pacing as an outlet for his emotions. Sleep, of course, was impossible. His body was strung too tight, his blood still singing through his veins as he envisioned Anna balanced on the porch railing.

He took the steps two at a time and gazed at his reflection in the bathroom mirror, wondering how Anna hadn't known him.

He chuckled. The possessive streak hadn't been beaten out of him. He knew how stupid it was to be jealous of himself, but he couldn't control it any more than he could control his desire for her.

Splashing cold water on his heated skin, he dislodged a contact lens. He'd grown so used to them he sometimes forgot they were even there. He removed them and threw them in their case, a little relieved to see the golden color he'd become attached to over his thirty-two years.

Jogging gingerly back down the stairs in sweatpants and T-shirt, he grabbed a drink out of the fridge and headed for the deck. Settling onto the lounger with a sigh, he rested his head back and let the utter peacefulness of the place seep into him. He'd actually gotten to the point where he could be outside without jumping at each cracking twig.

Not that he was unaware. The familiar surge of alertness never left him. He never forgot the danger that could be lurking or the threat his presence brought his family.

He'd weighed the possibilities in his mind so many times, but either way, dead or alive, he endangered them. His cover had been cemented by the government's best, and even his family didn't know him, but it was no guarantee. Information was leaked all the time, and there were people who were very unhappy about his being here. The same people who'd kept the knowledge of his children from him.

As much as he hated them for it, it was the one argument they couldn't shatter. Their guilt and his stubbornness were the only reasons they'd helped him.

Because either way he would have his family, and they'd known it.

He stretched languidly, feeling little pangs from areas not fully healed. The doctors told him he'd never have the full range of abilities he'd commanded so easily from his body. At least not without suffering for it. He needed to get back on a daily workout schedule and continue to strengthen his muscles. He wanted, *needed*, to be as close to 100 percent as possible.

He pushed his hair off his forehead, suddenly remembering

Anna's hands tunneling through it. She seemed to enjoy winding her fingers in the curls, and he'd felt relief he had something different from the past that she enjoyed. He'd always kept his hair buzzed short, even before the army.

Oh, Anna. What am I going to do about you?

A part of him wished for the thousandth time he'd done things differently. If he'd dealt with Rafe's death, if he hadn't been so afraid to love her and settle down, maybe he would be in bed next to her right now, holding her instead of dreaming about it.

Maybe.

Anna woke the next morning anything but refreshed. Her pillow was punched into a ball so tight she wasn't sure she could rescue it. She replayed the kiss, kisses actually, a hundred times, torturing herself. At first she'd wondered at the familiarity of them. When she'd dated two other men briefly, their good-night kisses hadn't evoked any of the desire she'd felt with Rico. Obviously, her mind connected desire with him, which explained the familiar sense of déjà-vu.

Sometime during the night, the guilt she felt over betraying Rico evaporated. In actuality, it was her guilt over her own feelings of love for him that still lingered. She had no reason to feel guilty about going on with her life, as he'd done so easily before his death. He'd discarded her love and all their years of friendship as if they were worthless.

Now it was time for her to let go of her anger and tuck her love for him away into a part of her heart where she could treasure the good he'd brought to her life. It was time for her to live.

Gage brought about this change. Suddenly she was thinking about spending time with him, doing normal day-to-day things. Spending her nights with him, doing all sorts of—

"Mom!" squealed Rafe, bounding onto her bed, his energy recharged after a good night's sleep. In his eyes she saw Rico, and for once didn't feel the reflexive clench around her heart.

She smiled at her son, grabbing him for a big hug and kisses. "I love you, buster," she said.

"I *love* you, Mom," he replied, a proud grin at his correct pronunciation.

"Good job!"

His grin widened even farther. "Mom? Where's Mr. Mohwan?"

"I imagine he's sleeping," she said, with an inward smile at the thought of Gage sprawled across a bed.

"Why didn't he sleep here?"

Out of the mouths of babes. "Because he has his own bed, at his own house, sweetie. Where's your sister?" she asked, getting them both off the subject of Gage and beds.

"Downstairs with Grandma."

"Why don't you go down and join them? I overslept, so I'll shower and be down in a few minutes."

"'Kay!" he yelled, giving her a high-five.

Anna watched her son tumble off the bed and out the door as fast as his short legs could carry him.

She took a deep breath. "Thank you for them, Rico," she said with a glance through the window at the blue, blue sky.

"Did you put everything you needed on the list?" Anna asked, tucking coupons inside her pocket.

"*Sí,*" Lina called from her room.

"We'll be back later then," she said, stepping out onto the porch to join the twins. Her stomach seesawed at the sight of them with Gage.

Oh, goodness. She wasn't ready to face him so soon. No, she could do this. All she had to do was act like a mature, sophisticated woman and keep her hands to herself.

Easier said than done.

"Mom! Mr. Moran's coming with us!"

She quickly sought Gage's reaction to her daughter's announcement. Only heated memories and desire lurked in his heavy-lidded eyes.

"Hope you don't mind. I was on my way there when I saw the kids." He shifted and shoved his hands into the pockets of his shorts, smiling at her with all the sincerity of a toothpaste commercial.

If he wasn't lying through his teeth, she'd eat her socks.

"I'll even help you carry in your groceries," he added with a heavy dose of charm.

Now she knew he was lying. What man on this earth volunteered to carry in groceries? Actually, his obvious ploy to spend time with her clenched her heart in a sweet fist.

Deftly removing a cereal box of potential cavities from Rafe, she glanced at Gage for the zillionth time. Expression grim, his regret over joining them painted his face in stern lines. Shopping with two children was always an adventure, and he obviously wasn't enjoying it.

Disappointment settled in her chest. If he couldn't spend this kind of time with her children, she couldn't even think of seriously dating him.

At the checkout, she caught him staring out the front windows at the parking lot. "What are you looking for?"

Startled eyes met hers. "Nothing."

She arched a brow at him and swung a packed bag into the cart.

Rico worked at hiding his growing unease. He didn't like the fact she noticed it. His first visit to the supermarket in years would have been fun if not for all the people, banging carts and ringing registers. They were too open to an attack. He needed to get them out of here now.

The group made their way to Anna's huge Ford Expedition, and the adults loaded it while the kids tried to help.

Only four other people were outside the small store. Two elderly women were making their way inside, a man busily counted his change while hurrying to his car, a harried woman dug through her purse before triumphantly pulling out keys.

Suddenly the small rubber ball Rafe had gotten out of the

store vending machine slipped from his fingers. As if in slow motion Rico watched it bounce across the pavement to stop against the store.

Rafe looked both ways before skipping after it. All at once the prickling feeling at the base of Rico's neck spread to his heart, and his pulse kicked into high gear.

From the corner of his eye, he caught sight of a black van turning into the parking lot. It inched its way in.

He gauged the distance between himself and his son.

A glance showed Anna buckling Rebecca into one of the child seats in the back.

"Come on, Rafe," he said, fighting the urge to yell as he walked toward his son.

Without warning, the van accelerated, a grinding sound that obliterated the peaceful morning. He ran the rest of the way, snatched Rafe up and held him tight to his chest. Turning, he ran back to the Expedition. The van sped by, and air buffeted his back. A quick look confirmed his worst fears. No license plates.

And the man who slammed the side door shut wore a black ski mask.

Anna spun around as the van roared by them. "He almost hit you!"

She hadn't seen the attempt to grab Rafe. "He's fine, Bella. Give me the keys," he said, while handing his son to her.

"What?" she asked, still checking Rafe for injuries. "Shouldn't we call the police or something? That maniac could have killed you both!"

With her arms around Rafe, he easily took the keys from her hand. "Why don't you belt him into his seat?"

When she only stared at him, he dropped all pretence and could hear the growl in his voice. "Now."

She hesitated, then appeared to make a decision and did as he asked. She climbed into the passenger seat and leaned over to pop the hood when he asked. His cautious check showed no one had tampered with the vehicle while they'd been inside.

He'd doubted it would have happened with so many people around, but couldn't afford assumptions. Grateful Anna held her questions, he sped home, constantly keeping a lookout for company.

Relief filled him when his mother greeted them from the porch. He'd been terrified they'd try to grab her instead.

"Did you get everything?" she called, before picking up on the tension between the adults. She pursed her lips and gave him a narrowed look. "*Angeles,* why don't we go play in the backyard?"

He checked the urge to order everyone inside. He would give the yard a look, but the upcoming conversation needed to be private.

Putting his six grocery bags on the table, he wondered how long before Anna hit him with questions.

He didn't wait long.

"Are you going to explain?"

"We have to talk."

She slammed the refrigerator door after putting the milk away. "Obviously."

He watched his children playing with his mother. After this failed attempt, it was doubtful they'd try again so soon. They'd need to regroup. Even so, there wasn't much time.

Dammit, he didn't want her to find out like this. But there was no other way. Someone had tried to grab Rafe. Did they know who he was? Or was this revenge against a "dead" man?

He turned back to her. "I think you should sit down." She needed to know the danger he'd put them in, as much as he wanted to protect her from it.

"That bad?" she asked, leveling him with a hard look as she sat.

"The driver of the van purposely headed for Rafe." The thought alone flooded him with rage. They wouldn't get his family!

They'd have to go through him first.

"Excuse me?" she said, a nervous laugh trailing off.

"Someone tried to take him. I saw the van door open and a man, dressed in black, reached out to grab him."

She shot to her feet, slapped her hands on the table and leaned across it. "And you didn't let me call the police? I can't believe this, Gage! You save my son from a possible kidnapping and then rush us out of there? We have to get them!"

"We can't call the police."

"Who are you to decide? Someone tries to take *my* son and you think you're going to keep me from calling the police?" She marched to the phone and had two numbers punched in before he seized it from her grasp. Infuriated, she made to grab it back, but he put the cordless on the counter and grasped her upper arms.

"Listen to me, Anna. Listen. You can't call them. There's too much you don't know and they can't help us, anyway."

She pulled away, backed up a few steps and studied him. Emotions fired across her face until only wariness and, thank God, anger remained. Anger he could deal with.

"Tell me why we can't call the police."

Proud of her for holding it together, regardless of the tremor in her voice, his view of her changed again. She might hate him for all this, but she wouldn't break.

"Because we can't tell them who I really am." He took a deep breath and sent a rusty prayer to the heavens. "I'm the reason they tried to grab Rafe."

"What?" she scoffed, but her eyes remained glued to his.

No matter how he told her this, she'd be confused and scared. "I think someone has found out who I am and tried to take Rafe for revenge."

The silence hung suspended before she burst out. "Well, who are you?"

He looked at the shiny floor, fighting himself. As badly as he wanted to tell her, he didn't want to see her hate for him.

"I'm surprised you don't know. I made a mistake with the yo-yo. I hadn't been thinking straight..."

He stopped talking as horror widened her eyes.

"Who...are...you?"

"You know. Your heart knows."

You know.

The ice trickling through her made it difficult to breathe, difficult to think, difficult to push the echoes from her mind. And she desperately needed to think, to make sense of nonsense, separate nightmare from reality.

Your heart knows.

Everything inside her abruptly went numb. Her mind became a blank space, incapable of conjuring up a response, her feelings deadened. She floated there for a minute, in that peaceful, white cloud of nothingness until she became aware of his voice and its urgency.

"Bella?"

With one word, he shattered her. It was like being frozen cold, then blasted with heat; pinpricks of pain raced through her body, bringing to life nerves long cold.

But she didn't welcome the familiar warmth following the thaw and strove for control in those tension-riddled seconds.

"What did you say?" Disappointment weighed heavy. She'd begun to care for him, coming alive with feelings that died with Rico.

"I called you 'Bella.'"

In a flash she remembered him using the nickname as he handed Rafe to her in the parking lot. "Don't call me that! You have no right!"

"I have every right. I'm the only one who's ever shortened your name to it."

Chest heaving, she fought her rising hysteria. With measured breaths, she pushed the words past her clenched teeth. "I want you out of my house. Now."

"I'm not going anywhere. I know this is hard for you. I know I sound crazy. But it's true."

She started taking sideways steps from the kitchen to the den's sliding glass doors.

"It's me," he burst out to stop her retreat. "Rico!"

She blanched and froze. "How dare you! What kind of sick game are you playing?"

"It's the truth. My name is Americo Stephano Carella, named for Papa's Italian relatives. My twin was Rafael Esteban Carella, named for Mama's Spanish family. We were born on Mischief Night...."

"You could have gotten that information anywhere!" she interrupted hotly.

"The first night we made love, you came out of the hotel bathroom in a short white nightgown you had saved up for. You wore your hair loose the way I loved it. You never knew how nervous I was, how scared I'd hurt you and you'd never want me again...."

"Enough!" she shouted, breaking into his relentless remembrance. "I don't know who told you these things or why you're saying them, but the proof you need is something you can never have! You look nothing like him. *Nothing!* How could you think I'd believe this insanity?"

In an abrupt move he tilted his head back and reached up to an eye. What was he doing? Maybe I should call the police. He could be dangerous. He could be...

Her thoughts ended as she realized Gage pulled a contact lens from his eye. Without looking at her, he removed the other and laid them on the table.

Then he faced her without blinking.

"Oh...my...God." She blindly reached out a hand and braced herself against the glass door, vaguely registering its warmth. Black dots swam before her eyes, and anger and a dizzying loss of blood added to her faintness.

Because glowing golden eyes watched her—not velvety brown.

Her son, Rafe's eyes.

Rico's eyes.

He took a step toward her. "No, stay…there," she choked out, needing the space separating them. Was it possible? Could Rico really be alive? Tears burned her eyes while unbridled hope grew, fueled by the many odd coincidences since Gage's arrival.

"Just sit down. I don't want you falling. I can't catch you from here."

Anna slid down the wall, lowered her head and began massaging her temples. She waited for the barrage of questions to hit, but curiously there were none.

Finally, she looked at him and then quickly away. It hurt too much to look into those eyes. With a deep breath she clenched her teeth and met his gaze. "This…you can't be alive." Her hands lay palms up on her knees. She had no strength to move them.

"But I am." His voice, huskier than usual, rolled over her in a gentle wave.

"How?" she barely whispered.

"How," he repeated. His chest expanded and eyebrows rose. "Let's break this down a little. Your question covers a lot of ground." As if afraid of spooking her, he lowered himself to the floor across from her. "My funeral was staged by the government for two reasons. One, they didn't believe I'd live more than a few days, anyway. Second, they wanted to protect my mother and anyone else associated with me."

Seconds ticked past. "From who?"

"From the people who did this to me," he said in a low voice, the bright sunlight highlighting the weaving pink and white scars on the hand gesturing to his face.

She shook her head and he hurried on. "I know this is going to be hard to understand, so bear with me. I joined a group after reenlisting. Our missions were covert, known only to the men who sent us on them. We went to different places all over the world to gather information or for surveillance. On one of those assignments, two of us gained access to the specified area and, after getting what we needed, we were caught leaving. Only one of us could get away. He did. The people who caught me were upset and wanted answers I couldn't give them. After I was rescued, I needed plastic surgery to fix all the bones. This is the result.''

Anna relaxed against the wall and folded her arms across her chest. Either this was shock or subconsciously she realized the truth a while ago, she admitted to herself.

The more he spoke, her astonishment about his identity transformed into certainty. His eyes were more than evidence enough, but his patronizing explanation reminded her of all the talks they'd had before about the military. He would give her the bare facts to placate her, and many times she had let him in order to avoid their opposing opinions over army procedures and ideas.

But not this time.

''I need a drink. Do you want anything?''

He shook his head.

She stood, stiffening against the unsteadiness until it passed. Skirting around him, she went into the kitchen and calmly, as if none of the past fifteen minutes had happened, she poured herself a Coke.

He's alive.

She squeezed her eyes shut, then opened them and glanced into the den. He was still there.

''This cannot be happening,'' she whispered, and took another sip. Maybe I'm dreaming. Or hallucinating. She put the glass onto the counter and pinched herself.

Damn.

Okay, get a hold of yourself, Anna. Now is not the time to get punchy. Dear God, someone tried to take Rafe.

She drained her soda and washed the glass by hand, all the while pushing away the questions from her heart. Her family was in danger and she needed details.

She dried her hands on a towel, then carefully placed it on the butcher-block island. Sucking in a fortifying breath, she strode into the den and sat back down on the floor.

She forced herself to look at him. *Rico*. Steeling her heart, she asked calmly, "Is that everything?"

His half nod, half shrug answered for him.

"Bull," she said.

He looked startled.

"I'm surprised you think I'd accept that."

"It's the truth," he all but stuttered.

She rested her chin on her bent fingers and gave him a stare designed to unsettle him.

"What exactly do you want to know that I didn't tell you?" he asked in guarded words.

Men. He gave her a story with more holes than Swiss cheese and expected her to accept it. Just comes back from the dead and expects her to smile and throw a welcome-home party.

She had questions now, plenty of them. And that didn't even count the ones about her and Rico.

"These people you went after...who were they? What did you get from them? Where were the rest of the men you were with, and why didn't they help you? Why didn't the other guy stay instead of you? How long did those animals use you as a punching bag? Why are these animals still running around after you if you're 'dead?' What other injuries did they cause? And don't downplay it, because I've seen you limp and wince when you thought no one was looking. Your hands are a wreck and your whole body shape is different. And last, at least for the moment, you say the government expected you to die and staged the funeral. So why haven't you gotten in touch with us sooner? What in God's name have you been doing for the last nineteen months?"

Rafe's voice floated into the den counting from one to ten and ending with a bellowing, "Here I come!"

"That's some list," he said at last, watching her warily.

"And you're going to answer each and every one of them," she ordered. "But first you're going to answer this. Why did they try to grab Rafe and not you, if they want to get revenge?"

He rubbed a hand along the back of his neck. "The only reason I can think of is to get to me. They can't do more physical damage without killing me. Kidnapping Rafe, taking my son, would hurt me far more than broken bones."

His son. Yet another issue they needed to discuss. One that took a bit of the wind out of her sails. How long had he known about the twins? Did he ever plan on seeing them or becoming a part of their lives? And what about her? Where did she figure into his plans? Those questions and many others would have to wait. Only her children's safety mattered now. She couldn't let violence touch their innocent lives.

Standing and facing the lake, she was surprised to see small swells rolling gently to the shore. Her children played hide-and-seek while Lina sat watching them. How could everything look the same when her whole world had been turned upside down?

Get a grip, she sighed, giving herself a mental kick. You can't fall apart now. And you definitely can't throw yourself into the arms behind you. Definitely not.

"Anna?"

Hiding her yearning and fear, she faced him. "How do we keep the children safe? Can't the police do anything?"

"We can't involve them. I'm not sure who the Balangerios are using as an informant. I'll call a few friends and have some men sent in."

His clipped sentences were like cold stakes, pounding the seriousness of the situation into her. "I see. So you think someone local, someone I may know, is working for these people?"

"Yes."

Oh, damn. "That's impossible. I mean, maybe they have someone watching, but to suggest I could know their informant is ridiculous." The revulsion of such an idea had her wrapping her arms around her middle. "The people I'm close to would never work for those monsters. No. Never. You're wrong."

"You may be right," he said softly, putting a hand on her arm.

She jerked away, bumping into the wall. The look on his face was terrible, and he slowly dropped his hand to his side. She opened her mouth to explain, to take away his hurt.

But how could she explain that she needed his touch as much as she feared it?

She cleared her throat. "When will you call your friends?"

"Soon," he replied tonelessly.

"Until then?"

"Keep the children in the house. Make sure everything's locked."

"What about Lina? Are you going to tell her who you...who you really are?"

Catlike moves had him at the kitchen door before she finished speaking. He halted and looked back over one shoulder, all but his eyes in shadow. The color of beaten gold, they regarded her with such pain that tears welled up and blurred his image but could not drown out his words.

"Why? Do you think she wouldn't wish me still dead?"

Chapter 5

Her protest swallowed by the sound of the screen door slamming, Anna dashed stray tears off her cheeks and ran to the door. Already across the road, he was inside his house before she could yell out.

He couldn't possibly believe I'd want him dead. He's the father of my children, the only man I've ever loved. He knows me better than that.

Her own words were a reminder that Rico hadn't known her at all.

Rebecca's high-pitched giggle jolted her. Striding into the kitchen, she rid her face of the traces of tears and called everyone into the house.

"But, Mommmmmm, I want to stay outside," Rafe whined.

"I was thinking you guys might like to watch the new Disney movie I bought today."

Five minutes later the twins were leaning against giant pillows in the den and drinking juice, already absorbed in the newest animation.

"What's going on, Anna?" Lina asked. "And don't you

give me that innocent look. Why would you pull them inside on a beautiful day like this?''

Opening her mouth to respond, she was interrupted.

"I think I can explain," Rico said from outside the screen door. Her pulse did a funny little skip at the sight of him, an eerie déjà vu feeling reminding her of her response to Gage. Which had actually been a response to Rico. Oh, Lord!

He opened the door and shouldered his way in, almost losing his sunglasses in the process. "I'll be moving in for a while."

Two duffel bags hit the floor hard.

"Excuse me?" she asked, incredulous. How could she keep from touching him if he lived with her? Better yet, how could she keep her heart from being broken a second time?

Lina watched the by-play with great interest. "Explain please. What exactly happened while I sat outside?"

Rico walked past them, peering over the countertop that served as a wall between the kitchen and the sunken den. The children hadn't noticed his arrival.

"Anna, is there somewhere we can talk?" he asked in a neutral voice while he walked back and methodically locked the screen and solid wood doors.

"Can't it wait until later when they're asleep?"

"No."

Just looking at him and knowing who he was made it hard to think straight. Taking a deep breath, she went into the other room. "Kids, we'll be in the dining room if you need me. Okay?"

They both nodded, never taking their eyes from the screen.

Spinning on a heel without looking at Lina, she led the way to the dining room, a shaky feeling in the pit of her stomach. She slid wood-and-glass doors from between the walls, closing them off in the room, but still enabling her to see in the direction of the den.

"What's going on?" Lina finally asked, anxiety threading her voice. "Why did Gage lock the doors?"

"Everything's going to be fine. Really," she said at Lina's suspicious look. She pulled out a dining room chair and gestured to it. "But I want you to sit down. There are a few things you need to know. It's all going to be hard for you to understand. I'm still having a hard time with it myself…"

"Anna! Tell me what's going on!"

"Lina." Rico pulled his hand away from the blue venetian blinds he'd been looking through. "I lied to you."

"What?"

"I lied. I'm not Gage Moran."

"What do you mean?" she interrupted. "Who are you, then?"

"I'm Rico. Your son."

Lina's dark-brown eyes darted from him to Anna and back, completely confused.

"No, you're not," she said with a nervous chuckle and looked at Anna. "What kind of sick game is this?"

"It's not a game, Lina," she answered.

"My sons are dead! How can you be so cruel?" Her white-knuckled hands pushed her out of the chair, and her lower lip shook from her shuddering breaths. "They're dead!"

"No, Mama. No. I'm right here."

Lina's head shook from side to side as she denied his claim and her own hope. Anna put her hands out to stop Lina's exit, when Rico broke out with a torrent of Spanish.

Lina stilled. Her eyes rounded and an unsteady hand lifted to cover her mouth. Anna eased her back down into the chair, worried by the shaking that swept through the older woman's body.

Rico slowly bent to his knees beside the chair, not quite hiding a wince.

"You're not Gage Moran?"

"In name only."

Lina's hands balled in her lap while a crazy hope lit her eyes. Reaching out with shaking hands, she gently removed his glasses. Even Anna held her breath as Rico opened his eyes.

"Madre de Dios!" she whispered, shock sweeping away her color as she hurriedly crossed herself a few times.

"Sí, Mama, es Americo," he whispered. "It's really me."

"How?" she choked out, anguish making her accent thicker than usual. "My baby, what happened to you? Who changed you?"

Placing his hands over hers on his face, he said, "It's a long story, Mama."

"I can't believe this. I can't believe you're alive!" Her tears dripped into her wide smile, but she didn't notice, so busy she was touching Rico. "You know then about the children?" She continued at his nod. "Then you must know the truth about what happened…"

Anna's heart clenched at the thought of Lina's confession, but Rico interrupted. "Mama, I know there's a lot to talk about, but there's something else I need to tell you."

"Wait." Leaning over, she gathered Rico to her, her arms surrounding him. Brushing the ebony hair away from his face, she whispered against his temple, "Just let me hold my son."

Anna stepped backward to the doors. Relief, love and even sadness haunted Rico's face. Remorse pierced her. She hadn't rejoiced in his return and thanked God. She hadn't hugged him or kissed him. She hadn't reached out to him and had pulled away the only time he tried to touch her. What kind of welcome had she given him, after all he'd been through?

None.

He may not know her anymore, but Anna wasn't sure she liked the person she'd become.

Carefully laying the cooked lasagna noodle in the pan, Anna tried not to look at the clock again. Rico and Lina were still talking in the dining room, and she wondered if her supposed infidelities had come up in the past half hour. Did he know yet there hadn't been other men? Did he feel guilty for leaving her or glad he'd gotten to see the world and not tied himself down in marriage with a woman he didn't trust?

The rest of the noodles in place, she spooned in the sauce and meat mixture, vaguely registering the Disney music crescendoing from the den.

What did he think of her now? She knew Gage found her attractive, so that meant Rico still wanted her. But was that enough? Passion and her love hadn't been enough to keep them together before. Besides, was Rico what she wanted?

She added a layer of mozzarella and ricotta cheese without looking at the ticking clock. What would happen now? Could they protect their children?

A nagging headache pushed her to the aspirin by the sink. Swallowing two, she looked out the window over the sink as the incredible realization swept through her again. Rico's alive! He's here, in my home, in my life. Alive. Every time she started to think of the past, the knowledge that he was alive would steal the breath from her and she would relive the disbelief and hope all over again.

The dining room doors slid open roughly, the sound causing her heart to beat at a dizzying level. She quickly picked up the spatula in a weak attempt to look busy. They came walking out, Rico's arm resting around his mother's shoulder, her own around his waist. Putting on a bright smile, she said to Lina, "How are you?"

"I've been given a miracle from God," she said reverently, smiling up at her son. "Thank the heavens I told my neighbors I was moving to Idaho with you. It would have been harder for him to find me!" She wrapped her other arm around his front and hugged him to her. "But hearing the rest of his news has me hoping it won't be taken away."

Anna finally glanced at Rico. The force of his gaze seared her and she looked away quickly, not wanting him to see the raw emotions running through her.

He hadn't looked for her. He'd been looking for his mother and found his children. Oh, God. Why should the thought hurt so? "I'm sure nothing like that will happen," she murmured, adding another layer to the lasagna.

"Here, Anna. Let me finish this. Why don't you and—" she chuckled over her hesitation "—you and Rico talk?"

"We have nothing to say," she said hollowly. "He needs to make calls before we'll know how to protect the children."

Silence followed her remark.

"We have more to talk about than the children."

A slight thrill chased up her spine, even as she tamped it down. Her body betrayed her even as her heart hurt from this newest kind of betrayal. Remember what he did in the past, she told herself. Remember how easily he walked away. Stayed away. "No, we don't," she returned, spinning to face him. "We have only the children to discuss."

Locked in visual combat, she heard Lina slide the lasagna into the oven and leave the room.

Rico crossed his muscular arms over his chest and leaned back on his heels, looking relaxed and dangerous. "Nothing to discuss," he repeated. "Who are you trying to fool? Me? Or yourself?"

"I'm not trying to fool anyone," she said through clenched teeth. "According to you, the twins are in danger. Because of you, I have to be worried my children will be hurt. Now, if you think this is going to be a grand opportunity for you to walk back into my life, after everything you've done, and pick up where you left off, you're wrong. There is no you and me. You made sure of that years ago. Now the only discussions we'll be having will be about the children."

She looked away from those disturbing eyes and started slapping place mats onto the table. His silence stretched for so long she had to force herself not to look at him.

His voice, when it finally came, was a cross between a growl and purr. "You and I are not over. Yes, we have a lot to talk about." He paused, and his voice dropped even lower as he turned her to face him. "I know I hurt you. But I promised I'd always come back for you. I'm keeping my promise, Bella.''

As if she'd stepped back in time, the unconditional love and tenderness she'd always felt for him washed over her, waves of it willing her to forget the past few years. She swayed, leaning into the strong hands on her shoulders.

''I even understand why you needed to...*be* with other men and I forgive you. You were young and you'd never been with anyone but me. I wasn't around enough.''

He forgave her.

''You're so tense,'' he said soothingly, his fingers massaging her neck and shoulders in circular motions.

Bitter fury bubbled into her throat like an acid, eating away the weakening tenderness. Lina hadn't told him. She hadn't told him about the lies.

But how dare he! How dare he come back into her life, as accidental as it obviously was, discover his children and still believe the lies about her! Believe she'd cared so little for him that she'd made love with anyone else.

And how dare he forgive *her!* Damn him.

''Get your hands off me.'' She concentrated on saying the words calmly, fighting the urge to scream them.

''What, Bella?'' he answered, absorbed in his massage techniques.

She jerked away from his touch and looked up. Again the impact of his strange, familiar face slammed into her defenses, but this time she didn't give in.

She wasn't a girl anymore. She wouldn't bow out of a confrontation or clash of wills.

Rico needed to learn how much things had changed. How much she changed.

''I am not, nor will I ever again be your 'Bella.' You are staying in my home to protect the children. You came back here, I assume, to protect them and your mother. While you are here, you are not to lay a finger on me. No more kisses, no more casual touches. And you are not to tell the children who you really are. Not until this is over. Is that understood?''

A muscle moved rhythmically in his jaw, keeping time with the ticking of the clock's second hand. ''Giving orders?''

She almost flinched from his whiplash question.

''I assumed you'd know how to follow them after all these years of training,'' she shot back with a sarcastic purr.

He took a step closer. His shirt brushed against hers. The insides of his boots bracketed her sneakers. His head bent down to her. She knew it was an intimidation tactic, and even as it worked it infuriated her.

''I agree to your 'terms.' But add my own.'' He lowered his head so close she could see the flecks of topaz glittering in his eyes. ''When we kiss, and I promise you we will, it'll be because you *ordered* me to. Is that understood?''

She sucked in a breath, pressing her lips together to hold back her instinctive denial. He knew she wanted him and had no problem using it against her. Damn him.

Don't react, Anna. Act. ''Is that a promise?''

The implication was not lost on him. He nodded, his nose brushing hers.

''Good. Because it will be a cold day in hell before I order you to kiss me. It's not like you're my only choice should the need hit.''

With what she hoped resembled a cold smile, she moved away, unintentionally brushing against him. His eyes flared with emotions she wasn't about to stay and figure out.

Even she knew when to retreat and regroup.

''Mommmmm! 'Becca threw her bread at me!''

''Did not!''

''Did, too!''

Had she ever been more tired in her whole life? Even working eight hours a day while pregnant had been easier than this emotional roller coaster she couldn't get off.

"Both of you stop. If you're playing with your dinner, then you're done eating it. It's time for your bath."

Ignoring the twins' groans, Lina's silent disapproval and Rico's blatant stare, she carried her plate to the sink. The children followed and saved her yet again from having to say anything to the adults. She wasn't trying to ignore Lina, but it was so hard to see the happiness on her face. It made her angry and jealous, of all things! He'd come for Lina, not her. Admitting it to herself made her feel even worse.

In a way she even hoped Lina wouldn't confess about the past. He hadn't tried to find her, and he still believed she had betrayed him. If he had searched and "forgiven" the past, she would have wanted Lina to shout her innocence. It would have helped heal things.

"Here, Mom," Rafe said, handing her his plastic plate, Goofy's face hidden under tomato sauce.

Rebecca followed suit before skipping back to Rico.

"Want to help us take our baths, Mr. Moran?"

Her daughter's voice scraped across her thin patience like nails on a chalkboard. As thankful as she'd been at the time, her children's unquestioned acceptance of Rico's moving in would make some things more difficult for her.

"'Gage,' remember?" As she headed for the stairs, she saw him scoop Rebecca up into his arms. "How am I going to help?"

"You have to make sure we don't splash too much or swim underwater too much. Mom says it's dan-ger-ous," she explained, mimicking Anna's warning.

"Your mom's right," she heard him answer from the twins' bedroom.

She turned on the taps, squirted in some bubbles and stood, pressing her hands against her back and stretching. She stopped dead when she caught her image in the mirror.

Oscar the Grouch had nothing on her.

Her hair was a mess from her frustrated fingers, her clothes bore remnants of dinner, hopefully from little hands and not her own, her paleness held a twinge of green and definite meanness pinched her eyes and mouth.

For a minute pride battled with feminine vanity. Let him see what she looked like after taking care of two energetic kids and a house. She wasn't a teenager who had all day to style her hair. Then again, days like today only happened in soap operas, she reasoned, and her personal makeup artist had split between takes.

My God, look what's happened to me. Just this morning, I was a sane, happy woman. Now I'm standing here, having a conversation with myself and I'm losing. So, okay, Rico has come back from the dead and someone tried to kidnap Rafe. You can handle it! You're strong. You're intelligent.

"If you stare at the mirror any harder, it'll shatter." The amused voice silenced her pep talk.

She turned to see Rico leaning against the door frame, his white dress shirt open at the bottom and anchored behind each pocketed hand. The small triangle revealed abdominal muscles that created rippling shadows down to his jeans, the gold metal zipper winking at her.

Realizing suddenly why the fly had become so obvious, she glanced up, hoping he hadn't noticed she noticed.

A small smile quirked his mouth, and eyebrows arched over heated eyes.

"Do you have a question to ask?" he cajoled, his husky voice causing unseen tremors in her.

Because she didn't trust her voice, she glared until he chuckled and left.

She looked back into the mirror at the added pink flush on her cheeks.

Now, you're drooling.

She sank into the mattress, the cool goose down pillows cradling her pounding head, the covers embracing her aching body. *Tomorrow I'll handle everything so much better. Tomorrow Rico can tell me about the people he's been talking* to on his computer since bathtime. He'll have a solid plan for protecting the children, with trained people to help. Tomorrow I'll talk to Lina, put my behavior down to shock and be happy she has her son back. Just a few hours' sleep, even if they aren't deep and dreamless, and I'll be able to handle Rico.

Checking the clock again, she realized her alarm would go off in thirty minutes. She would check the kids, peek through some blinds and try to sleep some more. This might not be the best plan, but Rico hadn't parted from his computer long enough to discuss the nighttime guard.

Rico.

No, stop thinking. Twenty-nine minutes till the alarm. Count sheep. Furry, white sheep jumping over a fence.

The loose floorboard at the top of the stairs creaked. Her eyes flew open. One of the twins? No, she would have heard them pass her room. Lina had moved upstairs into the guest room so they were all on the same floor. Rico was on the computer in the kitchen or asleep on the pull-out couch. She slid her hand up under her pillow and curled it around the handle of the hammer she had grabbed thinking she should have some sort of defense just in case.

Fear chilled her.

A large form, shadowed by the hall nightlight, filled her doorway. She relaxed.

"You can stop sneaking around," she growled.

"How did you know it was me?" Rico whispered back, moving into her room.

How did she? "I just did. How did you get up the stairs so quietly?"

"I skipped the ones that make noise."

She silently applauded that painful maneuver. He must have done two to three at a time to be so quiet. "Next time be loud. I'll assume it's not a murderer."

He didn't answer, and she closed her eyes, praying for unconsciousness. One sheep, two sheep...

"You've been amazingly calm about this situation."

Now he wants to talk.

"Would you rather I have a breakdown?" she murmured, wondering idly if she really was, while ignoring the fact that he sat on her bed. Sleep. Let me fall asleep.

"No. I expected more questions or yelling."

Ah. The light dawns. "You expected me to blame you, right?"

Silence.

"What do you mean?" he asked warily.

"You expected me to blame you and hold you responsible for Rafe's almost-kidnapping and the violent people who want to hurt my children." Three sheep, four sheep…

A half snort, half laugh, then, "You always did know what I was thinking."

Her fifth sheep crashed into the fence. "No, I didn't. Or I would have known you didn't trust me." She sat up and arranged the sheet and light blanket around her as he swung to face her in the semidarkness. She held up a hand and halted the words about to come from his open mouth. "No, now is not the time to argue about what happened years ago. If you're determined to ruin my sleep, you can tell me how we're going to keep us safe."

She could hear him grinding his teeth. So, who cares if he's mad?

"There are two agents outside right now watching the house."

"Wait a minute, I thought you said before that you moved in here to protect us, but that you still want everyone to think you're Gage."

"Right. I'm not positive the Balangerios know who I really am, so we're going to have to play this off as a whirlwind affair."

"The problem with that plan is everyone who knows me will find the idea suspicious. Also, if you really believe I could know the informant, don't you think he or she is going to notice two men in an unmarked car?"

He stifled his laughter and lowered his voice. "You've been watching too much television. You can look, but I guarantee you won't know they're there."

If her legs didn't feel like dead weights she would go and look. "So the good guys are skulking with the bad guys. I feel much better."

He ignored her sarcasm. "Tomorrow two others will take over. Our job will be to make a list of people you're in contact with. We'll go over them one by one until we figure out who's been watching you."

"I forgot to ask how you found out someone's watching us."

"I got an e-mail from Mike."

"Your partner," she prodded.

"Yeah. It was a sentence we came up with in D.C. to use if anyone started digging into Gage Moran's background. I've only given the name here, so I'm upsetting someone."

He'd showered. The scent of soap mixed with warm male wrapped around her. She took a deep breath, searching her blank brain for something to say.

He beat her to it. "Why would your friends become suspicious of my moving in?" A hand sank into the mattress next to her, bringing his leaning body closer. "I mean, you said you'd have no trouble finding another man should the 'need hit.'"

She really wasn't up to this right now. The only solution was to derail him. She sighed heavily and affected a bored tone, "Contrary to what you believe about me, I've never had men stay the night to be discovered by the twins the next morning, and my friends know this. Your moving in will look suspicious because we could easily have an 'affair' and you could walk home in the wee hours without the twins finding out. So why move in?"

She couldn't see his features clearly, but she knew he was angry. Very angry.

The silence stretched and she wavered on the idea of retrieving the gauntlet she'd thrown down.

"I see. So to convince everyone, we'll have to show them how impossible it is to keep our hands off each other. I moved in so we could be together all the time, which they'll correctly translate means having sex whenever we have a minute alone. Since your friends know you so well, they won't be surprised by your taking in a stranger to satisfy your insatiable *needs*, will they?"

It wasn't a question. With every word, he'd moved closer, his features coming into focus to match his hard, mocking whisper. Even though she played on his bad opinion of her, his insults hurt.

"And don't worry," he continued. "Our agreement still stands. I won't kiss you until you order me to. But," he added, a finger coming up to gently swipe her bottom lip, "we'll have to put on a convincing show for anyone who stops by. You'll have to act like a woman in…lust. I'm sure you've had enough practice."

She wanted to tell him where to put his act, but couldn't speak past the lump in her throat.

"Your voice when you talk to me, your body language, everything needs to show how in tune we are. Two people who know each other inside and out, totally familiar with each other's bodies. You know what kiss will weaken, which touch will heighten the pleasure. I'm sure you remember how it was between us, don't you, Bella?"

How could she be so hurt and seduced by him at the same time? He truly believed her to be no better than the women who walked the streets outside their old Miami homes. Where was the Rico who protected her, cared for her, dreamed with her?

And who were the women who'd weakened him with kisses and touched him so intimately? How many were there? Pain exploded through her chest as images flashed behind her eyes, hurting her far more than his low opinion of her.

Boy, he'd get such a laugh if he knew the truth about her experiences. She needed him out of her room so she could ease this incredible aching in her chest. She couldn't let him see what his words were doing to her. She cleared her throat and tried to cover it by rearranging the covers around her.

"Actually, I don't remember what it was like…with you. But I'm sure I can take from my other experiences and come up with a star performance. Now, if you don't mind, I need to get some sleep. The children get up very early."

She uncurled her legs, but his body stopped her from stretching out. She didn't meet his gaze. Couldn't. She reached behind her and fluffed her pillows, reset her alarm clock, praying he'd leave.

Finally he stood and walked out. She slid back down onto her side and pulled the covers up to her neck, a pillow to her chest. She waited for his feet on the stairs, afraid to even breathe and have tears escape.

All of a sudden he was back.

"We need everyone, children included, to believe we're together." He ignored her protesting noise and dropped two pillows onto the carpet, making his bed parallel to hers. "I'll stay on the floor tonight. I'm going to be up and down a lot, and one of us should sleep. By morning I'm climbing into that bed with you. They won't understand me sleeping on the floor. I don't want information like that to slip out when we have company."

He unfolded a blanket, knelt down, then hesitated, his head visible from where hers was buried in her pillows. For a crazy moment she thought his hand reached out to her, but then realized it was her imagination. She could hardly see him and prayed she was just as invisible.

If not, he'd see the tears she could no longer hold inside.

Chapter 6

She cried last night.

Rico slapped the pen down onto the table and sat back. The concentration he needed so badly was blown apart by the same recurring thought.

She cried last night.

He'd been hard on her. Too hard. He should've stayed away from her room, but he'd been frustrated by her evasive tactics. All night she'd avoided looking at him. The few times he'd caught her eyes, he'd been unable to discern the emotions in them. Then bam! Nothing.

And that made him want to shake her. And kiss her. He'd never had trouble reading her emotions before, but now he was lucky if he read one. Especially since she'd found out the truth.

He sighed and rubbed his hands up and down his face hard, ignoring the twinge along his temple. He dozed ten minutes at a time all night, then woke to listen to the house's sounds. When dawn slid into Anna's room, the silver light brought relief. He'd stood and watched her sleep, her small hand curled under her chin, and he fought himself. He'd almost given in to the unnecessary threat and crawled into bed with her, but he didn't trust himself. He wanted her too badly.

He had to protect her. But right now the danger to her wasn't unknown. The danger to her was him.

He chuckled softly. It was all too ironic.

"Lina, I don't want you to tell him about the lies."

"Why would you not want the truth known?"

Anna paced to the end of the hallway, away from the big ears in the bedroom. "I don't think it would do any good."

Shrewd eyes measured her. How could she explain this, when in truth, it didn't make much sense to her? She was sure of only a few things. Rico had not come here for her. He still believed she slept with other men while they'd been together. He desired her. He wanted to be a part of his children's lives. If he found out the truth, would he then want to be with her? Would he then assume they'd live happily ever after? Or would it be easier to walk away again?

"You want him to love you, don't you, *hija?*" The question, in the Spanish-accented compassion, made tears sting her eyes.

"I don't know. I just don't know. The only thing I do know is I want you and my children safe. Nothing matters more."

Lina puttered in the linen closet, rearranging folded towels. "Ignoring Rico will not make him go away. Even as a boy, he did not give up on things. The more I tried to stop him, the harder he tried." She closed the door. "I know you do not believe this, *hija,* but he loves you. I can see it in his eyes. I don't like keeping the truth from him, and he will not be happy with me, but I owe you." She smiled and reached out to caress Anna's cheek. "I understand your worry. I want you to believe in his love. Believe it is real and not based on lies. So, I will not tell him. Not yet."

Anna sucked in a steadying breath. "Thank you."

"Thanks for what?" a deep voice rumbled.

She swung around and saw Rico standing at the top of the stairs. How much had he heard?

"Did they teach you how to eavesdrop, too?" she snapped, her rudeness due more to the strange looks he'd been giving her all day. It unsettled her.

He didn't question the *they*. "Yes."

Nonplused, she stared at him.

"Gage! Gage! Can we go outside yet?" Rafe asked, a welcome distraction as he ran out of his room and wrapped himself around Rico's legs.

Anna caught his quick grimace, not knowing if it was caused by an injury to his legs or Rafe calling him by another name.

"No, not yet. We need to give it a few more hours."

Rico had told the children they couldn't play outside because he put chemicals on the lawn before they woke up. For some reason they didn't even ask why. God knows whenever she told them to do something they questioned it to death.

Death. Not exactly an appropriate word.

She worried her bottom lip, mentally chiding the morbid sense of humor she hadn't seen for years.

Rico and the twins had already headed down the stairs, and Lina stared bemused down the empty hall.

Anna remembered one of the promises she'd made to herself the night before. She turned and hugged Lina, then kissed her on the cheek.

"I'm so happy you have your son back," Anna whispered, realizing she genuinely meant it, regardless of what it meant for her own life.

Lina's eyes welled, but she blinked rapidly. Understanding lit her eyes. "I know you are, *hija*. But I thank you for saying it."

Anna hugged her again, wondering how Lina knew her so well. "I'm going downstairs. Remember what he said. Don't look out or stand by windows longer than necessary."

"I won't forget."

She nodded and left Lina straightening up the guest room she'd moved into. Although Rico hadn't pulled all the shades down or shut the blinds, he'd made it clear they should be careful. Daytime would be easier, but when they put on the inside lights tonight they'd have to avoid throwing their shadows.

The pounding on the side of her head increased, and she mentally kicked herself for not paying closer attention. She'd been calm all day, keeping the children occupied, answering the few questions Rico asked her while going through her address book. As much as she tried not to think about the danger around them, it was always there. A silent reminder that her once-peaceful home could become a battleground. The violence she'd tried so hard to leave in Miami had followed her here.

"Mom! Can we build somethin' in Grandma's room?"

"With Legos?" Rebecca said, ending her brother's question.

"Yes, but stay with her and sit on the floor to put them together."

They agreed and ran down the hallway. After listening to them explain to Lina what they wanted to do, she went downstairs to the kitchen. There was no sign of Rico, and she grabbed the aspirin bottle out of the cabinet.

"Are you okay?"

The aspirin bottle went flying, white pills bouncing around the counter and onto the floor. Swallowing her heart, she gripped the counter.

"Must you keep doing that?"

Footsteps audible, he crossed the kitchen. "I'm sorry. It's habit."

She glanced at him quickly, then back to the pills he was picking up. He apologized. Rico never apologized. Then again, they'd only fought once and never spoken again, but still, he wasn't the kind of man who admitted his mistakes.

"I jump at every little sound, yet I can't hear you! What if someone gets in the house? He could *skip* by me and I wouldn't even notice!''

He chuckled, the sound rumbling around in his chest without escaping. ''I want you aware, but the chances of someone getting by the men outside and me are slim.''

He knelt down, and the two of them picked up the sea of pills. Naturally, she'd dropped the brand-new, super-size economy bottle. A groan slipped from her when they dumped handfuls in the trash.

Just as they were finishing, he asked, ''Getting a lot of headaches?''

Of course he'd notice.

''Why?''

He gave her a look. ''The kids can't take these, and Mama avoids medication.''

''How do you know?''

The petty jab, born of frustrated anger, fear and heartache hit home. His face tightened, and he again became a stranger, making her realize how open his expression had been moments before.

''I'm sorry,'' she murmured. ''I didn't mean it to sound—''

''Forget it,'' he said, shoving himself up and moving stiffly to the table.

Self-disgust churned her stomach and did nothing for her head. She hadn't meant to hurt him, just push him out of her space. He walks back into her life and expects he can do anything, ask anything he wants. At the same time he'd been through pure hell, the depth of which she knew he'd never tell her.

''You're right. Your mother still avoids medication, but she does take vitamins.'' She poured herself water from the fridge and took three. She debated telling him more, but at this point it didn't matter. She turned and looked across the kitchen into his expressionless face. ''The aspirin are mine. Usually this is all I need, but sometimes I wait too long and have to take the stronger stuff.''

"For what?" he asked quietly.

"Migraines," she answered, capping the practically empty bottle and putting it away.

"You never got headaches before."

He looked angry, as if this change hadn't been approved by him.

"Well, I do now."

"Since when?"

She paused her folding of a hand towel. "Do you want the actual date?" she asked wryly, smiling a little in spite of her anxiousness.

"Yes."

She shook her head and glanced over at him. His arms folded across his chest, eyes narrowed and intent, he shouldn't have made her want to hug him.

She sighed. "I don't know. Years ago. Does it matter?"

"Do you realize you still answer a question with one when you don't want to answer it?"

She stilled. He was right. But why did he remember so much about a woman he didn't trust? Then again, why was he so curious about her?

"It started as headaches and the doctors thought they were a side effect of the pregnancy. When they got worse, they ran some tests to check for a tumor."

"A tumor!"

He'd shoved away from the half wall and approached her.

She held up a hand. "They didn't find anything."

He halted.

"Instead of getting better, they got worse and didn't stop after the twins were born. For a couple of years I gave myself shots."

Somehow she knew he held his breath and shrugged in a nonchalant way. It truly wasn't a big deal. At least, not something she couldn't deal with.

"You hate shots."

His flat announcement brought back a vivid memory. She,

Rico and Rafael had been sitting outside their houses. No breeze moved the summer night, forcing them out of their stifling homes. People milled about, and even though midnight had come and gone, cars drove by at a crawl while the passengers yelled and waved to friends. Everyone seemed intoxicated more by the humidity than liquor or drugs.

She'd been leaning on the porch railing, listening to Rico and Rafael argue sports when the bottles started flying from one of the cars. One hit her on the side of the head, another sliced her calf. Rico had been moving toward her as soon as it started and had scooped her up and into the house before the pain even registered. Rafael, true to nature, ran after the car with a bat, yelling curses the entire time. Rico took her to a medical clinic where they stitched her up and insisted on a tetanus shot. She'd always had a phobia about needles and argued persistently, but had been unable to talk the doctor out of it. She'd buried her face in Rico's neck and cried as he'd held her tight and murmured comforting words.

She'd remembered that, many times, while giving herself migraine shots. Many times she'd wanted someone to hold her when the needle pierced her skin and the pain in her head had her crying. But she'd learned well that when it came down to it, she could only count on herself.

"I still hate shots, but I didn't have a choice. Even though it's in pill form now, I sometimes need the shots if I wake up with one. Then it's too late for anything else to work."

He looked away from her, his lips flattened.

"It's really no big deal," she said, wondering why it bothered him so much.

He pinned her with an angry stare. "It is a big deal. They can't tell you why they keep happening?"

Sure she could, but oddly she didn't want him worried about something he couldn't control. The doctors felt stress was the biggest contributor, and she knew this situation would give her tons. She didn't need him to take on the Big Protector role again.

"Nope. They said one day they might stop. Now, let's work on these names," she said, and decided to grab a drink before they started.

"Have you seen an allergist?"

She sighed. "Yes."

"Neurologist?"

She fought to keep calm as she poured a coke. "Yes. She did a CAT scan and an MRI."

"What about—"

"What about," she said, slapping the empty can onto the counter, "you back off and drop the whole subject? You can't fix this. Even if you'd been around when I went through it, you wouldn't have been able to do anything."

An expression crossed his face too quickly for her to identify. He looked down and made piles of the papers and yellow legal pads he'd written on. Just as she was about to say something to break the tension, he spoke.

"But we'll never know if I could have helped, will we? Because, as you said, I wasn't here."

She opened her mouth to respond. His bitter self-recrimination should have been satisfying. After all, he admitted to not being around when he was needed. Then why did she feel so bad?

"Listen. What's done is done. You're here to help us now, right?"

He nodded, avoiding her eyes.

"Okay, then. Let's figure this out." She waited a few seconds to see if he would ignore her suggestion. Instead his shoulders relaxed and he nodded.

"Want a drink?"

"Yeah. Thanks."

She lifted her eyebrows at his tone and poured him a cola. When she turned to carry their drinks to the table, she saw him checking out the half-closed blinds—a chilling reminder to worry more about the danger they faced, rather than a past that could never be reborn.

"These are the people you said you see the most." He held up a pad, showing her the separated columns of names. She stood behind him and to the side, deciding it was the only way to keep enough space between them.

"These are the people you've worked with before and now. How many know about your life in Miami or about me."

"None," she responded flatly.

He stared up at her, disbelief and something else in his unfamiliar eyes. "No one?"

She shook her head.

"Why?"

She shrugged.

"Annabella…" His voice held an unspoken plea to confide in him.

"Don't call me that!"

He kept staring at her, making her stomach clench with all sorts of emotions.

"You didn't have to be embarrassed about telling people the truth. Single mothers aren't branded by society anymore. Besides, you know I'd have come back to you if I'd known about the children."

She sucked in air at the verbal slap.

"Wait, Anna. I just meant—"

"No! It doesn't matter what you meant. It really doesn't." The last she repeated for her heart, which was being cruelly squeezed by his words. She turned and took a few steps away, hurrying when she heard his chair scrape roughly across the floor. With the table between them, she reached across and pulled the legal pad to her.

"Which column do you want to start with?"

She ignored his curse. Staring at the names, but not reading them, she could see him out of the corner of her eye, raking a hand through his hair.

Finally he sat back down, and relief lowered her heart rate. She leaned on the chair with a one knee. Standing above him made her feel a little more relaxed.

"Start with the first one," he answered, coolly polite.

It was so easy for him to control his emotions.

She'd better start taking lessons.

An hour and a half later she pushed the pad across the table with more force than necessary. It glanced off his chest and gave her a childish satisfaction.

"This is ridiculous. That plumber was here three years ago! Don't you think he'd have done something by now?"

Rico massaged the bridge of his nose. "I'm not leaving anyone out. Have you seen him since?"

She had the strong urge to pout. "No."

"Then cross him off."

"Great. I'm feeling better already," she scoffed.

He ignored her. "I think we have a good preliminary list. Your aunt Clare, Brooke, Pete Joncaluso, Dana, your boss at the paper, your mailman and the Johnsons and the Burkes down the lane. They're the only ones who moved in after you.

"As far as brief contact, there are twenty or so possibilities…from the cashier at the supermarket to the woman who jogs by every morning."

Anna let her head fall back, the stretch loosening tense muscles. "Including Aunt Clare and Brooke is ridiculous. Couldn't it be someone I don't know who's watching the house?"

"Yeah, but it's unlikely. Whoever looked into my files started the day I arrived. Mike tried to track them, but they covered up well. He made sure it wasn't real estate agents for the house or insurance companies doing a routine background check." He leaned his elbows on the table. "We never figured someone would be suspicious right away. The odd thing is they started their check using my Gage social security number."

"How on earth did they get ahold of that?"

He rubbed the scar on his throat. "I don't know. I expected

it to start with that name or the license plate run on the Jeep. This changes things."

"I need the paper back," she said, reaching for the pen and catching the sliding yellow pad.

Before she could start writing, she saw him smile.

"What?"

"You always hated puzzles."

"Puzzles?"

"Yeah. Unanswered questions. Mysteries. They drove you crazy until you figured them out."

She shifted uncomfortably in her seat. "So?"

"So, you're doing it again. You're going to solve this. Not that I mind the help, it's just good to see some things never change."

His words tightened the cold band around her heart. "You're wrong. Everything changes."

She ignored what her words did to him and concentrated on writing down ways someone could get his social security number. After a few minutes she looked up to find his intent stare. "What have you used it for?"

"I can have Mike check the background ID again and see exactly what documents it's on. Offhand, it would be on credit card accounts, college transcripts, my driver's license."

She nodded and kept writing until a stray thought interrupted her. "How did you arrange to stay at Jim and Emily's?"

"Pure luck. Jim Henderson was in the military with my superior. He arranged it. They're at their daughter's, but they'll go on a month-long tour of England when they're ready, courtesy of the government."

"How...nice."

"The government can be generous."

She let that one go.

"All right, here's my list— Wait a minute. Why can't the person behind all of this be from the government?"

His eyes narrowed.

"Did you see *Clear and Present Danger?*"

He nodded.

"The secretary is having an affair with the drug dealer's right-hand man and inadvertently feeds him information. It could be someone in the office of your superior or someone with access to the computers."

She could practically see the faces of the people who worked for his boss as he mentally flipped through them.

"Could be," he murmured. "Girlfriend. Relative. Blackmailer." He flipped open his cellular, dialed and, after a few seconds of listening, punched in more numbers.

"Hey, Bonnie. Is Clyde there?" he said, a warm grin tugging his lips to the right. She fought the immediate questions that barraged her about the woman on the other end and concentrated on what was missing from his smile. New dental work. No, that wasn't it. Lips? No, the bottom was a bit fuller.

His mouth formed words, but she didn't hear them. He stopped talking, and the tip of his tongue slid along the bottom lip from corner to corner wetting it. The shine it left behind caused a blossom of heat to warm her stomach and spread to her toes and fingertips.

It reminded her of a night not so long ago, out on the porch, when moonlight had reflected off the shine on his lips after his mouth left hers.

The night she'd been wrapped in Gage's arms as he awakened her body with electric sensations.

Gage.

The name acted like a douse of cold water, and she realized Rico wasn't talking anymore. His face came into focus, his eyes watching her with heat in their depths. Somehow he'd known what she'd been thinking. Known one night she'd been on the verge of making love to another man.

"You okay?"

She nodded jerkily, her body still losing the effects of a memory.

He went to say something, then hesitated and cleared his

throat. "Mike wasn't home, Bonnie will let him know I called. I'll meet him online later."

She arched a brow.

"Bonnie is Mike's wife. She was pregnant when we were on the mission at the Balangerios. Every day Mike worried she'd deliver before we got home."

She took a shot in the dark. "He's the one you were with that night, isn't he? The one you made sure wasn't captured with you."

He nodded slowly. "He had a wife, a child on the way. A family. He had more to lose."

Seconds passed. A sweet ache spread up her chest, but she stifled it before it became tears. He let Mike go because Mike had a family. And because Rico didn't.

"I wrote to you when I found out about the pregnancy."

"What?" She wished he shouted the word. His stiff, hollow question made her wince even though the fault was not her own.

"I found out I was pregnant two weeks after...you left." She didn't say *fight,* didn't want to remind him of the other lie. She also didn't mention she'd been so violently ill from heartache and nerves, never realizing it could be due to something else. "I didn't know what to do. I finally wrote to tell you. I hoped you'd come back or at least help me decide what to do."

She forced herself to look at him. The naked pain on his face made her want to take back the words.

He leaned his elbows on the table and buried his face in his hands. Her heart fought the instinctive urge to reach out to him. Her head reminded her this wasn't her fault. She'd suffered for years because he didn't believe in her and couldn't forgive a lie.

He stood abruptly and averted his face, then walked to the bathroom off the foyer. The soft click of the shutting door echoed through the quiet like a shot. She looked around her kitchen, a room she'd spent years in every day and wondered why it looked so different. Why everything felt different.

She sat back in her chair, drained, and fighting righteous anger and tears. She wanted to feel only hate for the man who'd left her and never really loved her, a man just like her father. The man who'd come back searching for his mother. The man who lied and made her care and brought violence to threaten her children.

But she couldn't find any. She sat there searching her heart and found no hate, no joy in causing the same hurt she'd felt so many times. Instead, it was as though his pain had healed hers.

It was time to let it go.

He didn't love her. He'd left her. He'd found her only by accident. Then he'd lied to her and let her start caring for another man. One she could never have because he didn't really exist.

He walked fearlessly into violent situations and she couldn't watch the six o'clock news.

But he would have helped her had he known. She could see that from his reaction. He cared for her, if only because she was the mother of his children. He desired her, something she knew would not be enough. He would be a great father, and he loved his children.

He may not be husband material, but he was a good man.

The bathroom door opened and he walked out to the front of the house, moving silently into the living and dining rooms. Without looking at her, he walked back into the kitchen and into the family room, checking the windows. Unfortunately, the sun had set and the table light couldn't penetrate all the shadows and let her see his face.

He walked past her to the kitchen sink, leaning over to peer through partially closed blinds. Satisfied, he straightened, but kept hold of the edge of the sink.

Time ticked by, and Anna followed through with the resolution she'd come to. She pushed back her chair and ap-

proached him. Other than a stiffened spine, he made no move.
Staring at the middle of his back, she took a deep breath and
slid her arms underneath his, wrapping around to his front.
She laid her head on his warm back and hugged him, silently
trying to tell him she was sorry. That she understood what he
was feeling.

She didn't see the surprise on his face or see him look down
at the arms around him and close his eyes. She knew he held
his breath, but didn't know it was an attempt to control the
remorse and guilt and fear swirling inside him.

She had no idea how long they stood like that before he
spun in her arms and yanked her sideways to the floor, covering her body with his. Somehow he slowed their descent and
she didn't hit the linoleum hard. Just as she regained her
senses, he barely whispered, "Don't talk. Someone's on the
deck."

Fear flowed down her spine. He leaned up slightly, giving
her the room to tilt her head back to see his face.

What she saw chilled her more than the danger on the other
side of the wall. Alert, but otherwise tautly expressionless, he
was poised above her, listening intently.

Not three inches from her face was a gun.

Chapter 7

Rico's heart beat against her chest; his ribs pressed against hers. Fighting his weight, she pulled much-needed oxygen into her lungs. A peek away from the inverted *L* shape in his hand revealed no change in his expression, no relief for her panic.

Just then his hip started vibrating.

All kinds of unmotherly visuals colored her mind in scarlet waves. The heat of them flooded through her, ending in stinging flags across her cheeks.

He reached down, and she held her breath.

"It's okay now," he said, his hand coming back up with his beeper.

His vibrating beeper.

"What?" she asked, trying to appear coherent while relief left another kind of tension behind.

"It's safe," he answered, pushing a button and putting it back on his belt. Then he swiveled and put his gun in the back of his pants, the move pushing his hard chest into hers, making her fervently wish he would either get off or kiss her.

She barely bit back a groan as he finally started to get up, his hands on either side of her head. Then she made the mistake of locking gazes with him.

Noses practically touching, his breath teased her lips.

He's going to know, she thought, panicked. How pathetic am I to have these feelings when we're in danger?

"How do you know from your beeper that it's safe?" she said in a rush, while trying to squirm out from under him.

She froze as he answered physically. His hips, now aligned with hers, pushed down, effectively holding her and getting her attention.

Don't look at him. This is embarrassing enough.

"Look at me."

No.

"Anna."

The scent of cologne, magnified by his adrenaline, wrapped around her. Warm and utterly male, it enticed her to nuzzle the pulsing throat a kiss away. His weight settled down again, not crushing as before, but a welcome pressure to her swelling body. He whispered her name, a simple, torturous caress on the underside of her ear. She arched up, losing her mental battle in the rising need to be closer to him. One hand curled in the damp cotton between his shoulder blades, the other pressed flat and absorbed the beat over his heart. She turned and met his gaze.

Stunned, she stared, the expression on his face more erotic than the blatant, intimate pressure against her. Blazing, knowing, wanting eyes, a mirror of her feelings inside and out. He tilted his head to the side and lowered it. Breathing ragged, lips parted in reflection of his, she ignored the reflex to close her eyes. She wanted to see his desire, see what their kiss did to him and have her response doubled by watching it all play out in his eyes.

His lips skimmed hers, dry and smooth and way too brief.

One of them trembled.

He shifted onto his forearms and tunneled his fingers along

her sensitive scalp, winding them into her hair and tearing a moan from her throat.

She wanted to forget everything but the man in her arms. When his body jerked at her touch, she smiled to herself and pulled him closer, exhilarated that he shared this madness.

Then only the cool air kissed her as he levered up and freed himself from her embrace. Dazed, she recognized sounds in the background—banging on the front door and her name being called.

Rico stood, held out a hand to help her up and pulled out his gun with the other. His face was uncompromising, his gaze never left the front door. The only sign of his desire was in the profile of his jeans, while she couldn't even breathe normally.

Humiliation surged through her. She wanted to run to her room and forget the way she all but begged him.

No, Anna, she reminded herself, you're an adult. Deal with this.

Ignoring his hand, she stood and straightened her clothes, inwardly cursing her shaking hands.

"Fine. Be that way," he said indifferently. "But remember you did forget to *order* me."

Her hands froze then continued their chore. She'd thought she couldn't get more humiliated. At least he'd reminded her why she couldn't afford to be intimate, emotionally or physically, with him.

"Anna!" The voice outside grew more insistent, reminding her the children were upstairs. Something she should have heeded earlier.

Rico reached out to close the slate-blue blinds over the sink, then strode to open the front door while she hurried into the den to compose herself. Did he think he could pull a caveman routine now because she'd—

Wait, she hadn't even kissed him! Muttering in disgust, she jumped at another of Pete Joncaluso's bellows and went to face the music, just beating Lina to the door.

"Anna, who the hell is this guy?" His stubble-laden jaw tight and eyes narrowed, Pete brought with him the scent of rain and cigarette smoke.

"He's—"

"Her lover," Rico interjected smoothly. The arm he threw around her shoulder may have looked loving, but it tightened like a vise.

To Pete's credit, he controlled his amazement as he scrutinized them. She forced herself to relax into Rico's side to further convince him. "I see. This happened—" he swallowed hard before continuing "—suddenly."

Anna opened her mouth to agree, but Rico tugged her closer and kissed her temple. Anna caught Lina's silent exit back upstairs, whether to watch the twins or to stay untangled from the lies, she didn't know. She just wanted to go with her.

"These things usually do," Rico replied, his words reeking with satisfaction.

Shame scorched her. She could only imagine what Pete was thinking. He'd known her for two years, but that didn't guarantee he wouldn't think the worst of her for having an affair with a man she'd known less than a week.

She was going to wring Rico's neck for this.

"Can I get you something to drink?" As soon as she said the words she cringed. Now wasn't the time to play hostess.

"No." Pete took a deep breath and said more gently, "No, thank you, Anna."

"So, Officer, what brings you here tonight?"

Pete swung to face him, his leather gun belt creaking in warning. "I didn't catch your name."

Rico stiffened, but he continued to sound congenial. "The name's Gage Moran."

"Sergeant Joncaluso," Pete punctuated with a nod. "Someone called anonymously and reported a prowler."

"A prowler?" she asked quickly, looking at Rico then back to Pete.

"I didn't see anyone," Pete assured her. "But that doesn't mean someone hasn't been here."

"I'm sure it's a mistake," Rico said with a shrug. "You can always ask the neighbors. One of them had to be your caller."

"I already planned on it. So, tell me, Mr. Moran, what do you do?"

"I'm a computer security analyst."

"Where're you from?"

"Originally or since college?"

"Either."

"Born in New Hampshire, raised in Maryland, college in New York," he replied sardonically.

"Planning on adding Idaho?"

"Maybe."

"Ever been arrested?"

"That's it. You two want to continue getting to know each other, fine, but I'm going to talk to my neighbors." She untangled herself from Rico, gave him a shove and marched to the front door.

"You going to let her leave?" Joncaluso asked him.

"I'm not going to *let* her do anything. Anna's her own woman." Rico kept his expression even as the cop gave him another once-over, although he wanted to grab Anna and keep her from going outside. He'd give her ten seconds out there before he followed, but the uneasy feeling at the back of his neck told him he needed to be careful with this guy. There was more to him than met the eye.

And it had nothing to do with the fact that Joncaluso wanted Anna.

"Wait a minute," Joncaluso called as Anna stepped out the door. "Someone needs to stay here with the kids."

"Lina's here. Besides, you two aren't done grilling each other yet."

Joncaluso actually looked sheepish for a second, cementing Rico's theory about the cop's more than civil feelings.

"I'm done. For now," he added, sending Rico another of his icy stares.

If there wasn't so much at stake, he'd be concerned about being on Joncaluso's bad side. He looked as if he could bend steel.

With his teeth.

"Fine. I'll stay here." Anna gave in but pointed a finger at Joncaluso. "You let me know if you find out anything more."

"I will." He hesitated out on the porch.

Rico decided the looks he was getting meant the cop wanted to talk to Anna privately.

He leaned more comfortably against the wall.

"Anna, you need me, don't hesitate to call the station. If I'm off duty, you have my home number. I don't care what time it is."

"Thank you, Pete. But I'm fine, really. If someone is prowling around, Gage can take care of us."

Joncaluso pinned him with another look. "I don't advise you to play Rambo. You see someone, call the station."

"Sure, Officer," he said with a smile as he moved back into the foyer and put his arms around Anna's waist.

The cop read Rico's silent message and walked to the patrol car. Had he been warning him as a citizen or as one of the men behind the kidnapping and hacking? Was he the "prowler" the agents had beeped him about? The shadow outside the window? The timing of his beeps made it possible. He needed to get in touch with his men.

As soon as the door shut, Anna twisted out of his embrace.

"How dare you!" she said, seething. She planted her hands against his chest and shoved him hard, then swept past him into the kitchen. "That man is my friend! If he'd wanted to hurt me or the kids, he would have a long time ago!"

Rico leaned against the stair railing, struggling to control the pain circling up from his ribs and hip. Telling himself he was unprepared for the shove did nothing for his ego.

"You don't get it, do you?" she said with her back still turned. "When you leave again, I'll still be here. I don't want these people to think the worst of me."

"Who said," he began, his hands on his knees, "I'm leaving?"

"You always do."

She scored a direct hit. He straightened up, but a slashing pain went across his ribs, taking his breath away again. Reaching out, he grabbed the railing post to keep from falling on his face just as she pivoted to face him.

"Oh, my goodness," Anna mumbled, rushing to him and putting her shoulder under his arm.

"Kitchen."

"Okay, slowly. Slowly, I said! If you fall, I can't pick you up. Oh, I shouldn't have pushed you. I wasn't thinking about your injuries."

He settled in a chair, grateful the pain was receding. He must have an old fracture that hadn't been ready for the pressure. He stuck a hand under his shirt, feeling around. Whatever it was, the damage didn't feel permanent.

"I'm okay. I don't need your pity," he said in a painful growl.

"You are an impossible man! I hit you and you can't even accept my apology…" Her words trailed off and he glanced up to find her staring horrified at the skin his hand inadvertently exposed.

He dropped the shirt, but she was already on her knees by the chair. She reached out to lift his shirt, and he grabbed her wrist.

"Let me see," she said softly.

"No."

"Yes."

"I don't want or need your pity."

"Good, because I'm not offering any."

Taking in the stubborn tilt of her chin, he let go and looked in the other direction. He focused on the newest drawing hanging on the refrigerator. She lifted his shirt up, then stopped as she made a distressed sound. He knew what she was seeing. Thick scars, uneven flesh tone, dents where skin hadn't anything smooth to heal over, smaller bumps from the metal they used to put him back together. For a man who'd been so body conscious, it wasn't easy to accept he would never look better than this. Nor was it easy to let her see him.

He'd seen Anna's embarrassment and regret over their mind-numbing intimacy on the kitchen floor. He hadn't helped by letting it provoke him into insulting her.

Finally he gave in and turned back to her. What he saw took his breath faster than her hard shove. Devastating sadness knit her brows and rounded her eyes.

He experienced a swift déjà vu. Her sadness reminded him of a woman ecologist he'd met in South America. She'd stood surveying the latest destruction of the rainforest she'd fought so hard to save. He remembered feeling uncomfortable and helpless and giving her meaningless platitudes. She'd shaken her head and smiled sadly at him. "Your words can't help," she'd said. "This is too deep for words."

In Anna's eyes he saw the same pain.

"I'm so sorry." She let his shirt drop, gently smoothing it over his ribs and stomach.

"It doesn't hurt anymore," he lied.

"What kind of monsters could do this to a human being?" He could hear her tears as she gestured with both hands.

"It wasn't a picnic."

"Don't be flip about this!"

"How do you want me to be?"

"I don't know. Upset. Depressed. Angry." She stood and walked to the blinds, sealing them shut even tighter.

"I've been all of those things. Still am to some extent. They told me I'd have to let go of it to fully recover. I found that I'm still left with some."

"Who told you?"

He mentally kicked himself. "The psychiatrists."

"You went into therapy?" she asked incredulously as she turned around.

"No, I was dragged into therapy." The sadness was easing from her features, replaced by curiosity.

It's better to answer her questions than see her pain.

"I kept having nightmares and couldn't relax. I couldn't handle being alone for the few first weeks, after they reduced the meds and I was more coherent." He flexed his fingers, almost feeling the restrictive bandages he'd been mummified in for months. "They call it post-traumatic stress disorder."

"How are you now?"

"Better every day."

She stared at him the same way she had when she'd accepted his real identity. "Will you tell me about it?"

"I don't know." He continued when her gaze dropped to the floor. "Maybe. Yes. Someday."

She took a deep breath and nodded. "Well, now that we've settled a few things, we need to talk about the prowler and where you're putting that gun before the kids come down for dinner," she said briskly, bustling around and getting out plates and glasses.

"What things?"

She arched him a look. Probably for his annoyed tone.

"One, you won't hang on me and embarrass me like that again in front of my friends. Two, you aren't going to shield me anymore as if I'm a fragile child and three, you're going to tell me what happened to you."

"Oh." Great, he thought wryly. I'm glad we settled so much. You'll just have to understand that I'll do anything to keep you and the family safe. Even if that means discouraging your potential boyfriends.

He smiled at that thought, turning it into a cough when she gave him a dubious look.

"This one I keep on me," he said, shifting to pull the 9mm

Beretta out of his waistband. He secured it in the holster that attached to his jeans on the inside of his right hip, but kept the holster hidden. Anna watched as he pulled out his loose shirt so that it hid the telltale bulge.

Putting their drinks on the table, she propped both fists on her hips. "I don't like it."

"You don't have to."

"Don't let them see it. I mean it! I can't talk about how bad guns are if their hero is wearing one."

She whirled away and went into the pantry, marching right back out with a loaf of bread.

"And get that stupid grin off your face. You know they adore you!"

"Actually, I didn't."

They took the wind out of her sails. "Oh. Well. They do. So don't do anything to make me knock you off your pedestal."

He chuckled, then sobered. "About that prowler. It must have been a crank call. I'll know more when I get the relay from Mike, but I'm assuming their alert was for Joncaluso."

She frowned into the pantry, her hand deep in a box of animal cookies. Pulling a handful out, she faced him.

"But if it was Pete, why didn't he just knock on the kitchen door instead of going around? And don't you think he would have mentioned seeing you push me onto the floor?"

He hoped his amazement didn't show. He hadn't thought of the cop knocking on the back door. "Whoever was outside the window wouldn't have seen us hit the floor. I saw a shadow, not a body."

"The door?" she reminded.

"I don't know."

This was not going as planned. They should have grabbed the kids long ago and not trusted that informant. Rico Carella was dead and would unfortunately not suffer the loss of his children.

Now two agents kept the house under watch at all times, which could be due to the background computer checks. Worse, Anna's lover was more than a roll in the hay. That much had been evident when he'd thrown her to the floor and pulled out a gun.

It was time for the backup plan.

"Dim a light in every room, but turn it off when you go in. I don't want anyone throwing shadows against the windows."

Lina went to take care of that order.

"I need you to get out a couple of candles for the den, in case the television doesn't give off enough light."

Anna nodded, flipped on the TV and headed for the kitchen where the twins sat creating their collages. They looked so sweet and innocent, freshly bathed and in their summer pajamas.

She couldn't lose them.

Backing off from that thought, she grabbed several thick vanilla candles from above the stove and placed them around the den. Rico set up his laptop computer on a mahogany end table and unplugged the phone, plugging in a line from his computer.

"What's this?" In his hand he held up one of the plastic edge protectors left over from the twins' toddling days.

"It covers the sharp corner of the table in case one of the kids bump into it. Even though they're past the toddler stage, they still have their accidents. Rafe cut the side of his head on that one not long ago."

"It takes a lot to protect children, doesn't it?" he mused, staring at the cream-colored plastic he turned over in his large hand.

He was talking about more than the plastic.

"Yes, it does."

He bent and fitted it back on as Lina herded the children into the room. She beamed at her son, making Anna smile in response to the pure happiness on the woman's face. She had a pretty good idea how Lina felt.

Rafe and Rebecca settled on an old plastic tablecloth Lina put down in the middle of the floor, and Anna gathered the bags of already torn-up mail and glue. Within minutes the twins were engrossed in their joint project.

Lina sat in her corner rocking chair and worked on her latest needlepoint. Rico's computer hummed to life, and he was soon typing furiously.

Anna sat on the couch with a pad of paper for idea sketches and watched the cozy family scene. It looked so right and so strange at the same time. An entertainment show brought the sounds of the latest movie into the room, Rafe and Rebecca talked in fragmented sentences. Rico, whose scarred torso was imprinted on her mind, had obviously picked up typing and computer skills along with his deadly combat skills. Yet he fit so naturally into the picture with his mother and children.

No one stumbling across them would realize the danger they were all in.

"Bella, are you okay?"

She didn't have any excess energy to pounce on him for using her nickname.

"Yeah, I'm fine," she said lightly, abandoning her work to join the art project on the floor.

Rico studied Anna covertly as she lay on the floor. Stretched out on her stomach with her sock-covered feet in the air, she shouldn't have looked so sexy. But she did.

She laughed at something Rafe said, and he leaned forward and kissed her nose. God, he wanted that. He wanted to crawl over to them and get sloppy kisses and hug their beautiful mother.

Somehow she'd managed to raise two really great kids. The more he was around them, the more he realized how much went into taking caring of one child, much less two the same age. She'd done it by being both the mom and the dad, a commodity neither of them had growing up.

Speaking of which, what had happened to her mom?

Glancing at his screen, he replied to Mike's suggestion to meet in person. Although they met in an online service where they could change nicknames daily, it was time for more in-depth discussion.

Mike had spoken with the two field guys, and they'd reported they sent the alert beep when Joncaluso had pulled up and walked around the house. They'd beeped back when he reached the front door. Frowning, Rico brushed his fingers on the keys without responding. Joncaluso hit the front door a few seconds after the safety beep. He needed the exact time frame from the men outside to find out if the cop had been on the porch or just around the yard. They damn well better have had someone stationed by the side fence to watch, or heads would roll.

Because if Joncaluso hadn't been on the porch, he wasn't their prowler.

They decided on a different method of communication between him and the agents that would rely more heavily on their beepers and cell phones. Mike agreed to pass on the codes to them.

He sent Mike Anna's insights and bit back a chuckle at the quick reply. No, he typed in caps, Anna does not want a job with the agency.

Mike then said he had run a check, but the cop had come up clean as a whistle. Possibly too clean. He'd make the arrangements to fly in tomorrow with that report and the pictures he'd gathered from old Balangerio surveillance files.

He also said he'd bring the new protective identities he'd finagled from their boss.

Anna was going to hate him for the rest of her life, but he couldn't allow them all to be sitting ducks. Mike's latest news confirmed his worst fears. Two men had been caught trying to dig up Rico Carella's casket the night before.

Like a magnet, his gaze was drawn back to Anna. She'd changed positions, giving him more of her profile. He could see from the lower lip she was biting that something was definitely bothering her, reminding him of her earlier expression. It had tested every ounce of his control. He'd wanted to crush her to him and promise her everything would be fine.

But he knew touching her was the one thing she didn't need. A lifetime ago it would have been. Today it would only add to the purple shadows bruising the skin under her eyes and the paleness she tried to hide beneath makeup.

Rafe grew tired of his gluing and joined him. Standing next to Rico's leg, he leaned one small arm on it.

"Is that a 'puter?"

"Sure is," Rico said, finishing his sentence to Mike.

"Can I press a button?"

Rafe stared so earnestly at him, Rico forgot what he was going to say. Ruffling his son's hair, he pushed away the bittersweet memories of his brother.

"Ummm."

"He asked if he could press a button," Anna said from the floor.

Compassion softened her features, and in the muted light he couldn't even see her irises. Only impossibly large, soft, perceptive eyes.

He knew then that he loved her.

Not like before, although that was a part of it. He loved the person she'd become. The woman who bore his children when it would have been perfectly understandable had she not. The woman who stood up to him, who'd played tag with their kids and ended it with a water hose fight. One she let them win.

He loved her.

"Gage," Rafe patted his leg. He tore he gaze away from Anna's very pale face.

"I'm sorry, son. I was daydreaming. You can hit a button, but only the ones I tell you. Deal?"

Rafe stuck out his hand, much the same way Rico had done

to his son days ago. Had he taught him that? Pride surged through him as he shook his son's hand.

He heard a sniffle and looked up. His mother ran the tip of her finger under each eye and gave him a watery smile.

Two hours later it was the twins' bedtime. Going through the routine, Rico felt more like he belonged.

"What's that?" Rebecca asked from behind him, tapping on the bulge in his back jeans pocket.

"My wallet," he explained, pulling it out. He flipped it open, and Rafe scrambled out of the bed Anna had just tucked him into. He sent her an apologetic glance, and she shrugged with one shoulder as if to say, "It happens all the time."

He reached out and pulled a blue credit card from his holder. "Hey, Becca. This 'yooks 'yike Aunt Dana's cards."

Rebecca nodded. "But she had more than Gage."

Anna gave a tired chuckle. "Sweetie, some people have too many. Rafe, *looks like*."

While Rafe dutifully mimicked his mother, Rebecca pulled out a card.

"This has three colors."

Rafe reached for another.

"This one has a tiger!"

Pretty soon every plastic card lay on the bed.

"Why do you have different ones?" Rebecca asked.

Rico reached out and tugged one of her curls, loving the way it bounced back up. "They do different things. Those two buy gas for your car, and the other one can buy anything you want. You don't need that many of them."

"Aunt Dana does," Rafe said while he smashed two of the cards together, then proceeded to pretend they were race cars and vroom them around the bedspread.

"Enough stalling, you two."

"You can stay in my bed, Mom," Rafe offered generously.

"What a sport you are. But where would you sleep?"

He shrugged. "With Gage."

She rolled her eyes and sighed. "I don't think so. Come on, it's going to be morning soon."

Rafe imitated her sigh and handed Rico the plastic cards. "She always says that," he confided.

"She's right."

Rafe smiled at him as if sharing a private joke, then sprang into his bed. Rebecca handed him the rest of the cards and, still on her knees, tried to hug him. She only managed his neck and right shoulder. Her cheek pressed against his for a second before she pulled away and kissed it.

"Night, Gage," she whispered too loudly in his ear.

He closed his eyes for a second, kissed her forehead and walked out. He held the words in until he got into the hallway.

"Good night, love."

"He forgot to kiss my head," Rafe complained.

Anna hesitated, still seeing Rico's suffering. She knew it hurt him when the kids called him Gage. "He didn't forget, honey. He saved yours for when he comes in to check on you later."

"He checks on us?" Rebecca sounded awestruck.

"*I* check on you both every night."

"Yeah, but you're 'posed to," Rafe explained.

"I see." She stood between the beds and smiled at both of them. "Well, I'll make sure I keep doing my job."

They giggled, and she kissed them, tucked them in and checked the locks and blinds on their windows before she left the room.

Thinking about Rico's last expression, she started down the stairs. She could hear him talking to Lina and stopped halfway down on the shadowed staircase.

"I moved here after your funeral. It was a very bad time." Anna could hear Rico's mother bustling around the kitchen, opening cabinets and drawers. "I found out much and I grieved more."

"What do you mean?"

"Losing my only other son, it almost killed me. Anna and your babies were my salvation."

Anna hurried down the last two steps, sliding on the ceramic foyer tiles in her haste. She shouldn't have been surprised that he sensed her presence.

She hoped he didn't ask why Lina would grieve more after finding them. She didn't want him to find out about Lina's deception yet.

When he faced her, she unconsciously braced herself for the condemnation she would see there. What she did glimpse surprised her. A dark kind of suffering and a sardonic twist of his lips.

"We've all paid for things in our own way, haven't we, Anna?"

Instinctively stiffening in preparation for an attack on her past wrongs, she was thrown off when he straightened up from his lounging against the island and strolled to the refrigerator.

What was this? She inched into the circle of kitchen light and looked to Lina for guidance, but she was busy constructing a Dagwood-size sandwich for him.

"Hey, Mama," he said, putting down his already emptied glass and refilling it. "Did you notice little Rafe has the same speech problem as Rafael did?"

Lina gave him a warm smile that chased away the shadows of their conversation. "*Sí,* I did."

"You never mentioned that to me," Anna said a tad indignantly. If her son had an inherited speech problem, she should have been told.

"*Hija,* don't be alarmed. I don't know why I didn't mention it before, but maybe it is because Rafael's was gone by the time he was six or seven." She put Rico's monstrous sandwich on a paper plate, sliced it easily and reached over to pat Anna's hand. "You do all you can by correcting him."

That may be, but she was going to keep an even sharper eye on it. Not that she expected her son to be perfect, but if he needed help, she was going to make sure he got it.

"It's amazing how much he looks like Rafael," Rico said, chasing down a bite with some milk.

"I know. Except for Anna's lighter brown hair, he's all your brother," Lina said, leading Rico to the table with her own plate of vegetable munchies.

An idea formed, and Anna slipped out of the kitchen and into the living room. Moonlight filtered through her sheer white drapes, allowing her to gather her loot without flipping on switches. Hugging her precious collection to her chest, she realized she felt somewhat giddy at what she was about to do.

Walking back into the kitchen, Lina spotted her before Rico, and her face reflected her approval.

"I thought you might like to see these," she said, easing them onto the table next to him.

He looked at them in confusion, then stilled.

"Are these…?" His hand reached out to them, wavering before lying on the top.

"Yes. They're the twins' baby albums and others. It was my one extravagance back then," she chuckled. "I'd buy film whenever I could."

"It is too bad you did not have one of those video things," Lina teased.

"Yeah, someday," Anna said, unaware of her wistful tone. She began sorting through the pile and put the albums in chronological order. "I'm just going to have to splurge."

Rico's warm hand settled on hers. "Thank you."

Jolted by his touch she looked at the word emblazoned on the cover above their hands.

Love.

She dared a peek at him and was snared by the naked emotion on his face. For the first time she recognized him, Rico, and saw the boy she'd loved. She tried to look away, but his hand tightened on hers.

It was the first time since he'd returned that she experienced their old connection.

"You're welcome," she said, and smiled.

* * *

It was her first genuine smile.

He turned another page, smiling at the snapshot of his children's laughing faces covered with chocolate icing, birthday hats tilted to the sides.

He'd been poring over the albums for hours, seeing Anna's smile in his mind over and over again. His mom had abandoned them not long ago, then Anna had excused herself to go finish work in her office. Her reluctance to be alone with him had been obvious.

Knuckling his scratchy eyes, he glanced at the clock. One-thirty. He closed the last album and added it to the stack before taking another walk around the lower floor.

A look toward the shadowed living room windows reminded him of his second conversation with Mike. His friend had been in touch with the agents, and their relay had confirmed the worst.

Joncaluso hadn't been on the back porch. He'd shone a flashlight around the backyard and walked the length of the fence to the lake and checked behind it. But he hadn't been on the porch.

Unfortunately, when the cop showed up, their positioning had been focused on him at the front of the house. Which meant whoever had been at the back of the house had left unnoticed.

Or had that been the plan? Call in a tip and then sneak out the side? He frowned, walking back into the dark kitchen and opening one of the blinds so slivers of moonlight spilled in. Maybe their visitor hadn't left walking.

The moon's likeness bobbed on small, tranquil waves. No tall reeds crowded the shore. The only unnatural parts of the lake were three docks. Anna's neighbors' docks anchored sailboats while hers stood empty.

Little place to hide. Which meant their visitor would have needed a distraction, at least, to avoid being seen. Which also meant they knew the timing of the patrols.

Damn. Hopefully he was wrong. If not, he prayed their luck would hold out one more day, until he could get his family safely away.

Closing the blinds, he headed for the stairs and the twins' room. He couldn't hold back a smile at the glowing, green galaxy blankets they slept under. Bracing himself on their nighttable, he knelt down between their beds.

Here in the dark, with silence wrapped around him, he looked at them, touched their hands and cheeks and kissed their foreheads. He acted like a dad.

Pulling in a deep breath, he rose and left to check on his mother. Finally he headed for Anna's room, mentally preparing himself for the sight of her asleep with the sheets twisted around her, her legs bare.

She wasn't there.

Heading back down the hallway, he walked through a doorway and climbed the wide wooden attic steps and wondered idly why she didn't set up her office closer to the children.

When he got to the top of the stairs, he knew.

Three massive skylights dominated the ceiling. Even as he appreciated them, he wished for solid wood instead of flimsy Plexiglas.

It would be hard for someone to get to the roof without them noticing, but not impossible.

Anna slept under a circle of light, leaning against the huge, slanted drawing table. Roughly sketched pictures and words crowded the edges, and an unfinished strip lay beneath her arms. Crossing to her, he bent and fought the impulse to trace the purple circles beneath her eyes. Her eyebrows came together in troubled twitches, betraying her distress even in sleep.

Fists of guilt and regret pummeled him. When she found out about the witness protection program, any ground they'd made the past few days would be gone.

He stared at her. So many times he'd pictured her face: laughing, smiling, daydreaming. Never had he pictured her this way. Her eyes never curved into the half-moon shapes he'd loved to tease her about. Back then, his teasing had only made her laugh harder, until she ended up in the only place that mattered. His arms.

He crossed those arms across his chest, warding off the emptiness. If he picked her up now and carried her to the bedroom, he wouldn't let her go.

He winced as he straightened, cursing the metal construction that held his body together. Constant souvenirs of his lost identity, his lost life.

Pictures on the opposite wall caught his eye. Anna still slept deeply, and he gave in to his curiosity. He'd stayed out of this room on purpose, trying to give her some space in her own home.

But now he was here.

Frames held some of her earliest strips. In them the twins still held their conversations in her womb. Other frames held awards. Stunned, he walked the length of the wall, counting seven.

She'd done so much. He had gone away—no, run away—to experience life, learn more, accomplish more, than all the people he left behind.

Oh, yeah, he'd succeeded. And what did he have to show for it? Two children who didn't know him, a crazed lunatic out for revenge, a broken-down body and a woman who had once loved him but could barely look at him now.

He rubbed a hand on the back of his neck, noticing for the first time a blue blanket covering something in the shadowed corner. Stopping in front of it, he warred with himself and lost.

The blanket hid a stack of canvases and a pile of sketchbooks. The kind he used to tease were attached to her body.

He clicked on one of the track lighting lamps that lined the wall and picked up the top book. With an unsteady hand he touched its cover, scenes from yesterday racing before his eyes. In a comfortable move, he braced it along his forearm and flipped open the cover.

His stomach freefalled.

It was his face. Rather, his *old* face. His touch upon his own cheek startled him until he realized he'd reached out for the larger jaw he saw on the paper.

Is this who Anna saw when she looked at him? Did he still look like a stranger to her?

He turned the page, examining the back for a date. Nothing. Then he faced the new picture he'd exposed. Another sucker punch. The picture took him back to the neighborhood. So incredible her drawing, he could hear the kids yelling and playing, smell the stale poverty that clung like the heat of a South American jungle. She'd drawn him standing on the porch, in a corner, watching over his brother and mother. Lina sat in her favorite rocker, more chunks of paint missing than covering it, and Rafe was laughing at something she'd said.

He kept turning pages, seeing his memories of those years played out by her talented hand.

He went through all the books until only one remained. On it was a date he knew as well as his own birthday.

The date he reenlisted.

The metallic taste of dread made him hesitate. He glanced up at her. She hadn't moved. He checked his beeper. It still glowed green and ready.

In an abrupt move he got up and decided to check the house again, even though he could hear his mother's soft snore and the kids occasional movements in their beds. He rechecked every handle, lock and window. All secure.

Recognizing his reluctance didn't make it easier to deal with. He stood at the bottom of the attic stairs, gripping the railings, then took careful steps. The creaking didn't disturb her exhausted sleep.

The pads of paper still lay spread out on the floor. Only the last one stayed closed, its date blazing off the cover in a red warning flare. Avoiding it, he went for the stack of canvases.

Picking up the first, he unwrapped it from its thin sheet covering.

Colors attacked him. Reds, blues, purples. He didn't know the names of all the different shades. He set it down and stepped back.

He remembered her first attempt with paints. She'd hated it because it was too broad, too abstract, she'd said. She liked the thin, controlled lines of her pencils.

The painting before him was done in huge slashes of color. All stemmed from the center swirls of black. He took another step away. It bothered him. How could this have come from Anna? Soft, gentle, loving Anna.

This was brutal and ugly. It hurt to look at, yet he couldn't look away. There was something else in there, but he couldn't pinpoint it.

He raked his hand through his hair and tugged hard enough to bring a sting his eyes. He was the farthest thing from an art critic. In fact, he'd made fun of people they'd seen in a museum one day, people who'd stood there and seen scenes and emotions on the wall. He'd seen paint thrown and splattered and selling for thousands of dollars while he barely earned minimum wage.

He lowered himself to the floor without taking his eyes off it. Confusion. Rage. It screamed at him.

Wait a minute.

He shifted closer. Two thin lines of blue swirled down from the middle and then all around until they blended with other colors.

The longer he stared, the more that color stood out. Which didn't make sense. She used it the least of all others.

He moved closer until he could reach out and touch it. There was something about—

Then he saw them.

The blue swirls weren't lines. They were drops of paint placed close together. Drops.

Teardrops.

Pain.

Chapter 8

Anna heard a groan. She slid back down into the deep comfort of sleep only to be disturbed again.

Her eyelids flew open as reality slammed into her. She didn't move. The crimp in her neck helped that. Scanning the room from her sideways position, she saw nothing unusual. Then another noise, not loud and right behind her.

Why had she let herself fall asleep?

"It's me," Rico said, his voice remote.

Relief relaxed most of her muscles, allowing her to move. Stretching up, she swiveled on her chair and froze.

Her heart lay in pieces on the floor. The old Rico, in all shades of gray, surrounded them on sketch pads. Paintings paneled the wall and Rico sat in the middle, his head bent over a drawing in his lap.

Panic held her immobile. If he'd crawled into her body, she couldn't have felt more exposed.

"How dare you," she said in a wavery whisper that fell short of anger. "Those are mine! They were covered for a reason…"

He raised his head, and she was speechless. His cheekbones shelved the light from above, throwing the bottom of his face into shadow. A perfect frame for his vulnerable anguish.

"I didn't know," he said. His hand smoothed the page with his likeness over and over.

"You didn't know what?" She slid out of her chair to the floor and peered at him. He ducked his head into the shadows. Wide shoulders lifted, then sagged back down when he didn't answer.

"What didn't you know?"

"I didn't know that you hurt, too."

Her mouth formed the word *Oh*, but no sound squeezed past the lump of surprise in her throat.

"That sounds stupid," he said, sucking in a deep breath. He carefully closed the drawing pad and added it to a stack on his right before dragging both hands through his hair. "When my mom told me you cheated, I lost it. I was mad. And…I was hurt. All I wanted to do was get as far away from you as possible."

She jerked back as he lumbered to his feet and brushed past her. The sudden movement caused a breeze to lift the loose hair around her face.

He strode across the room as if pursuing the past, only the room ended too soon for answers. He stood without speaking, and she twisted her fingers together, searching for words that wouldn't come out as anger or accusations.

"You betrayed me." The soft growl floated across the room as if from the mouth of a cave. "You cut out my heart and left me so torn up I bled for years. I would imagine you in another man's arms, in his bed, his life. And I wanted to kill both of you."

"I didn't—"

"No!" He stepped out and his eyes speared hers, slicing her with their clear fury. "I don't want you to apologize or explain."

She tried again to tell him the truth when his quiet voice interrupted her.

"I should be apologizing."

Shocked, she tried not to gape and failed. She could only stare at him as he came closer and lowered himself in front of her.

"You were so young, Bella. *We* were so young. I should have forgiven you!" His impassioned words were reflected in fever-bright eyes. "You'd waited all those years for me and I left the first time we had problems. I don't know if we could have worked it out, but I should have tried, especially for the twins."

He missed her wince as he eased himself back and leaned against the wall. "*God!* I should have been there! I know how hard it was for Mama to raise us alone."

She stared at her lap, seeing all the hard times she'd lived through.

"Bella, look at me. Look at me!"

His strong, scarred fingers grasped her chin and forced her gaze upward.

"I'm sorry," he whispered.

She knew the pain in her heart showed on her face, but she couldn't move away. She tried to use her hands as a shield, but he shifted closer, pulling her between his legs.

He released her chin and gently grasped her wrists. She felt her palms against his warm, rough cheeks and was startled into meeting his eyes.

"I'm sorry I left you alone. I'm sorry for not forgiving you."

He pulled her palms away and kissed both centers. Her fingers were still curling when he put them together, wrapped his own around them and leaned his head down.

"But most of all, I'm sorry for the danger I've brought to you and the kids. When we used to talk about getting married, you said you wanted a safe neighborhood to raise our children in."

He lifted his head. "You did that, Bella. You found a safe place to raise them, and I've ruined it."

She was denying it, even as she tried to absorb the fact he apologized for it all. Well, almost all. But right now she had to take some of this guilt from his face. He'd already suffered so much.

"Did you know you were bringing the danger here?"

"I knew there was a chance."

She sighed, the whole situation lying heavily on her shoulders. "Why did you invent a fake background and come here?"

"Someone tried gaining access—"

"No!" She shook their joint fist of hands and tugged him close enough to see his expanding pupils. "*Why* are you here?"

"To protect my family."

"Exactly. To protect us. You thought the danger was already here." A thought had her pulling back. "What were you going to do if there was no danger? I mean, what if they hadn't tried to kidnap Rafe. Would you have ever told us?"

He glanced away.

"I'm not going to get mad. I'm trying to understand what you were thinking before you came here."

A corner of his mouth kicked up.

"What?"

"Nothin'."

She pursed her lips and studied him.

"Stop it," he said gruffly, casually bending his neck side to side.

"You still pull that little delaying tactic when you're uncomfortable with the subject."

He froze, then straightened his neck to pin her with a stare. Finally he released a wry chuckle. "I spent years learning how not to give anything away with body language. Yet you see right through me. Just like you always did."

She made an agreeing noise. "You're still dodging my question."

He sighed heavily. "I don't know. I didn't think that far. Too many things could happen. I wasn't going to do anything that would put any of you in danger. So, I tried not to think about telling you the truth."

"It couldn't have been easy."

"It wasn't. Although I don't know how I would have lasted weeks or months without claiming my place." His hands tightened. "And don't take that the wrong way."

He dropped a kiss on her fingers and absently rubbed his chin against them. Suddenly he straightened and looked right into her soul.

"I still care, Anna."

She jerked back, but he wouldn't release her hands. Her chest caved in as if someone had stepped on it.

"Don't do this. Don't throw words around." She was babbling as she concentrated on releasing her hands from the vise. She yanked them sideways in a weak attempt to dislodge them.

"I'm not throwing them around. Please, stop! Listen to me. I do care. It's not like before. It's deeper."

She stopped struggling.

"You were like my little sister, then my best friend, then my girlfriend and lover. But those last few years, we were together only through the phone and letters. We never had time to date or do other normal things. Looking back, whenever we were together, I was always on my best behavior, afraid to be in a bad mood or fight because we never saw each other.

"This past week I've seen you in every mood. I've seen you as a mother and a daughter, happy and sad, scared and angry. You actually got in my face!"

She couldn't keep from smiling with him.

"You'd never done that before. Whenever you didn't agree, you'd talk it out, but when we started getting into it, you'd shut down and let it all go."

"I hate fighting."

He nodded. "From the way you grew up." He hesitated. "Not to get off the track, but I've been wondering something. Where's your mom? Why isn't she here with you?"

"She's dead."

"Awww, Bella. I'm sorry."

"Don't be. I hadn't seen her since I told her I was pregnant."

"What?" It was more of a statement than a question.

She sat back.

"No, don't pull away from me. Talk."

"When she sobered up enough, I told her I was pregnant." She flexed her fingers, staring at them unseeingly. "She wasn't happy. I wanted to talk to her about it, about what I should do, about school, about you. I didn't even know if I should go to a doctor right away or if the changes that had already happened to my body were normal. Instead, she left the house. She came back the next morning hung over, but with a new bottle for that afternoon. Then she ripped a piece of the brown shopping bag from around it and wrote a phone number on it. Then she told me to call my aunt and beg for help if I had to. She'd met a man and she was leaving Miami with him. So I'd have to take care of my problem myself because she didn't need any more mouths to feed...."

She snorted indelicately. "Which is kind of funny when you think about it, because she never cooked anything, and here she was kicking out her chef and maid."

"Don't. Don't make a joke out of it," he whispered.

"How else should I deal with it? Tell me. Should I pity the fact that she never got to know her beautiful grandchildren? Or should I forgive her because she had such a hard life and didn't know any better? Maybe I should feel guilty I didn't even know she'd been dead for three weeks before they identified her."

She tried to shake off his hands again and failed. Instead, he yanked her into his arms.

"Let me go!" She pushed against his chest, stopping short at the thought of reinjuring him.

"No. I wasn't here before to do this. But I'm here now. So let me hold you."

She was starting to lose sight of why she shouldn't relax into his arms, but she gritted her teeth and tried again to free herself.

"Why? It's too late. Just let me go."

"I can't. Don't ask me to."

His husky whisper, sincere and determined, punctured her armor of anger and pain, leaving her boneless. He gathered her closer, tucking her head against his shoulder. The curve of her nose fit perfectly against his neck, her ear snug against his strong heartbeat.

For the first time in years she felt safe and unburdened, as though someone was there to share the weight with her. She felt small and feminine and strong, able to handle anything life handed her.

She felt like a woman.

She closed her eyes, inhaling the moment with every cell so she could add it to her memory box.

Then she opened her eyes.

"You care?" she asked quietly.

She felt his nod and murmured response through his chest.

"Then you don't care about the other men."

He pulled away and looked down at her. She searched for anger, jealousy, any of the old emotions, but could find none.

"I'd be lying if I said I didn't care. How can I explain this so you'll understand?" He hugged her close again and leaned his cheek against her head. "The worst part for me wasn't even what you'd done, although that was hard enough. It was that you didn't love me anymore. I never questioned your loyalty because I believed in your love."

"You thought I didn't love you?" Outraged hurt colored her words.

"Yeah. You've always followed your heart, so I knew you wouldn't be with someone else if you still loved me."

"If you believed I loved you that much, then why did you believe the worst? Why didn't you question it? Or give me a chance to at least explain?"

"I didn't want the details! I didn't even want to hear you admit it. God, Bella. Just hearing Mama say the words killed me."

Seeing it from his point of view, she could almost understand why he'd run. Would the young girl she'd been have done it differently, had their positions been reversed? Could she have listened while he told her about other women he'd made love to? Just the thought splintered her heart and she knew now, years later, she still wouldn't want to hear the words.

"But now maybe I've finally learned something. I'm human. I'm not perfect. Not at warring or loving. So how can I not forgive others for making mistakes?"

The tension in her eased. He would forgive Lina when she told him the truth.

He tightened his arms around her as she relaxed against him. He'd said the right words. The way she nestled against him told him she understood.

The urge to laugh and shout his thanks to the heavens made him pull her closer.

"I guess it's my turn," she said, straightening in his arms, the move throwing back her shoulders and outlining another area in which she'd changed. Sweat beaded his upper lip, and with difficulty he focused on her profile. It revealed her nervousness, even if her altered breathing pattern hadn't given her away. She pulled in her lower lip and worried it with small, white teeth.

Apprehension mixed with desire and settled uneasily in his gut, but he fought the urge to rush her.

"I think I understand better why you left the way you did. All these years I've been so angry that you didn't question your mother or give me another chance." She shrugged and slanted him a quick look from beneath the fern-like fan of her lashes. "But now I realize I might have done the same thing."

"Probably not."

"Well, we'll never know," she said, her tongue peeking out and wetting her lips. He shifted her out of the cradle of his legs and onto his thigh so she wouldn't notice his reaction.

"You can tell me anything, you know."

She shot him a quick smile and nodded. Sucking in a deep breath, she looked him dead in the eye and told him.

"Lina lied."

Of all things he expected, this was not one of them.

He chuckled without humor. "What?"

"She was trying to protect you, so she lied about the other men."

"Anna, what are you saying? Mama wouldn't lie to me! Look, it doesn't matter anymore, you don't have to do this."

Two slim fingers against his lips halted the words. She returned his accusing stare with sadness and understanding.

"No." His shaking head dislodged her fingers. He wished he could brush away the growing suspicion with the same ease.

"She wanted you to stay enlisted and away from Miami. She didn't want you to go back and die there."

Like Rafael. He heard the words she didn't say. Like an old movie, he saw himself running to his twin's lifeless body sprawled in the trash-littered street.

Mama exchanged one jungle for another, without giving me the chance to choose. How could she have thought this was right? How could losing the only other person I loved make my life better?

Anna tensed, causing him to lean away or get her head slammed into his chin. She cocked her head to one side and faced the attic stairs. "Do you hear something?" she asked as she scrambled to her feet.

He was right with her.

Adrenaline and fear surged through him. The twins.

He drew his weapon and held Anna behind him with one arm as they crept down the creaking steps. Anna leaned against them, urging him faster, but at least understanding they needed to make as little noise as possible.

His rational side knew there was slim chance anyone made it inside, but he found this new parental protectiveness didn't allow for logic.

In less than fifteen seconds they made it to the bedroom, and he hoped his tight squeeze on her arm indicated she should stay in the hall. A rosy glow from behind a Disney nightlight illuminated two slumbering children.

A quick check showed no danger.

"Mom?" Rafe twisted in his bed and made a small sobbing sound. Anna rushed past Rico, almost knocking him over to get to the bed. As much as he wanted to stand there and give comfort, he knew he had to check on Mama and the rest of the house.

"I'll be right back," he whispered, and Anna nodded without looking away from Rafe.

He checked on his mom, who surprisingly enough slept on. A walk-through of the house showed no changes, but he paged the agents, anyway, and was slightly reassured by the all-clear numeric response.

The adrenaline rush faded as he walked upstairs to the twins' room. Rolling his head to loosen his neck, he flipped the safety on his gun and returned it to the small of his back.

Peering around the corner, he was surprised to see Anna gone and Rafe already asleep. A slight shuffling sound drew him to the attic, and he realized she was closing the sketchbooks.

Standing at the bottom of the stairs, with only the soft light from above pooling around him, he looked to his left. His mother's partially closed door couldn't block the sound of her breathing. His eyes squeezed shut as he let himself think about

Anna's confession, as if he could block out the truth. What had his Mama done?

Feeling old not only in body, but in soul, he climbed the stairs. Order restored to her office, Anna gently recovered the pile of sketchbooks, smoothing the blue blanket across the top.

"It still makes no sense," he said, even though she didn't acknowledge his presence. "My job in the military was more dangerous than staying in Miami. Wait a minute! Why did she think lying about you would keep me safe? What does one have to do with the other?"

She turned to face him, staring at him with an expression he couldn't read.

"What?"

"You believe me."

"Of course I do. I don't understand it. I'm angry as hell about it. But I know you're telling the truth."

She flashed him a brilliant smile, and his heart lurched in his chest.

"Um, I know you're upset with your mother. Believe me, it took me a long time to understand. But I know now that she believed this was the only way to protect you. She'd lost one son and the thought of you going back to Miami, marrying me, being stuck there and maybe dying there was too much for her."

"Whoa! First off, what gave her the idea we'd stay in Miami and be stuck there? And how did lying about you guarantee I wouldn't stay? How'd it guarantee I'd reenlist?"

"I don't know all the answers. You'll have to ask her." She threw her hands up. "Maybe she knew you wouldn't want to be in the same city as me anymore. Maybe she knew how much you enjoyed fighting."

The conversation resembled a minefield. Every time he negotiated one, he'd spot another trip wire.

"I didn't *enjoy* it. I was good at it. If anything, I enjoyed being good at something," he said carefully.

"Whatever," she said, shrugging. She lowered herself to

the floor and leaned against a filing cabinet. He joined her, sitting so he could watch her face.

"You know I didn't have the money for college until after the army, so school wasn't an option."

She nodded, but it was to shut him up, not an agreement.

"You think I reenlisted because it was more fun killing people?" he asked, amazed and trying to keep it from fueling his anger.

She flinched and stared at him with the same caution she'd always reserved for Gage. "I didn't say that."

"It's not like the death we saw in Miami. Just go in, open fire and run. This was different. Bombs or face-to-face. Sometimes it had to be done by hand. Either way, I never enjoyed it. I never laughed or got off from it."

Offended, she glared at him.

"That bothers you?"

"Your wording leaves a little to be desired."

He snorted. "I guess there's a lot I won't be sharing with you if you offend that easily."

"I'm a civilian. Isn't this supposed to bother me? I'm not able to handle the cruelties of the world because I've been so sheltered. Isn't that what you always told me?"

Her counterattack was so unexpected he leaned back on his arms, using the position to stretch his protesting muscles.

"I don't remember saying you were sheltered. I was there. I remember what you suffered."

She looked away and studied her teardrop painting. He wondered why she hadn't put it away.

"You didn't need to know what I did. Not that I was allowed to tell you, anyway."

She laughed, but its vibrancy was gone.

"Yeah. I remember. A huge portion of your life I was allowed to know nothing about."

"That bothered you?"

"Of course it bothered me!"

"You never said."

Her jaw set for a moment. "And if I had?"

His turn to pause. "I don't know. I'd have tried to tell you more. To be honest, I thought you hated the army. You never asked a lot of questions."

"Why should I? I knew the answer. It was *classified*."

He blew out a breath slowly, wishing he could reclaim the closeness they'd been sharing before Rafe cried out.

"I guess I should have realized how much it was hurting you. Maybe I could have handled it differently. I'm sorry."

Her head tilted to one side as she studied him. The gesture stabbed at him. Innocent yet cautious. The differences in her kept hitting him at odd times, but he'd never realized until now how much those changes were due to him. She was stronger than he'd given her credit for, but she was also much warier.

Because of him.

How was he going to be able to break through all these barricades between them? Especially when it was his actions that had put them up.

His mother's words whispered in his ear. Earlier that night she'd pulled him aside before Anna came downstairs.

There's only one way to heal the past, hijo. *You must open your heart to her.*

He took a deep breath and jumped, going airborne in an area totally foreign to him. He should have been confident.

But he was scared to death.

"I take full responsibility for what happened to us. But I can't be held accountable for things I didn't know about."

She watched him, her distrust narrowing her eyes.

"I want, more than anything in this world, to be with you for the rest of my life. I want to wake up next to you every morning and go to sleep holding you in my arms. I want to be a husband and a father and spend every day trying to make you and the twins as happy as possible."

He tried to gauge her reaction, but too many emotions were

flicking across her face now. Better than nothing, he thought. Praying, he plunged ahead.

"I can't do it by myself. I can't read your mind, Anna. When something upsets you, you need to tell me. Because I can't be held responsible for it unless I know about it and get a chance to fix it.

"Last week, when I caught sight of you for the first time in forever, I couldn't believe I'd walked away from you. Now, looking at you and knowing you haven't been with anyone else, well…I almost wish there had been," he murmured.

"What? I thought you'd be happy about it," she said, throwing the sarcastic words at him.

"Sure, a part of me is happy. But I thought I had a chance to make up for running out on you. To find out I ran for no reason and left you pregnant *and* alone. You'll never be able to forgive me."

Her silence confirmed his suspicions.

"I can't believe Mama did this to me. To us! Why didn't she write me about the twins?"

"She didn't know about them. I left not long after you."

"You didn't tell her?"

"She wouldn't speak to me! I thought it was because she believed I'd been unfaithful to you, but now I know it was because she couldn't face me."

The anger simmering beneath the surface erupted. "So here you were, pregnant, and you lost me, your mom and Mama all at the same time? Why are you even speaking to us?"

The saddest smile curved her lips and tightened his throat. "You're my children's family. I hate what happened, but I understand why you both reacted the way you did. Lina punishes herself far more than I ever could."

"You could keep her away from her grandchildren."

"Oh, sure, I could keep her away from her only living family, and my children would go without a wonderful, loving grandmother. That would make everything wrong turn magically right."

"You're a bigger person that I am," he grumbled.

"If I hadn't gone to your funeral, I never would have seen your mother. If I hadn't spoken to her, I never would have known the truth, and a part of me would still hate you."

He flinched.

"I'm not saying this to hurt you."

"I know."

She sighed heavily. "Lina did what she did because she wanted to protect you. Can you imagine what it's been like for her, thinking she sent you to your death? Thinking she'd deprived her grandchildren of their father?"

His gaze shot to hers. As her words sank in, some of the anger drained.

"No, I can't imagine it. You know, when I told her who I was, she said she had something to tell me. Do you think she was going to tell me the truth?"

"Yes."

"You sound certain."

"I am. I asked her not to the next day."

"Why?" His head reared back in disbelief.

"I had my reasons."

"Tell me."

She frowned at his command. "I wanted you to forgive me and let go of it. If you found out right away, then you'd be feeling like you are now—guilty. I don't want your pity."

"You don't want my pity," he said slowly, trying to sort through her confession. "You could have gotten your pound of flesh by throwing all this in my face. But you didn't. Which means you didn't want revenge, you didn't want to hurt me and you didn't want my pity. What do you want?"

Her lips parted, then closed, and a mutinous look crossed her face. She resembled Rebecca during a pout, but she was definitely all woman. *His* woman if he had his way.

"Remember, I can't read your mind."

"It doesn't matter—"

"It does!" he interrupted. "What do you want? You're the one who's suffered the most! What is it *you* want?"

Tears welled up in her eyes, and he forced away the instinct to hug her to him. He could feel her tension, knew this was too important to back down from.

"When I met 'Gage,' I was so confused. For the first time since you I was attracted to another man. I wanted to spend time with him, make love to him, maybe have a future with him. I started to believe I could let go of you and love someone else and have someone love me." The words tumbled out of her, and she was oblivious to the tears sliding down her cheeks. "I've had to be the strong one all the time and I wanted to share some of it. I wanted to be held and supported. I wanted a man to share my life and be proud of all I've done and will do. I like my independence. I've worked hard for it!"

She'd been leaning forward as she delivered her passionate answer. Now she slumped back down and swiped the tears from her cheeks with both palms.

"You wouldn't understand," she finished.

He pulled his knees up and rested his forearms there, staring at her.

"I think I do. You wanted me to love you."

Her eyes and mouth rounded before she tried to hide her reaction. He was right.

"I think that because you distrust me so much, you wanted to know how I felt before you told me the truth," he said the words lightly, trying not to sound accusing. But he had another truth he needed to uncover. "You haven't been with any other men at all, have you, Bella?"

She stared hard at him, shoulders back and arms folded against her chest. "No!" she burst out. "There's been no one else!"

She reminded him of the stray kitten he'd found behind his house. Prickly, defensive and totally adorable. She would hate the comparison.

"I see," he said calmly, focusing on the one small light

she'd left on in the corner of the attic. Inside him, though, a storm of emotion besieged him. He wasn't proud of it. In fact, a sadness filled his chest along with tenderness and his body's other, more insubordinate, responses.

Then he made the mistake of looking at her, and all his good intentions were blown away. Pure male satisfaction clashed with hot need and set off thunderous results he no longer had hope of controlling.

"You know how I feel. I told you before I knew the truth. So the question is, What are you going to do with me now?"

Chapter 9

His eyes blazed with warning and promise. The air she held in her lungs burned, reminding her to breathe.

"'Do with you?'" The words rushed out on her exhale, but she was proud of the breathless, offhand tone.

She might as well have pulled a tiger's tail.

A slow, bone-melting smile answered her. He leaned close, bracing his weight on his hands. It took little to bring him within inches of her.

"Yeah. 'Do with me.' I'm all yours. You decide."

The desire that exploded in her stomach stunned her. Grateful she was already on the floor so she couldn't fall, she felt a sheen of sweat break across her face.

All mine. He's all mine. This beautiful man, who looks like he should be posing for one of those calendars with half-naked men in it, is offering himself to me. To me. And it's Rico. My Rico.

He remained still, waiting for her to decide, and in that moment the most powerful feeling broke over her. She could leave right now or she could stay here, with this man, this ghost of her heart.

The uncertainty disappeared, and her fears calmed. No matter what their future, no matter what happened with the danger lurking around them, she had tonight. All for her.

So she smiled and watched in fascination as his nostrils flared and his eyes glowed impossibly brighter.

"Are you sure?"

She nodded. "As long as we're safe. From the outside dangers, I mean. It seems absurd to even think of this when…"

"We're okay. I checked in ten minutes ago." As he spoke, his lips moved closer until her own tilted in response and felt his words puff against them.

She nodded, the movement brushing her lips against his, and she heard his breathing stall. His tongue came out to wet his lips and brushed against hers. She sucked in a breath, its pass over her wet lips another kind of caress.

"Just once," he whispered before leaning into her. His lips joined hers slowly, and she watched in fascination as his lashes lowered against his cheeks. Something about seeing him unguarded tugged at her—a fragile emotion mixing with the passion he called up with a touch.

The exquisite movement of his mouth on hers made tears sting her eyes. He cherished her without being overwhelming, giving her the space to pull away.

As much as she enjoyed being a recipient, she wanted to share the incredible feelings he inspired in her. She put her hands on either side of his face and deepened the kiss, trying to tell him without words what he meant to her.

He pulled away timeless moments later and stared. A small smile quirked his lips, and with a scarred finger he traced a path only he could see from her temple to her lips.

"I'm going to take another check of the house," he said, his voice husky. He paused. "Meet me in the bedroom?"

She heard the question within his question. He was giving her a chance to choose more than the room.

She nodded, and he searched her face intently before he nodded back. Then he left on ghost-silent feet, and she stared at the empty doorway, wondering if she was dreaming.

Rico checked the house once more. He paged the agent again and waited for all-clear back. While he waited, he tried to ignore his body's throbbing urgency to return upstairs. He tried to forget the expression on Anna's face after they'd kissed. The need and the fascination.

He strode into the darkened kitchen and hurriedly drank a cold glass of water. The glass still in hand, he wiped his mouth across his forearm and caught sight of the glass's decoration.

"Snow White and the Seven Dwarfs."

What the hell was he doing? He couldn't make love to her tonight. Yeah, they'd answered a lot of questions. But there was more. Maybe he was expecting too much, too soon, but he could see she was still holding back.

Making love might get past the last of the walls. Or it could backfire in his face.

He squeezed the glass, wishing he could throw it. Trying to mend fences with his family and catch this psycho were taking its toll on his nerves. He was so tense that even the healthy parts of him were beginning to ache.

He got another glass of water and rolled his neck.

Making love to Anna would relax him.

He chugged the water, forcing the thought from his mind. Besides its effect on their relationship, he couldn't ignore the real danger they faced. Agents or not. And when just looking at her made him deaf and blind to everything around him, he could just imagine how he'd be with her lying naked in his arms…

He groaned aloud and forced the image from his mind. There would be time for them later, after this whole mess was over.

But how could he not make love to her? How could he go back up there and keep his hands off her?

His beeper vibrated, and he checked the green glowing numbers on its display. All clear.

He'd let them all down once before. He'd be damned if he failed them again.

Anna walked out of her master bathroom and stopped, digging her toes into the soft carpet. She'd seen in a movie that the repetitive motion was relaxing. Her stomach reminded her of a ride she'd gone on at a fair last summer. A violent combination of excitement and fear that came too close to nausea.

When she'd come down from the office, she'd felt only the excitement. But in the bathroom nightlight she'd looked into the mirror and seen a mother of two with more stretch marks than sexual experience.

What would she wear? Should she be waiting in bed?

She knew the candlelight would hide the stretch marks pretty well. Then again, this was her, and those marks were from his kids! He'd need to accept her for the woman she was now. Not the young girl she'd been.

She'd taken off her clothes and looked into the full-length mirror on the back of the door. Well, the lights being off the first time couldn't hurt.

Naked, she thanked her lucky stars that she'd shaved her legs that morning and slapped on some lotion. Teeth and hair brushed, she realized she only had her normal nightshirt in the bathroom. That wouldn't do. Seduction in Snoopy wasn't quite what she'd envisioned. She wrapped her bath towel around her and went in search of clothes.

So, here she stood. Wrapped in a towel, doing ridiculous toe exercises in her carpet that weren't working. And he'd be here any second.

Her stomach shifted into overdrive as she hurried to her dresser. She dug to the back of her underwear drawer, past the utilitarian white undies until her fingers hit paydirt. She'd bought an ivory lace and satin camisole to wear with an outfit and it had come with matching tap panties. They would have to do.

She slipped them on, the slide of satin only doubling her nervous goose bumps. Now, in bed or out? She folded down the sheet and light blanket. There. With the three fat candles burning strategically around the room, it looked welcoming.

Jeez, Anna, this isn't the hospitality suite!

She started to pace, wringing her hands, while the panicked mantra, "I can't do this, I can't do this, I can't do this," raced through her mind. She wasn't a seductress. She was a tired mom, for goodness sake!

Just then she heard a creak on the stairs and froze, halfway between the door and her bed. Mentally she was scurrying around the room for a suitable place to lounge. None were working.

Forget it! I'm under the covers, she thought and moved to the bed.

"Wow." Rico's deep voice paralyzed her mid-dive. "You are not making this easy, lady."

She didn't turn around, although she could only imagine the kind of view she presented.

"I came up here to tell you our timing is off." She felt, more than heard, his stepping closer. "But seeing you, I'm thinking to hell with timing."

If she leaned back a tiny bit, she'd be against him. She fought the urge as she tried to sort through his words.

"You don't want to?" she whispered.

He skimmed his mouth against her nape, sending uncontrollable tremors throughout her body. Then his warm hands captured her waist before sliding across her quivering stomach to pull her flush against the front of his body.

A sigh shuddered out of him as he buried his face in her neck. The feel of his warm, male skin threw the butterflies in her stomach into a heated frenzy. No inch of her collarbone escaped his mouth, and she was trembling helplessly by the time he reached her ear.

Like a puppet whose strings only he pulled, her body responded to his touch and wordless commands. His palms skimmed up her sides, causing her camisole to wave upward in a cool tide against her heated face. He halted, and the satin pooled on top of her breasts. Outlined in ivory perfection, the satin was stilled only by the nipples hardening in anticipation.

"Beautiful," he breathed, and she saw that he too watched the satin's undulations across her chest. In deliciously slow movements, his fingers skimmed the skin below its waving edges, avoiding the berried tips begging for his touch.

She gripped the muscled forearms that banded across her chest, and her head fell back against his shoulder. Eyes squeezed shut, she silently willed his fingers to end the throbbing torture. She arched forward and drew a sound from him, although the relentless teasing continued.

She rolled her head and watched him watch her. He dragged his gaze up to hers, his so hot with need that the ball of warmth in her stomach melted, a liquid consent that needed no further interpretation.

"Kiss me," she whispered, her fingers curving around the back of his neck and pressing him closer.

He groaned and mumbled something, but she was beyond trying to piece together words. Their mouths met in an explosion of need in the same moment his hands captured her breasts.

Nearly incoherent with sensation, her knees buckled, tightening his grip on her. She didn't realize he'd flipped her to face him until he stopped kissing her. She raised heavy lids to see him dragging his shirt over his head. Without embarrassment, she copied him, slinging her camisole onto the floor.

He froze, then stared at her, shaking his head with an expression of awe as his gaze traveled over her. When his eyes met hers, confidence and a vivid happiness gathered in her, burning off the last of her insecurities.

He held out a hand, and she twined her fingers with his, remembering a night not long ago when he'd shown her how sensitive fingers could be. With a tug she was against him, chest to chest, skin to skin, heart to heart.

They hugged, breathing in sync, each marveling over impossible dreams becoming reality. Time passed, and for once neither counted the lost seconds and minutes.

Because they were together.

Finally he leaned back, and she couldn't prevent the smile spreading across her face.

"What?" he asked gruffly, a matching smile starting.

She snuggled her chin into his chest and tried not to stare at his mouth. "I'm half-naked, shaking with lust," she giggled as he pinched her rear end and then continued, "and so happy I feel like I could burst."

A devilish light lit his eyes but as he opened his mouth to answer her, his expression became shuttered.

"Are you?"

Her smile faltered. "Are I what?"

"Happy."

The glow of it filled her, and she knew it was in her smile. "Impossible as it seems. Yes. Totally, completely, absolutely."

He sighed and brought his hands up to frame her face. He dipped his head to kiss her with overwhelming tenderness. Then, in a move that belied any physical limitations, he swung her into his arms. She curled her arms around his neck and shoulders and took advantage of the skin before her.

"Hey," he said, nudging his shoulder against her lips. She realized they weren't in the bed, but in the big rocking chair in the corner.

Confused, she shifted into a comfortable position on his lap. Then she saw his shirt over the arm.

"Hands up," he said, avoiding her eyes. She started to lift them up as he fumbled with the shirt. Why had he stopped? He still wanted her. She was all but sitting on the evidence.

But then...why? Mortification seeped into her and she froze, fighting it with the knowledge of what they'd just shared. Sensing her stillness, he met her eyes and proved how strong their connection still was.

"Don't even think that," he ordered, gathering the shirt to slip it over her head.

She yanked her arms down, pulling his gaze to her breasts. He looked away, then back at her face.

"Here, put this on."

"No."

He raised his eyebrows at her tone. "What?"

She grabbed the shirt from him and hurled it across the room. It hit the wall with a satisfying smack and fell in a crumpled heap. Then, with hands braced on the chair arms, she rearranged her legs so she sat astride him.

"Now that I'm more comfortable," she proved it with a wiggle, "Why don't you fill me in on what happened between the last kiss and here?"

Eyes wide since her wiggle, he stared at her in disbelief.

She sighed and leaned into him.

"Wait!" His hands gripped her shoulders, holding her away from him. She bit back a smile at his obvious dilemma. Hold her away so her breasts aren't touching him, but that left him a huge visual problem.

"Anna, listen, I know I'm handling this all wrong, and you have every right to slug me, but I can explain. *If* you put something on first."

She thought about it for half a second. "No."

He threw his hands up and focused his gaze on a candle across the room, his face turned resolutely away from her. Considering she'd been panicking about her nakedness not—she looked at the clock—not thirty minutes before, it was amazing that she felt completely confident sitting here. And for a big, macho guy, he was acting incredibly childish.

She smiled a little, then a devilish thought tickled her into a full-blown grin. Stretching her feet out until her toes sank into the carpet, she pushed, sending the chair rocking.

He whipped his head around and clamped her hips in his

hands, pushing them back onto his thighs. "Knock it off, Anna. You're not playing fair."

She arched a brow at his growl and knew her grin wasn't helping matters.

"You don't want me," she said evenly.

"Oh, yeah, you got proof of that," he said sarcastically.

"I did something wrong," she said in the same mild tone. She didn't put it in question, because she knew she wasn't the problem.

He looked at her quickly, shaking his head side to side. His gaze skipped down her body, and with a muffled groan he let go of her to grip the chair's arms with white-knuckled fists.

"You're killing me and sitting there laughing about it. Dammit, Anna, we can't do this!"

"Why not?"

"Why not? Look at me! Look what you do to me! What good would I be if someone did get in here?"

"But you said before that it would be fine."

He sighed. "Yeah, I know. Then I went downstairs and my sanity returned. I'd be crazy to risk everything for this."

She pulled back a bit, and he looked at her. "Damn, I knew I'd screw this up. That's not what I meant." He pulled her closer. "When I look at you, everything around me sort of disappears. When I touch you, nothing else exists for me, except you. I can't be ready to protect us if I'm not aware of the outside world."

His eyes beseeched her to understand, and she could see the obvious effort it was taking to rein himself in. She thought of every vile curse and then screamed them in her head.

"You're right," she said as she untangled herself from his lap. She refused to think of how ungraceful she looked. "I hate it, but you're right. Dammit."

He chuckled and she marched into the bathroom. In a few seconds she lounged against the door frame in her green Snoopy nightshirt.

"So, hot stuff, wanna cuddle?"

* * *

Rico lay on top of the covers, his right arm between his head and a pillow. Anna curled against him but under the covers, so he couldn't feel any body parts that would destroy his control.

They'd been talking about the kids and her work, but stopped a few minutes before to lie in silence. Her head rested on his shoulder, and his left hand played with the ends of her hair.

She was amazing. Never failed to surprise him. He'd walked into the room earlier, determined not to touch her. When he'd seen her standing there, all ivory satin, shadows and candlelight, he'd known he was lost.

She'd been nervous. He'd felt it in her tense posture against him. But the chemistry between them was too strong for even her to fight.

If she hadn't smiled at him, radiant and happy, he may not have come to his senses in time. It had slammed into him how much he stood to lose, and the thought had twisted his heart.

"What's wrong?" she whispered, wrapping her arm tighter around him.

He smiled in the darkness. It should scare him how easily she picked up on his thoughts and feelings. But it didn't. It comforted him and chased away the loneliness he'd carried for so many years.

"I was thinking about when you told me you were happy."

She shifted to look at him. In the candle's yellow glow, she looked even more beautiful. He didn't know if he could continue not touching her.

"It's okay," she said, once again turning into him. "This isn't easy on me, either."

They just stared at each other. The desire was there, but another emotion overpowered it. She hadn't said the words yet. She didn't need to. He could see it, feel it.

She gave him a small smile and winked. "We're going to have to suffer through this together."

He tried to smile back, but knew it fell short. The emotions running through him didn't allow for easy bantering.

She sighed. "Okay. What were you thinking about me being happy?"

"That I wanted you to always be that way. I was worried that if we made love tonight, you'd pull away again."

"Why?"

"Because of our past. Because there's still a lot we have to talk about."

"True. But I'd consciously made the decision to make love with you. It's not as if we'd gotten carried away without thinking it through."

He mulled that one over. "You thought about it? What did you think would happen tomorrow, in the light of day? Would you kiss me in front of Mama and our kids like I thought about you doing?"

She stiffened.

He pulled his arm from beneath his head and wrapped her in his arms, dropping a kiss on top of her head.

"Don't," he said, nuzzling her hair.

Her troubled face tilted up to his. "I didn't want to think about those things. I just..."

"You just what?"

"Well, now it sounds stupid and irresponsible."

He squeezed her, a silent urging to tell him.

"I just wanted to be with you." She shook her head. "Do you know how many nights I dreamed of you here, in my bed, holding me, believing me? Then to have even a part of that dream coming true. How could I not grab it?"

"Hell with it," he said, getting up and yanking back the covers. "I have to hold you."

Surprised, she hesitated and then held the covers up so he could slide between them more easily. Instead, he walked around the bed and climbed in the other side behind her.

"Here, turn over. I just want to face the door."

They both sighed as their bodies came together, face to face and sharing the same pillow.

"One kiss?"

She nodded.

A mere melding of lips, as much closeness as they could allow, and his heartbeat sped up.

He broke it off and gave her a mock-stern glare and order. "Don't make this any harder than it is. No pun intended, of course."

She chuckled, and the tension lowered to a tolerable level.

"So, would you like to hear about the great Chocolate Icing Caper?"

"Of course."

"I'm really to blame. After all, in a child's eyes, icing is only a tiny bit thicker than paint. Why wouldn't it look good all over the hallway walls?"

He laughed.

And in that room, sheltered by darkness and dreams, they filled in the holes of the past. For a little while there was no pain or anger, no regrets or sacrifices.

There was only an unspoken love.

Chapter 10

"**No!**"

The guttural denial blasted her awake. Her heart slamming against her breast, Anna struggled to focus.

In the nightlight's soft glow, she could see nothing out of the ordinary.

Then a fist slammed into her back. She flipped to face Rico as he let out an agonized moan.

Asleep, with his face twisted by the demons tormenting him, he lay rigid on the bed, his covers kicked off.

"Wake up. It's okay, you're safe," she whispered, and made a crucial mistake.

She touched him.

In a blur of movement her arm was bent back to the breaking point, her face forced into her pillow in a futile attempt to escape the pain. She tried to call him, wake him up by yelling his name, but the pain had robbed her breath.

"No more."

The words sounded as if they'd been pulled out of his chest. She sucked in enough oxygen to croak, "Okay."

Abruptly he let go.

"Oh, God, Anna. Jesus! Did I hurt you?"

Once again she was flipped, only this time as if she was porcelain and not a bag of cement. Her arm protested the movement, and she used her other hand to hold it close to her body.

Rico continued to murmur broken apologies around his rapid breaths. As the shrieking in her arm lowered to a holler, her ability to speak returned.

"You take the term 'bed hog' to new heights."

Dredges of his nightmare darkened his face, stole all softness from it. Jaw locked, lips sealed and eyes raging with guilt and horror, another stranger had revealed himself.

"Sit up. I'm checking your arm."

Before she could refuse, he'd levered her up. Clutching her arm to her, she closed her gaping mouth. It was obvious he wasn't going to listen to her.

"Does this hurt?" he asked, carefully raising her arm even with her shoulder.

She shook her head and bit back a moan.

"This?" His shaking voice belied his attempt at being medically impersonal. He rotated her sore arm then probed the muscles and bones.

"Yeah, it hurts, but I don't think anything's broken," she assured him. "I've strained it worse after carrying one of the kids through the mall."

She smiled ruefully at him, trying to draw him out of the terrible intensity that gripped him while ignoring the throbbing that pulsed from wrist to shoulder.

He continued examining her arm before nodding, as if answering his own question. He lowered it back down and, in a swift move, sat on the edge of the bed, hands gripping the mattress.

He said nothing.

She waited impatiently, then let go of her tongue.

"Are you going to tell me about it?"

He stared at the floor as if it possessed answers.

"Hey," she said, leaning to the side and trying to get in his peripheral vision.

No response.

"Warning, I'm about to touch you," she said, half kidding. She reached out and laid her hand on his bare shoulder.

He was shaking. Not obvious, violent tremors. Intermittent currents like tiny vibrations. "I could have killed you."

Close enough to see how bloodless his knuckles were, she scooted nearer on the rumpled covers and put her other hand over them.

"But you didn't. You let go right away."

He didn't respond.

"Look at me!" She tightened her hold and shook him lightly.

His head turned, and she almost wished she could take back the order.

Devastation. She closed her eyes against it, praying the laughing, loving Rico would return.

He did not.

They'd come so far that night, bared so much. She'd known, deep down, that she couldn't bring up his capture, and she'd avoided it. She'd been afraid to lose the magical ease they'd discovered.

Maybe she should have pushed earlier.

"Talk to me," she whispered, scooting forward until the knees of her crossed legs touched his side. "I want to know what happened to you. I want to understand it and help you if I can."

He abruptly shook his head.

"Please don't shut me out."

Not again.

This time it was he who closed his eyes, as if he'd heard the silent words.

"I respect your need for privacy, but I don't think you should keep this inside. It's eating away at you. I can see it.

I can't believe you've kept it hidden, but now that I know, I'm going to push until you share it. Dammit, let me help you!''

Another emotion flickered, but he looked away before she could name it.

"It wasn't so bad at first. Threats, beatings." He stood and went to the windows, peeking out. She knew instinctively that he didn't want her touching him while he opened these wounds. So she clenched her hands in her lap and forced herself to remain on the bed.

"I could take their fists. I'd had worse in Miami." His voice held as much emotion as his expression—none. "But they'd push all the right buttons. Beat you until you prayed you'd pass out. Then haul you up and talk about America and what I could be doing instead, if I'd just tell them where my men were meeting. I'd refuse. The beatings would start again. With whips or pipes or chains. Whatever they got their hands on. Then they'd talk some more. Then electric shock. Then beat me some more. Got to the point I could time it."

He chuckled without humor. "I kept refusing. I don't know how. The more they pushed, the more I vowed to not give them what they wanted. Then they brought in Carmen."

Abruptly he turned away from the window and began pacing the room. She didn't want to hear his next words. The horror in his voice told her enough.

But she'd listen. Even if she ground her teeth down to the nerves, she'd listen.

"She was our informant. A member of the local rebels. She was beautiful. Exotic, but natural. Different from anyone I'd ever seen before.

"She was also the oldest teenager I'd ever met. Seventeen years old with eyes that had never been young. I don't know what she'd lived through. I only know our lives looked like a walk in the park next to hers.

"We're still not sure how they captured her. Or how they

even knew she'd helped us. But a little money goes a long way down there, and information is easy to get.''

He stopped, and she knew he couldn't avoid it any longer. He began to ramble, completely caught up in the past.

"They gave me one more chance to tell. I looked at her, as much as I could. My one eye was blinded by blood. The other swollen shut. But I could see her. They hit her. Over and over. And she kept glaring at me, screaming at me not to do it. Not to tell them. They ripped her clothes off and still she looked at me, so brave and proud—''

His voice broke and she covered her mouth with both hands to hold back any sound. She didn't want him stopping because of her reaction.

"I knew that if I told them where my men were they'd kill us. And I couldn't tell. They'd have sent a small army after them. That night was the pickup, and hopefully the reinforcements would arrive with it.''

He stopped pacing and stared down at the flame of the candle.

"They could see I was wavering, so they chained her against a wall and left us alone. She stood there, shivering, naked, bruised and bleeding and told me she'd never forgive me if I told. That her whole family had been killed by the Balangerios and she would do anything to bring them down...that being raped was nothing, it had happened before.''

He shook his head and looked at her. "Can you imagine? Rape being a way of life? This girl stood there begging me *not* to help her!'' He heaved a huge sigh, and Anna could clearly see the weight he carried. "Carmen knew the men were meeting the helicopter and said maybe things would change. I knew she was referring to the brief chance help would arrive. Then she said she knew it wouldn't be easy for me to watch, that I reminded her of her dead brother, and he too would have done anything to prevent her from being hurt.''

His voice had become progressively quieter as he spoke. He

turned to face her and it took all her strength not to go to him. A tear rolled down the candlelit side of his face.

"They raped her. The whole time she stared at me, and I never looked away. I wanted to will every ounce of strength I had left to her, and she knew it. It sounds ridiculous, but I think I helped her. And because she didn't fight back or scream or cry, she took away their pleasure in it. When they realized their plan backfired, they stopped and let her up. She walked out of my cell and gave me a small smile. It was victorious. Like somehow she'd won a battle."

Anna couldn't stay on the bed. She went to him and took his face in her hands, but left space between them. "Don't carry this guilt. You can't. Carmen made a decision, and like you said, if you'd told, they might have killed you both."

He exhaled, more of a sob than a breath. "I can't stop seeing her. I couldn't *do* anything, Anna. I couldn't help her!"

She realized that this situation only aggravated the deep guilt. Here he was in a situation without any control.

"Where is she now?"

He reached out to her and pulled her close, cradling her the way she wanted to do for him. His warm, naked skin was slick against her face, and his heart beat fast in her ear. "I don't know! That's just it. I don't know where she is. About six hours after she left the cell, all hell broke loose. Reinforcements had arrived, and against orders, my men came back for me. I told Mike to look for her, but no one ever found her."

He hesitated, and she knew what his next words would be, so she spoke quickly. "That's no reason to assume she's dead."

"How can I not? They wouldn't have just let her walk away. She should have been on the grounds somewhere. And even if by some slim chance she managed to get away, where would she go? She had no one! It kills me to think of her being left with nothing after risking her life."

Anna sighed, unsure of what to say. "Maybe you didn't leave her with nothing. The Balangerios were taken down, just as she wanted.'' She hugged him to her. ''I understand what you're saying about her being alone, but surely she had friends.''

He shrugged and spoke with his lips against her hair. ''I hope so. I hope someone's taking care of her.''

Anna held him and sent up a prayer about Carmen. Then she led him back to bed and pulled him to her.

It was time someone took care of him.

''Why do ya think he's seepin' with Mom?'' asked the whisperer.

''Maybe she had a bad dream,'' said whisperer number two, in a matter-of-fact tone.

''Or maybe she needed a hug,'' said the first one.

''She still needs one.''

The sleep-warmed wall behind her began to shake. Having had more experience, Anna was able to keep on her sleep face. Usually she heard the most interesting conversations between the twins when they thought she still slept.

Just when she was about to crack open an eye, another hushed voice entered the room.

''You two come out of there. It's barely dawn. Let your mother and R— Gage sleep.''

If the cat was ever in the bag, it was surely out now.

On their way out, Rebecca asked Lina why Gage had no pajamas on. All they heard of Lina's answer before the door closed was, ''He only wears the bottoms.''

Anna and Rico burst into quiet laughter, neither realizing Lina stood on the other side of the door, a matching smile lighting her face before she followed the twins to their bedroom.

Rico leaned over her shoulder. ''I get the feeling this is a morning ritual.''

She let her lids drift shut, refusing to figure out the minutes of sleep they'd grabbed between Rico's frequent house checks, his nightmare and the twins' arrival. ''Every morning. I listen to them and then pretend to wake up. It's better than a loud, beeping alarm clock.''

She squinted a scratchy eye open, thankful the blinds prevented the sunlight from piercing her brain. Rico's shadowed jaw and sleepy, deep-yellow eyes came into a blurry focus, causing a knee-jerk reaction of disbelief.

He was in her bed.

Unfortunately, morning was not her best time, regardless of the motherhood prerequisite, and she didn't think before saying, ''You're not going to kiss me, are you?''

''I'd been considering it.''

''Don't. Bottle my morning breath, and the government would have a lethal weapon.''

Something between a snort and a laugh made her realize that this wasn't the usual morning-after type chat. Too tired to be completely embarrassed, she buried her face in her pillow and mollified herself with the thought that this was not a usual morning-after, either. The bed shifted as he got up and as she gave in to the pull of sleep, she heard him in her bathroom.

Much too soon a voice said, ''Here, princess,'' and something was pushed into the hand dangling off the bed.

She opened her eye again to see her toothbrush, prepped with toothpaste.

''Hey, hurry up. I want my kiss,'' he said around his own toothbrush. ''Hope you didn't mind, I found this new one under your sink.''

''I've heard of breakfast in bed, but not dental hygiene,'' she mumbled as she pushed herself into a sitting position. Even knowing she'd be embarrassed about this later, when the rest of her brain cells woke up, she couldn't push away her normal morning grouchiness.

At least, she rationalized, he now knew mornings were not her best time.

With her empty hand she slung her mass of tangled hair off her face and started brushing. As he stood there brushing his own teeth and looking far too pleased with himself, her grumpiness escalated.

Around her toothpaste bubbles, she grouched, "I have to get up now to spit."

He smiled around his orange-handled toothbrush, and bent gallantly at the waist, gesturing to the empty bathroom. Anna walked past him as regally as the situation allowed, finished up and returned to bed.

"If you're not running for the door now," she said, half seriously, "Nothing's going to scare you away."

"I told you before, I'm not going anywhere. I already knew you weren't a happy person in the morning, remember?"

She frowned.

"Who had to wait every morning for you to get ready for school? You were never ready on time and usually didn't speak until we got halfway there."

"I forgot about that," she mused.

"I didn't. I figure I can handle it. Even if I have to bring you toothpaste in bed every morning." He grinned, looking far too devastating for someone who hadn't showered yet.

She sighed, wondering if this was another one of God's little jokes. She must look like something a tornado spit out, and he could pose for a magazine cologne ad.

"The things I do for one of your kisses," he teased, crawling back onto the bed. "Is it safe now?"

She squinted her eyes in a pseudo glare, then ruined it by smiling. "I don't know, you tell me."

He did, but much later.

"I'm so happy for you both, *hija,*" Lina said, giving Anna a rib-crushing hug.

A sliver of disquiet whispered through her, but she shoved it away. "We worked through a lot last night, but there are some things left."

She looked over Lina's shoulder to see Rico on the floor

with the kids. They'd all finished breakfast, and he'd been occupying them with a puzzle while the women did the dishes.

"I told him the truth," she said, sliding in the bottom tray of the dishwasher and closing the door.

The fork Lina was putting away dropped to the floor.

"And?"

"And he took it well. I explained things and he was confused, angry. But I think he understands."

Lina nodded, both women remembering the long hug he'd given his mother earlier that morning.

"Does not mean he will forgive me."

Anna folded her dish towel and hung it from the stove door. "He'll always look at you as the mother who loved him enough to try to protect him. And he'll always love you."

Lina pressed her lips together and nodded briskly. "I hope you are right, *hija*."

"Grandma!" Rafe called as he skip-jogged into the room. "I'm hungry."

"You just finished breakfast, little one. How can you be hungry?"

"Gage says it's cause I'm a growing boy," he answered, stretching on his tiptoes to try to grab a banana.

"Oh, wait just a moment," Lina said, putting down her dish towel and getting the banana out of the fruit bowl. "You are going to turn into a monkey with all the bananas you eat."

That had Rafe itching his sides and hopping around making monkey noises. Anna rolled her eyes at Rico, who'd paused at his puzzle making to stand and watch his son's theatrics. His dark, contact-colored eyes still managed to dance with mirth as they met hers.

Suddenly he looked down at his beeper, and all humor disappeared. She regained her breath as his expression calmed.

He walked up behind her, one hand taking advantage of the island counter's cover to slide down her right hip. The shivers went straight up her spine in a slow, heated blush.

"That was Mike," he said low in her ear, obviously uncaring of his mother's delighted glances. "He's here."

"Here?"

He linked his fingers with hers and led her into the living room at the front of the house.

"Don't panic," he said, keeping away from the windows and gathering her in his arms. "He has pictures and information we need to go over. I don't want him coming to the house."

"Why not? Wouldn't it be safer if you stayed here?"

He pressed his lips together and cradled her face in his large palms. "I'll be fine and so will all of you. We'll have one agent tail us and leave three with you. I won't be gone long. I promise."

It was absurd to feel so scared; she knew that. After all, this psycho wasn't going to storm in here without being stopped by their government caretakers first.

"Are you sure Mike can't just come here? He's a friend of Gage's, so why would it make any difference?"

"Whoever is looking into my background will find Mike. Probably already has. We started out in boot camp together and were in the same units for years.

"Look, this guy has every marking of a professional. A professional would know everything about their target, even things their target doesn't know about."

She searched his eyes, looking for something to lessen her growing fear. The determination she found didn't help.

"You're talking about Rafe."

He nodded. "I never gave information about the twins. How could I? Yet this guy knows about them. Which means he's known about you and Mama for a while and has been waiting."

The chill in her manifested into a shiver. He sighed and rubbed his hands carefully on the outside of her arms. Even though she suffered no bruises from the arm twisting last night, he was absurdly gentle.

"I don't mean to scare you, Anna, but I want you to understand what we're up against."

"I do," she said into his shirt. "I just don't like it."

"Neither do I," he whispered, planting a kiss on her temple and cocooning her in his arms.

"How long will you be gone?" she asked, pulling away to look up at his face. If she could keep looking at him, he was still here.

"An hour, tops."

They stood there, holding each other. Along with her fear of his safety and theirs was another deeper dread. He might not return.

Again.

"The sooner I leave, the sooner I return," he coaxed, rocking side to side.

The chill in her iced. She'd heard those words before. Her father had said them as he uncurled her small arms from around his waist.

Only he'd never returned.

She nodded, the jerky movement hurting the tight muscles in her neck. Searching for more strength from her ever-depleting reserves, she faced him, memorized him.

"Be safe."

He cocked his head to the side and brought her hand up to his lips. The emotion in his eyes caused the lump in her throat to burn even more.

"I'll be safe, Bella. I've got too much to live for this time."

His words replayed in her mind long after he'd left. *Too much to live for this time.* If they survived this hell, could the two of them actually have a second chance? Could she trust him enough to stay, even though she hadn't been the reason for his return?

Glancing up at the clock for the hundredth time since he left, not thirty minutes before, she slapped the playing cards on the table and fell back against the chair.

"A watched pot never boils, *hija*."

Lina sat across from her at the kitchen table while the twins sat engrossed in an educational television show.

"I know, I know."

"He'll be back."

Anna glanced up at the confident tone. "You seem sure."

"*Sí,* I am."

Ridiculous as it was, the tension in her eased a bit. Why Lina's belief would make a difference she didn't know. It just did.

"I need to do something," she announced, standing to put the cards away.

The doorbell rang.

The cards flew out of her hand, tumbling around her like old leaves in a fall wind. She met Lina's serious gaze.

"Stay with the twins."

"*Sí.*"

Inching into the foyer, she tried to use the afternoon sunlight to see a shadow on the porch. The long, thin windows on either side of the door were covered with sheer curtains, and usually a person's silhouette could be seen.

Not this time.

The agents wouldn't let anyone unknown get close to the door. So who could it be?

Skirting the door, she came up close to one of the small windows just as the knocking started.

"Anna, I know you're home. Hurry up! This cake's heavy!"

Relief clashed with the adrenaline in her system, and she swallowed to push back the nausea. She took labor-reminiscent pants to slow her heartbeat and swung open the door.

"Dana! I'm sorry about that. I was downstairs doing laundry and Lina was on the phone."

Dana's big grin widened further. "You're out of shape, my friend, if you get that winded running up the basement steps.

You know, maybe I should keep this cheesecake all to myself.''

"Don't you dare!" Anna said, swinging her friend into the house with one hand and closing and subtly locking the door with the other. "I need to indulge, and this is perfect."

Dana laughed, leading the way to the kitchen.

"Hello, Lina," she said, leaning over to give the woman a kiss while she set the cake on the table. "I made this extra special today. In fact, I think it's my best attempt yet."

"You need to leave your recipe alone! Always changing it, when every time it is perfect."

"I love this woman," Dana said, sober. "Why can't my men friends say the same thing about me?"

Anna laughed, feeling relaxation seep into her for the first time since Rico's return. This was exactly what she needed. Girl chat with her friend over fattening food.

"Don't just stand there, you dope. Get the plates while I go kiss those beautiful children."

Shaking her head at the funny face Dana made, Anna gathered the necessary supplies.

"I've made a decision," Dana announced, walking back into the room. "I'm going to get myself frozen, you know, that cryo-thing they do, and in twenty-five years they can wake me up. That way, I'll be the perfect age for Rafe."

"You're insane," Anna said, chuckling.

Lina was smiling, too, as she deftly cut the cake.

"No, I'm not. That is one gorgeous boy you have in there. He's going to be breaking hearts before he's nine."

Anna shuddered. "Please, don't even talk about it. I'm not ready."

"Moms are never ready for their kids to leave the nest," Dana said, opening the fridge and grabbing a can of soda.

"That is true," Lina said quietly.

Anna busied herself by getting a drink.

"Hey, Anna, by the way, I need some posterboard for work. Where do you buy the stuff you used for my comic strip?"

"That board I picked up at the arts and crafts store, but any office supply store sells it. How much do you need?"

Dana held up her hands, measuring in the air.

"Do you need a color?"

"No, it's for work. I just need to have a sturdy background for a sign we need to post. Why? Do you have some?"

"Yeah, I think I have that size in blue, green and white. Let me go check."

"You are a lifesaver!"

She took the stairs two at a time and as she jogged past the bedroom, she thought of Rico.

Please God, let him be all right, she prayed. Please.

Rico studied his friend in the confines of the car. Unflappable, with the kind of intelligence that made even the highest government officials nervous, he'd seen the man rattled once. At the time, Mike had been half carrying him from the Balangerio estate while their buddies unleashed the full force of their fury on the guards. Mike's disjointed apologies amidst the gunfire, combined with his being unable to look at Rico, had made him realize just how hurt he'd been.

"We're missing a piece," Mike said, his low, distracted voice pulling Rico from his mental jungle.

"What are you saying? That we still have no clue who's behind this?"

"Something's not adding up," Mike said, flipping through the papers in his lap. "Whoever masterminded this is doing so for personal reasons. No one made a move to pick up the reins of the Balangerio's businesses, and now it's been split up and given to the other families. So, the only other motive is revenge. The question is, who's still alive to want it this bad?"

Rico leaned an elbow on the door and pinched the bridge of his nose. The only living member of the Balangerio family was Enzo Balangerio, the ailing patriarch who'd been bedridden since his massive stroke two years ago.

"What's Enzo's status?"

Papers shuffled and glossy black-and-white photos landed in his lap.

"Those were taken two days ago. He hasn't left the hospital since admission. He's completely paralyzed on his left side, his speech severely limited. The doctors are giving a week. Two, tops."

Rico nodded, still looking through the pictures. There were aerial shots of the massive family compound he'd been held in, as well as at least one shot of each Balangerio family member. Some pictures captured one or two members together. It was those that he kept going back to.

"Who's she?" he asked, holding up a picture with two men he recognized and a woman he didn't. With his other hand he slid one more picture from the pile.

Mike arched a brow, and a sharp gleam entered his eye. "Figures you'd pick her out. She's the only one we don't have a full dossier on. She's a friend of the family, and not one background search turns up more."

Rico opened the file Mike gave him. Cecilia Jordana Sciozzi, twenty-three years old, five-seven, 110 pounds, blue eyes, blond hair. Very pretty, probably more so when smiling.

"How long ago was this one taken?"

"Four years. That's our last good picture of Joseph and Mario together."

She had on sunglasses and was listening attentively to whatever Joseph was telling her. Joseph, second in command of the Balangerio family, stood to the left of her, and Mario, his eldest son, stood to the right.

Rico looked again at the file, reading what little facts Mike had found.

"She's Mario's type," he mused. "Right age group."

"Maybe," Mike answered, tapping his fingers on the bottom of the steering wheel, checking the side and rearview mirrors religiously. "Maybe she's a friend of one of their daughters."

Rico stared at the two pictures, looking back and forth between the two images of the young woman, trying to find a scar or identifiable mark. The pics were taken from too much of a distance to be completely reliable but—

"Oh, no." It couldn't be.

"What?" Mike bulleted the question at him.

Please, God, let him be wrong. He looked at the pic again and back at her dossier picturing her hair black. Please let it be a coincidence. His heart thundered, pushing heat into his face. He felt light-headed.

"Dammit, Rico! What?"

"It's Anna's friend. Her neighbor."

He'd let them down. He'd let his family down.

"It's Dana."

Chapter 11

"You're sure?"

He ground his teeth. "It didn't click until I saw her middle name. Jordana. Dana for short. I don't know her connection to them, but I know it's her."

The cell phone rang and his heart dropped.

Mike said one word. "Who? When?" Long silence followed. "Who is? How many are down?" He bit out a curse. "Stay with her. No! Don't let that woman out of your sight. We'll be there in ten."

He ended transmission and looked at Rico, simultaneously starting the car. "An ambulance just pulled up in front of the house. Anna met the EMTs outside and said something about your mother."

"Son of a—" He bit off the curse and gripped the dashboard as hard as he could until pain made him ease up.

"Rico?"

He looked back, turning cold at the grim look in Mike's eyes.

"Dana's there."

As the car screeched into gear and swung into a 180, Rico pulled out his Beretta and checked his ammo.

"Back seat. Blue gym bag." Mike drove as he spoke. No wasted time or motion.

He twisted and reached back, pulled the bag up front and rifled through the assorted clips and rounds as the car sped through the mountainous back roads.

"You going to be able to handle this?" Mike asked, and Rico knew what he really meant. Would he be able to handle the violence?

He only nodded, and began to pray.

"An-na," Lina gasped, her hand grasping Anna's with bruising strength. "Some-thing wrong."

"I know, Lina, I know," she soothed, jogging to keep up. The paramedics wheeled the gurney over the front lawn with surprising speed. Lina's skin glowed with a sheen of sweat, pasty-white, her eyes burning like coals. "No...Anna."

"Ma'am. We need you to try not to speak. Relax the best you can so we can take care of you." The young paramedic spoke calmly, helping to put the gurney into the back of the ambulance.

"Can I go with her?" Anna asked, wringing her hands and looking back over her shoulder at the twins. Rafe stood beneath Dana's sheltering arm. Rebecca stood crying silently in front of them.

"Actually, I think it's a good idea. We need some help calming her down."

"Anna! How about I bring the twins? We'll follow the ambulance."

Anna's mind whirled. She looked around, but Rico was still not back. How could so much have happened in such a small amount of time?

She couldn't see the agents, but they must have notified him. He was probably on the way.

"Ma'am, we only have room for you and we need to go. Are you coming?"

A crash came from inside the ambulance. Lina had swung out an arm, toppling a basket of supplies.

"Dana, thank you. I need to be with her. I'll meet you all in the emergency room, okay?"

Dana nodded, and Anna stooped to give the children a hug. "Don't worry, you guys. The doctors will take care of Grandma."

They nodded and the paramedic's "Ma'am?" had her spinning toward the ambulance and jumping inside.

Please let Rico show up. Please let him see the ambulance. I need him right now. I need him so much.

She sat on the vinyl bench, gripping Lina's hand and praying, as the piercing wail of the ambulance's siren broke the silent peace of the neighborhood. How much more could her family survive?

Two police cars sat facing each other in front of Anna's house, lights off and sirens quiet. Curious neighbors had returned to their homes, leaving the two deputies to discuss the unusual situation.

Mike braked to a stop next to the first car.

"Where is everybody?" he asked, looking down at the young officer's chest. "Lansing."

"Who are you?" the rookie asked. His bright-red hair, freckles and wide eyes gave him an Opie-like appearance and screamed his inexperience.

"FBI."

The other deputy, standard-issue toothpick traveling around his lips, slapped the rookie on the arm. "See, told ya they'd call in the Feds on this one."

The rookie's awe as he stared at Mike had Rico biting his lip to keep from yelling.

"Give me a report," Mike ordered.

"Our sergeant is at the car around the corner if you want

to check it out. We've cut off all access to the side road. Three men were DOA on our arrival. They were discovered by some kids when the ambulance showed up at this house for a heart-attack victim.'' He jerked a thumb toward Anna's house.

"Thanks. We'll check it out. Any idea who they are?"

"No, it's weird, man. No IDs, parked back on one of the old mountain access lanes. One guy on the ground behind the car, one in the trunk and the other in the back seat. They were up to no good, that's for sure.'' The voice warmed to its subject. "We haven't had a homicide, much less a triple around these parts for over twenty years!"

"Anna's car's still here," Rico said, he and Mike exchanging looks.

"Maybe Dana's driving."

Mike took off with a brief thanks, swinging into a driveway and turning around. They roared down the lane and were at the hospital within eleven minutes.

Anna rubbed her aching right hand, still amazed at Lina's strength. The loud beeping of the emergency room monitors bothered her aching head, adding to the churning in her stomach.

They took Lina up to the cardiac unit for more tests, but at least she was stabilized. Now Anna needed to comfort the twins and hopefully find Rico.

Her sneakers squeaked on the shiny floors as she wove her way out to the waiting room. She expected to find her children either crying or running around the room checking everything out.

She found neither. Immediate panic hit, and she had trouble catching her breath. Feeling people looking at her, she saw only a young couple, an elderly man and a young man with a bleeding hand sitting in the deliberately cheerful room.

She approached the couple, trying to appear calm.

"Excuse me, have you seen a woman with two small children? A boy and a girl?"

The woman, her friendly brown eyes sparkling said, "Twins? Oh, I'm so hoping we'll have twins."

Anna noted the flush on her cheeks and her husband's hand lying over hers on the woman's still-flat tummy.

"Yes, they're twins and they're a double joy as well as a double handful," Anna said quickly, then added a smile.

"No, we haven't seen them. I wish we had, we've been here for so long already." The husband smiled at his young wife, his whole expression adoring.

I wish Rico had been around to look at me that way when I was pregnant.

"Thanks, anyway," Anna said, barely managing to control her panic. "Best of luck to both of you."

The couple beamed, and Anna headed for the rest room. Her heart beating double time, she searched the bathroom, calling their names. Nothing.

Stay calm, she told herself. Maybe they'd been rambunctious and Dana took them out into the sunshine. If she was right, there was a small park area on the side of the church next to the hospital. She should have told Dana to keep them inside no matter what! What if the people watching them tried to grab Rafe again? Or maybe both of them this time.

She threw open the door and halted, blinded by the piercing sunlight. Shading her eyes, she began walking quickly, then jogged to the park, searching the grounds at the same time. Halfway there, a blue car screeched to a halt in front of her. She didn't recognize the man in the driver's seat.

Blondish-brown hair, military short. Light skin tone, wide mouth. Dark glasses hid his eyes.

Run!

She pivoted and took a step back toward the hospital, adrenaline soaring.

"Anna!"

She knew that voice! Whipping back around, she stared at the man standing on the passenger side of the car.

"Anna, it's me!"

Rico! Relief rushed through her. Combined with the emotional upheaval of the past few hours and her abrupt spin, little black spots floated across her vision.

Rico caught her as she swayed, and she vaguely wondered why she didn't notice him running toward her.

"Here, sit down," he said, gently pushing her down onto a curb and forcing her head down against her knees.

"I'm okay, I'm okay," she protested. "No, let go. I'm fine. I have to check the park."

"For what?"

"The twins. I think they're out here. Then you need to come in and see your mom. Do you know everything that's happened?"

"Anna, who's with the kids?"

She looked at him then, at the white tightness around his mouth and the lack of any expression in his eyes.

"Dana. Dana's with them."

"Damn."

She looked around Rico to the unfamiliar voice. "Anna, this is Mike."

The man from the driver's seat. "Yes, hi. Why did you say that? What's wrong?"

Rico took both her hands in his. "Dana's the one we've been looking for."

She shook her head no. "Are you sure? How can you be sure?"

"Do you trust me?"

"Of course, but I still—"

"Anna, I don't have time to go into it all, but we think she killed the three agents watching the house. We have to find her."

"Oh, God. I gave her my babies!" The panic took over. "She offered to follow the ambulance. I should have known. But Lina needed me and—"

"Hush. It's not your fault." Rico pulled her into his embrace and stood, then walked them quickly to the car. "If it's anyone's fault, it's mine. I shouldn't have left you all alone."

Mike's cell phone began to ring.

"Yeah. Who's this? What?" Mike began pacing and listened with a contained scowl. "Yeah, I'm glad you're there, but someone's ass is going to end up in a sling. Hold. Anna, do you know where the old maintenance building is on Shreveport Road?"

She focused her chaotic thoughts. "Yes."

"She knows. Give me directions starting from there, then." Mike pulled out a small notebook and scribbled furiously. "Okay. Stay put and I'll make some calls. We'll be there ASAP, but if that plane moves, I don't care what you have to do. Good, I'm glad we understand each other." He flipped the phone closed and faced them.

"Who was that?" Rico asked, still hugging Anna to his side.

Mike looked at her. "Your friend, Joncaluso. He's a bit more than a small-town cop. He's FBI, undercover."

Rico shook his head. He should have known.

"We'll get into the details of all that later, but the good news is he saw Dana turn off instead of following the ambulance, and he followed her. Our man had been tailing her when his engine blew up. Apparently the car flipped over the median. I suspect Dana had the cars rigged in case one of the men lived."

Mike was shaking his head, obviously unnerved by the downfall of trained agents. Terror filled Anna as she realized the extent Dana was willing to go to get what she wanted.

"Joncaluso was behind him, radioed the accident in and stayed on Dana's tail. She's at an old airstrip outside town. She has the kids on a private plane."

"Are they okay?" She didn't realize she'd reached out and gripped Mike's forearm.

"He says they look a little scared, but they're unharmed."

"Thank God."

"Now I'm going to make a few calls and get us some help. Rico, you need to see your mom?"

"How is she?" Rico asked, looking down at her, concern and regret in his eyes.

"She's stable, and they're running more tests. I don't think they'll let you see her for a few hours."

He nodded. "Mike, let's go. I'll drive. Anna, sit in the front and give me directions."

His withdrawal into impersonal, military mode startled her and then filled her with a sense of relief. He knew what to do.

He would get their children back.

Rico needed to drive. He needed to control something, and controlling the car as they sped along snake-winding roads through the back country would have to do for now.

He wished the wheel was Dana's neck.

Anna sat beside him still as stone. Her instructions clipped, she didn't ask a question or worry out loud. Her silence confirmed what he already knew.

This was his fault. He'd brought this danger into their lives. Now he had to remove it.

"Rico, I want to get a take on Dana for the negotiators," Mike said from the back seat. He'd been busy on his cell phone, ordering authorities to the site, calling in favors and making promises of retribution to those who'd kept him in the dark about Joncaluso. "If Dana's just a friend of the Balangerios, why would she take the children? What would be the purpose?"

He ground his back teeth. "Damned if I know. It makes no sense. She's not a family member. She doesn't kill my children. How is that revenge?"

"How do we know she won't kill the children?" Anna asked, turning in the seat to face them. Her face was white but composed. In her eyes he saw the need for reassurance and the fear that she already knew the answer.

He didn't want to answer, but knew she needed to be prepared.

"We don't."

Rico slowed the car beneath the forest's thick, emerald umbrella of leaves, small branches and underbrush popping beneath the tires. All around them the forest grew wildly, untouched by man. Unable to drive further on old ruts that were once a ranching road because of the denser trees and high grasses, Anna looked around in amazement.

Where on earth was the plane?

Pete walked out of the shadows and stood in front of the car, a long, black rifle cradled in his arm as securely as an infant. His gaze met hers and locked. After a moment he nodded once, as if in greeting, or acknowledging her lack of emotion toward this revelation.

At the moment he was her least concern.

They all got out of the car, Rico catching her eye as he and Mike swung the doors shut with only enough force to make them click. She followed suit.

"Everything's quiet," Pete said, leading them deeper into the woods to a thicker area. "I don't know what they're waiting for, but there's been no movement around the outside. She's got two men with her. I'm assuming one is the pilot."

The plane sat at the end of the cracking asphalt runway, more than two football fields away. Even from their distance, Anna could see where clumps of wildflowers and grass had pushed through the untended strip.

Birds started chirping again, recovering from the disturbance of humans. All around them nature grew wildly, forming a stadium-like bowl around the small, private jet.

A vulnerable plane that held her children.

"The twins looked fine physically," Pete said, directing all his attention to her. "I don't think they realized what was happening, although Rafe looked more upset than Rebecca."

Anna glanced at Rico, and he quirked a small smile at her,

neither of them surprised that Rebecca showed the stiff upper lip. But she knew her sensitive little girl was frightened. Her children's trust had never been shattered by an adult, much less one so rooted in their lives. They loved Dana. The disillusionment alone would be heartbreaking.

Lioness anger surged from her heart, the force of it surprising but fortifying. Her pseudo friend had crossed a very dangerous line.

"Where are all the people you called, Mike?" she asked, avoiding Rico's concerned gaze. She could feel the power of it all the way to her toes.

"Some are already here," Pete answered instead, his eyes scanning the dense forest around them. She copied the movement and saw nothing, although his slight nods indicated locations. "I've had a few people on standby the last couple of days and called them as soon as I realized Dana wasn't going to the hospital." He looked at the men. "They're already in place."

"Good," Mike replied, giving Pete a narrow glance of approval. "The others should be here soon."

He turned to Rico. "I've got the rest of our team on their way."

Rico's eyes widened slightly before he looked away toward the plane.

"You know they'd want to be here. Plus, they'd kill me after it all comes out," Mike said with a grin, startling her with the change it brought to his face. Initially, he'd struck her as a quiet man who belonged in a library or lab with other superbrain types. His wide smile brought vivid life to his face and curved his eyes in the most attractive way.

"After what all comes out?" Pete asked suspiciously.

Rico and Mike exchanged a look.

"What details were you given with your orders?" Rico asked, leading them back across the small hill to their cars. Anna realized he was afraid of voices carrying and wanted them out of sight and hearing range.

"They told me a Ranger named Rico Carella was the leader of a team responsible for wiping out the Balangerio family. And that even though they were dead, there may be people wanting revenge on Anna and her children. Not long after I got here, Lina arrived and was added to my protection."

Mike nodded, then looked at Rico again. Rico turned and stared at Pete for long seconds. "I knew you were more than a town cop."

Pete nodded, not looking away.

Rico stuck his hand out and Pete grabbed it reflexively in a shake.

"I'm Rico Carella, pleased to meet you."

A tingle ran from the back of her neck down her spine, a giddy feeling from hearing him introduce himself by his real name. Pete had paled and searched Rico's face, eyes wide, hand still clasped.

"Anna?" he asked her without looking away.

"It's true."

Pete withdrew his hand and rolled his shoulders. "Well, this I didn't expect, but it explains a lot. I'm assuming it's a long story?"

Rico returned his smile. "You could say that."

Pete jerked his head to the side. "Does Dana know?"

"Not that we know of," Anna answered.

He turned to Rico. "Maybe it would be best if Anna stayed at the house and waited for contact or at the hospital with Lina."

Rico never looked at her. "Anna knows the risks. If she wants to stay, she stays."

A wave of emotion hit her. He was letting her decide and letting them know he believed in her. He turned to look at her, and she hoped he could see what she was feeling. His expression gentled and a slow quirk of his mouth told her he did.

The silence around them was broken by Pete's wry question. "So, what's the plan?"

* * *

"Rico, I know you want to go in there and get your kids, but if there's even the slightest chance she knows who you are, it could set her off," Mike said logically.

Eight minutes had passed with the four of them throwing out ideas. Mike remained steadfast in his belief they should allow a negotiator in—just like any other hostage situation.

"I agree with you to a point. This whole operation of hers went into effect when I came onto the scene." He paced, trying to control the anger and frustration racing through him. They were wasting time talking, and he couldn't think about what his children were going through. "I'm the trigger, regardless of my identity. I should try and talk her down."

"You and I both know that's exactly why you shouldn't talk to her. You're too close to this and have too much at stake."

Rico sighed, knowing Mike was right.

All of a sudden the peace of the forest was broken by the sound of jet engines starting up. They all ran behind the nature-made blind. Within seconds the jets stopped.

Joncaluso's radio squawked. "I have a clear shot on the pilot. Take him out?"

Joncaluso paused, his large hand wrapped almost completely around the two-way. "You're running this show, Mike."

Mike nodded and took control. "Negative, no shot, no shot."

He addressed Joncaluso. "How good are these guys?"

"Two out of four have their marksmanship medals."

Mike smiled, and Rico shook his head at Mike's expression. The man loved it when a plan came together.

"Excellent. Rico, we should hire this guy. I like his style."

Joncaluso's one brow rose, but he turned with them and returned to the car. Mike addressed the men again, telling them a negotiator was on his way and to stand by.

Anna leaned her rear against the front of the car, facing

them with her arms folded across her chest. Surrounded on
the front and sides by the forest, she stood in their shadow.
As Rico walked slowly toward her, he kept reminding himself
that this wasn't a rain forest and he shouldn't feel suffocated.

This wasn't South America.

"Come here, Bella. I need to hold you."

She rushed to him, and he held her tight, trying to absorb
her hurt. Her warmth and perfume settled around him like
strong hands.

He didn't want to let her go.

"I'm so sorry," he whispered into her hair. "I promise you
I'll get them out safe."

"I know. I'm just scared. They're so little! They must be
terrified and confused. What if they both start crying? Dana
never could handle their tantrums, and I can't imagine how
she'll handle genuine tears."

"She probably won't hurt them." He stroked her back, feeling her relax against him. "She needs them right now, so all
she'll end up doing is scaring them a bit."

Anna tipped her head up, her huge eyes wet and her mouth
trembling. "Unless she feels trapped. Then who knows what
she'll do?"

He wished she wasn't so smart. It would be easier for her
if she couldn't play all the angles.

"We'll have to let her think she has a way out, but not with
our children."

Anna nodded, then settled her head against his chest. "She
was my friend."

Her small voice cut him. Another betrayal for her.

"I know she was, honey. She's sick. She must be to think
this will work."

She squeezed him, hard enough to make his ribs ache, but
he didn't mind. As long as she was still willing to hold him,
he could stand anything.

Chapter 12

"The cavalry has arrived," Mike said, joining them by the car.

Anna leaned away from Rico and looked around.

Mike smiled at her confusion. "Can't you hear them?"

Rico did but knew she couldn't. He watched her expression, seeing her eyes go unseeing as she focused all her senses into hearing. Finally her face cleared.

"I hear something, but it doesn't sound like an engine. It's more of a hum."

"Not bad." Mike winked at her, and Rico appreciated his attempts at distraction. Not that they could keep Anna from worrying, but she'd handled so much already he feared she was close to the breaking point.

And this standoff had the potential to last hours.

Two dark sedans pulled around the curve below, and Anna's face darkened. Her respite from worrying was over.

Both stopped and a total of five men climbed out. Less than one hour after Mike's call, five of the best the military had ever turned out arrived in little Coeur d'Alene, Idaho.

All of them his friends.

"Were they training in the area?" he asked Mike.

Mike's smile was secretive. "Something like that. After the attempt at Rafe, I informed them your family was in danger. They've all been en route since. And, Rico, I'm going to tell them who you are."

"We have time?"

Mike nodded. "Not enough for details, but they need to know. If they don't believe it, fine, we'll convince them later."

Rico looked back at the men walking up the slope. Cal. Runt, Kid, Irish and Lucky. His friends. Here to protect his family because they thought he couldn't. Although, he knew, they'd have been here for Anna and his children no matter what the circumstances.

His first real friends after Anna and Rafael, these men had become his brothers in everything but blood. But, if you counted being wounded and bleeding on each other as a tie, then they were blood brothers, too.

Wearing green fatigues and carrying their weapons of choice, they looked lethal.

And they were.

"Thanks for coming, guys," Mike said, getting lost in the circle of handshakes and back-clapping.

The men looked at Rico, then to Anna and back to him, their stares serious.

Grateful didn't cover what their friendship, even after "death," meant to him.

As his friends turned their attention back to Mike, Rico registered the familiar kick in the gut at being ignored by those who knew him. He should be used to it.

"How are the kids?" Cal asked, and Rico bent his head against Anna's. Big, surfer blond "California" or "Cal" above all knew what Anna had meant to him. He'd listened when Rico talked about the dreams he'd planned with her. The children he'd wanted with her.

"Physically they're fine. But we've got two four-year-olds

who just watched their grandmother have a heart attack, and now they've been kidnapped. I'm not sure how they're acting in that plane or how Dana will react to them.''

"How's Rico's mom?" Runt asked. At seven feet tall and pushing three hundred pounds of muscle, he intimidated everyone he met, except the twin brother who stood taller and wider. The circle of short hair on the top of his head was dyed dark-green, and small, gold hoops hung from his ears. He was the Dennis Rodman of their team and tested every military rule just to see if he could.

He was also deathly loyal, a marshmallow with kids and animals and absolutely brilliant.

"They stabilized her."

All the men nodded.

"Who's got an eye on the plane?" Kid asked, and Rico hid his smile. The past few years hadn't helped the Kid look any older. He still looked eighteen, although he was pushing thirty. Their sharpshooter, he practically vibrated with the need to get out his scope. For all his energy, Kid had the patience of a predator and the hands of a hunter.

"Joncaluso," Mike began as he turned and gestured to the man who'd walked up behind him, "already has men out."

He quickly filled them in on Joncaluso's part in the whole scenario, and Rico used the time to study his men.

They all looked more at ease and, if he was right, hadn't seen any major action in over six months. They didn't have the intense alertness seen after time in the jungle or on a mission for months at a time. And although they were eager to help, they also looked ready for action.

"Now, even though none of you have officially met Anna, I'm sure you recognize her from Rico's pictures."

Those wearing hats tipped them at her and smiled, the others nodded in greeting. But as polite as they were, they held back. As Rico wondered why, Cal spoke.

"Ma'am, we all want to apologize for what happened to

Twice Upon a Time

Rico. Each and every one of us takes full responsibility for his...for what happened to him.''

He felt Anna take a deep breath to speak, and Mike interrupted.

''There's a bit more to this story, guys, and as tempting as it's going to be to celebrate, we'll have to wait until after the kids are safe. Take a look at this guy holding Anna.''

Their gazes swung back to him.

''He looks totally different, but that is, beyond the shadow of any doubts you might have, Rico.''

Amazement and disbelief widened the eyes scrutinizing him. He wished there was more time to explain, but like Mike said, time was something they didn't have. Heads swiveled between him and Mike, and he knew that the men believed it if only because Mike said so.

Rico dropped his arm from around Anna, removed his lenses and dropped them temporarily in Anna's cupped palm. Then he looked at his men, friends who had saved his life and mourned his death.

''Holy Mother of God,'' Runt said.

''Rico?'' Cal whispered, taking the few steps to him. He stopped inches from him and their identical height made them eye to eye. ''It can't be...but the eyes are the same. Exactly the same.''

Just then a loud metal scream ripped through the forest. En mass they ran, following Joncaluso's lead. The same noise, only shorter in duration, came from the plane.

''That doesn't sound good,'' Cal murmured from his position between Rico and Mike.

''They may not be getting off the ground, but they're going to try, and I don't want my kids on that plane when they do.'' Around him, heads nodded. He quickly popped his contacts back in, then Anna's hand curled into his. Gaze locked on the plane and lips pressed firm, she looked fierce.

And his heart ached for her.

* * *

"We're not sure what the status is on the plane, only that it's started up three times in the last hour, then shut down. It could be a mechanical problem or they're running the air-conditioning for a few minutes. The side door of the plane is open, but our men don't have any visual. As soon as the negotiator gets here, we'll contact Dana."

"I'll be the negotiator," Cal said calmly, his Southwest accent slowing the syllables.

Mike looked at him, evaluating.

"Since you've gone administrative have you forgotten what we're capable of?"

"No, I haven't forgotten. I've been concerned with keeping everyone with an emotional stake on the outer limits of this thing."

Runt cracked his knuckles, then rested them on his hips. From Anna's view he completely blocked the sun, reminding her of Paul Bunyan.

"We know how to do our jobs. That's why you called us, Mike."

"I agree," Rico said. "I'm not the right one to talk Dana out, but Cal would be perfect. He has enough inside knowledge to figure out her angle. Plus it helps that he's handsome as sin. If I recall, Anna, Dana's prone to good-looking men."

She forced a smile.

"Fine, then," Mike said. "Cal, you know not to let on about your involvement in the Balangerio mission. I'm sure that would send her over the edge. Obviously our priority is getting the twins out safely."

Everyone nodded.

"Now, the one down point is we have no idea if she has tried to contact the house. Layton was sending a crew there to tap the line just in case and forward the calls here."

Anna recalled Rico mentioning Layton as their former superior and the only other person besides Mike and his wife who knew Rico still lived.

"We're going on the assumption that she expected to get out of here without anyone stopping her. Cal, how do you want to handle this?"

"How much more daylight do we have?"

"Maybe two hours," Pete answered.

"I don't want to wait that long for sundown. And I don't want to wait for the rest of the people Mike called in. It's going to become a zoo. I'd rather have some control over this situation, wouldn't you, Rico?"

Rico nodded. "No question on that. All we need is an excuse to get you out there."

"What if you wear my uniform? Go in as a cop stumbling over something suspicious?"

"No," Anna said quietly.

All heads swiveled to face her, and it was difficult not to shrink back from the wall of maleness now focused on her. She licked her lips and stuck her hands in the back pockets of her jeans. "It's not a bad idea, but Dana knows just about every cop around here, *especially* the good-looking ones. And if she's been planning this, she'll have made it her business, don't you think?"

Rico sent her a small, pleased grin. "Next idea?"

Irish leaned back against a tree, one leg pulled up with a boot resting flat against the trunk. Anna couldn't help noticing how attractive all these guys were, but Irish tugged at her. All she could attribute it to was the dancing lights in his eyes. There was something about grown men who showed signs of the little, mischievous boy in them. And it was such a contradiction to the image of death he portrayed.

He would be perfect for her hard-to-interest cousin, Brooke.

"I'm thinkin' we may be lookin' at this from the wrong angle," he spoke, the lilt in his voice beguiling.

His accent clinched it. Brooke would love it.

"Men killed the Balangerios," he said, drawing out the *O*. "If it be revenge she's lookin' for, she's goin' to kill anyone military or official that stands in her way."

This set off a whole round of discussion, and Anna prayed the plane would stay quiet while they argued it out.

Feeling the stare of someone, she turned her head to find Irish studying her. The stare held no anger, no teasing or sexual interest. He examined her, and her chin rose on its own in challenge.

He nodded slowly. "Aye, lass. I'm thinkin' ye have a bit of the Irish in ye."

"And I'm thinkin' ye have a bit of the blarney in ye," she said, punctuating it with an arched brow.

Behind her, the argument died and someone guffawed. She couldn't identify the person who said, "I like her, Rico."

But she knew his rough timbre. "I like her, too."

Lucky had joined Irish by the tree, and the two of them talked in low voices.

"What are you two planning, Lucky?" Mike asked.

"Something you're not going to like."

The serious cloud settled back over the men. Anna could feel their tense readiness and knew if she reached out to Rico, she would feel the muscles of his arm wound tight.

Even though they could laugh at the drop of a hat, all of them were like cats ready to spring.

"We've got enough men here to protect anyone who approaches the plane. We can get more into position. But we need someone who won't set this girl off. Someone she'll trust."

Anna ticked off the possibilities in her head, but none would work. Unless...

Her head snapped up and met the bright-blue gaze of Irish.

"Aye, lass. I knew you'd be figurin' it out 'fore the rest of 'em."

"No." Rico couldn't read Anna's reaction in her wide-eyed gaze, but his came from deep in his gut.

"We don't send someone with no training into a dangerous situation like this. Especially a woman whose children are being held hostage. If anyone has a huge emotional stake in this, it's Anna.''

None of them said a word.

"Mike, tell me you don't agree with this?''

Mike gazed unseeingly into the trees, but you could see him going through the pros and cons.

"We'd need solid planning. But it's an option.''

He focused on Rico's face, then looked around at the men. "I say we go with Cal first.''

They all agreed, but Irish caught Rico's eye.

The bad thing about getting to know the men in your unit so well was that silent communication worked even when you didn't want it to.

Irish felt Anna was the best choice.

Well, Rico hadn't had much good luck in his life. He wouldn't risk Anna for anything in the world.

The words would come back to haunt him.

The metallic sounds of guns being checked shot her blood pressure up a few notches. These weren't the guns from TV or the play ones Rafe always wanted as toys.

These were the ones from her past.

Rico stood before her, yet another stranger. Mike had brought extra gear for him, again proving to be the detail planner of the squad. Rico wore the same fatigues as the other men and a headset, heavy black belt laden with a gun and other weapons and big black boots that added an inch or so to his height.

He looked big and dangerous.

He looked like a soldier.

A pain clenched her heart, and she waited for old scars to reopen. After a few breaths it eased and she looked at him again, trying to see through the curtain of the past.

Still a soldier. Not the old Rico, not Gage. But a new man whose ease in the uniform told her how much he'd missed it.

Mike gave him a gun, and Rico's hands went over it like a

lover's. He checked the chamber, pulled out the clip and slid it back in, aimed it away from them and sighted down something in the forest. His nod and small smile said it all.

She hated it. She hated his ease with the weapons, his absolute comfort in a situation that terrified and enraged her even though another part of her recognized his ability. She wanted to scream and cry and rush into that plane and grab her children.

Instead, she stood silent. Apart from the group and their weapons check, she closed her eyes and continued to pray.

"Is she going to make it?" Kid asked him. Rico put his gun in the waistband against the small of his back and followed Kid's gaze. Anna stood under a huge oak tree, her eyes clenched tight and lips moving silently.

"I don't know. She's strong, but I don't know many parents who wouldn't break going through this kind of fear."

Kid assessed him and his lips thinned. "We'll get your babies, Rico."

"I know we will, Kid. We have to."

Each man confirmed his readiness through the headset. Anna learned by observing and bit her lip to keep from asking questions, although it proved difficult when they fell into their lingo of acronyms.

Cal stood in the middle of the big circle of men. He'd changed from his fatigues into jeans and a somewhat loose plaid shirt with the sleeves cut off. His arms, tan and muscular, bulged with every movement and would hopefully distract from the disguised bulk of his bullet-proof vest.

If he was going for the construction-worker-stripper look, he had it down. Unless her appetite for men had been an act, Dana would fall for Cal the moment she laid eyes on him.

"Cal, if you get in trouble and need backup, say, 'It sure is hot out here.' Otherwise use the old codes."

Cal nodded.

Anna couldn't hold back her questions any longer. "What if Dana doesn't believe Cal's the owner of this land? Don't you think she knows who owns it?"

Mike, whose patience with her knew no bounds, answered while the men finished checking their equipment. "I'm guessing she's researched the property. Thing is, it's in holding companies so deep, it would be difficult to find out who actually owns it. If she found the correct name, it's a corporation. It doesn't matter if he's an officer, he can be looking after the corporation's interests. If she doesn't fall for that…"

Cal interrupted with a huge grin and exaggerated wiggle of his eyebrows. "All hell breaks loose."

As much as she wanted her children safe, the thought of Cal or any of these men dying, horrified her.

"Hey, Anna, don't worry," Cal added, obviously seeing her dismay. "I'm a professional."

With a jaunty salute and a blown kiss that had the others shaking their heads, Cal led the group away and into their positions.

Rico didn't follow, he stood watching her, as he'd done continuously as the minutes wore on.

"Mike will stay back here, coordinating. You can stay by him, if you'd like. Or, you can stay with the cars and meet the rest of the men. They should be here in fifteen."

She nodded, trying to sort out the emotions going through her and the ones she saw on his face.

He tilted his head and smiled at her. She wondered if he knew how sad it looked.

"Hug?"

She walked into his arms, burrowing into him. "Don't die."

He rubbed his hands up and down her back and with his forearms, pulled her into him, revealing the soreness of his hands. "I won't. I already told you I have too much to live for."

She gritted her teeth and willed back tears. "Don't do anything stupid!"

He grinned, although it didn't hold its usual impact. She could tell it was all for show.

"Hey, you know I love to be a hero."

His words brought back the kind words of comfort people had said at his funeral. *War hero. Hero for this country.*

Not again. Please, not again.

"What did I say? Bella, look at me!"

"Nothing, nothing. Just be careful. Get all of you back safe," she said, unable to speak in other than a subdued tone.

He nodded, looked as if he would say more, then turned away. Five steps later he stopped and faced her.

"I love you, Anna."

His words pierced her, ripping through old hurts and new hopes. Her mouth opened and closed and her mind raced, trying to say what her heart wanted and fighting what her mind urged.

"Don't say anything. It doesn't matter." He smiled the sweetest smile and the utter honesty on his face undid her. "I know you love me. I don't need the words. Not yet, anyway. But someday you'll say them again, and they'll be one of the greatest gifts of my life."

And he walked away.

Anna stood by Mike, both of them using binoculars while Pete directed what looked like a small satellite in the plane's direction. Cal walked from the woods in front of the plane, from the direction of a homestead on that side of the ridge. Hands on his hips and brow furrowed, he walked to within ten feet of the door.

Anna gasped, shocked to see Dana. Even though she'd known, it surprised the part of her hoping her friend wasn't responsible. Long black hair in a ponytail at the base of her neck and a small white top plastered to her stunning figure, she presented quite a picture hanging out from the airplane's doorway.

Cal stopped and grinned, the tilt of his head flirtatious and inviting her to play.

Pete adjusted the sound up a notch so she and Mike could hear their conversation.

"Well, well. I have to admit, finding a plane here was a surprise. But finding you, pretty lady, tells me the Lord answered my prayers this mornin'. I asked for an angel and he gave me one with her own wings."

Dana's smile bloomed. Mike switched his headset to Anna's head for a minute and all she could hear was gagging noises. One of the guys, she forgot which one, had another listening device so that from his angle, it could be pointed inside the plane.

"What's a gorgeous man like yourself doing in the middle of this field?" she asked, stepping out of the plane and onto the top step. Jeans encased her legs, and the hips she always complained about held up the belly-baring pants.

"It's my job," he shrugged.

"Your job is lookin' at fields," she flirted, flashing him a wide smile.

He ducked his head. Anna thought he was doing a wonderful job pretending to be sheepish and caught off guard by a beautiful woman.

"Sort of. My boss owns this spread and I have to make sure the local kids don't use it for their Friday-night hangout."

Anna kept the binoculars focused on Dana's face, looking for any hint that she might be figuring out the truth.

"Oh. I thought it was abandoned. Unfortunately we had to do an emergency landing and I was so grateful to see this here," she flashed another smile and made a show of swiveling her hips as she went down another step.

"Can I get you some help?"

"Oh, no! We have a mechanic on the way. We'll be out of your hair in a few minutes."

Cal smiled at her, and from their angle, to the back and right of him, it looked as if he turned the charm on full force.

"Can't say as I'm too happy about that."

She smiled again and this time added a sultry gaze and lick of her red lips.

"How about you keep me company until the mechanic arrives?"

"I'd be honored," he teased and followed her into the plane.

Anna held her breath. It seemed as if the entire forest around them waited, suspended in hope and fear.

A gunshot blasted the silence.

Followed by the tiny sounds of her children's screams.

Chapter 13

My babies!

Anna was up and running through the trees without conscious thought. A strong arm encircled her waist after only a few steps and pulled her back against a huge body. A quick glance up showed Pete's attention fixed on the plane although he easily held her suspended with his left arm.

"Wait," he ordered, subduing her struggling and pulling her down into a crouch beside him.

"Pete, let me go!"

He never looked at her and his hand remained clamped around her wrist.

"Hold on, Anna," he encouraged, his whole being focused on the plane.

They stared at the small jet. All noise had stopped abruptly within seconds after the gunshot.

Oh, please. Please let my babies be all right. Please let Cal be all right.

All of a sudden Rebecca appeared in the doorway. Anna

backpedaled clumsily, half looking over her shoulder as she made her way back to Mike.

She picked up the binoculars, and her precious daughter's face filled her view.

As well as Dana's, peering over her daughter's shoulder.

She was using Rebecca as a shield.

Terror rushed through her, and she couldn't catch her breath. Her view started shaking and she tightened her hands, holding on to the binoculars as if they were a lifeline to her daughter.

Tear tracks were visible on her small face. As well as something else. Her little lips pressed together, she stared into the forest with narrowed eyes.

Dana said something to her and she shook her head.

That's when Anna realized her daughter was furious.

That fury, combined with the tears, gave Anna strength. Her four-year-old stood there with more courage than most adults.

She would not fail her by breaking down.

Rebecca shook her head again and then she wiggled like a rag doll. Dana had shaken her.

The anger in Anna built so rapidly her vision blurred and deafened her to Mike and Pete's hushed whispers.

Rebecca lowered her little chin and took a deep breath before letting out one of her earth-shattering bellows.

"Mommmmmmmyyyyyyyyyyyyyyyyyy."

Rico thought he'd known fear. Thought he'd known terror. He'd been wrong.

Seeing his daughter held in the grip of a madwoman literally weakened him. A madwoman who'd just shot Cal. He couldn't imagine how Anna was dealing with it.

Lucky lay flat next to him amidst the bushes, arms bent and elbows supporting the hands holding his binoculars. Rico didn't need the extra vision. Close enough to see the color of his daughter's eyes, he stayed frozen.

If Dana saw them now, there was no telling what she'd do.

A megaphone stuck out above Rebecca's head.

"You must think I'm very stupid to fall for that," Dana said in clipped words. Rebecca's hands shot up to cover her ears and as she tried to crouch onto the floor away from the noise, Dana's hand on her neck pulled her back up.

Rico wanted to kill.

"Anna, I know you're out there. I'm not sure who's with you, but I'm sure you're there. You have three minutes. If you're not down here in the plane, you'll be very, very sorry."

She shook Rebecca again before dragging her into the plane's darkness.

Pulling the mike closer to his mouth, he asked, "How's Anna?"

"Holding her own. She wants to go."

Rico racked his brain.

"We don't have a choice here. Cal's probably dead," Lucky said emotionlessly. But Rico heard the rage in the carefully spaced words.

"There's always a choice," he responded. "Mike, put Anna on."

After a few seconds of rustling, her soft voice reached him. "I'm going."

Reassured about her emotional well-being by her angry statement, he wanted to argue, anyway. "We'll find another way."

Dana's voice echoed from inside the plane. "Two minutes."

"There is no other way," Anna said.

"Yes, there is. She wants me. I'll go."

"She'll kill you before you get in the plane," Anna said, sighing. "If you do get inside, what are the chances she'll let you get the kids out?"

"I can't let you—"

"You're not letting me!" Her furious voice whipped even at a whisper. "She asked for me, she's getting me."

Irish's voice intervened. "Anna, try and maneuver her to the back of the plane with you and the children up near the door. Also, if ye can open one of the window shades even a crack to give us visual.''

''Done,'' Anna said, and he could tell from her voice she was moving around.

''We're getting a vest on her,'' Joncaluso said.

He could hear Mike talking to her, telling her how to hold her body, how to talk Dana down.

''One minute!'' Dana's shout stepped up the urgency.

''Anna.'' He paused, searching for something that might give her courage. There was nothing. ''Don't be a hero, love.''

Her soft chuckle vibrated in his ear. ''Hey, I'm leaving that to you guys. I know you won't let me down.''

In her words he heard her reassurance to him, her understanding that he would be there.

More rustling in his ear.

''Does anyone have a visual inside?'' Rico asked, hoping.

All answers were negative.

Then he heard Anna's voice from far away.

''...me a gun.''

''No!'' he said into the mike, keeping the scream in his head down to a mere whisper.

''Think about it, man,'' Joncaluso whispered back.

''She's never fired one.''

''Dana probably knows that. It may give Anna an advantage. If nothing else, it gives her a chance.''

He sighed heavily. There wasn't even time to give her detailed instructions.

Movement on his left caught his eye and Anna appeared from the trees, walking with long strides. Hands closing in fists, then opening into claws and closing again, Rico wondered if Dana had invited the most dangerous of them all.

Pride and fear filled his chest.

Dana's laughter from the megaphone didn't affect Anna's stride. She reached the steps, taking the four of them two at a time, and ducked into the plane.

Lucky whistled soundlessly. ''She's one brave lady.''

Something he'd known, but never truly seen until today. Bella had grown up, become a courageous, strong-willed woman. He had a feeling her strength outmatched his in the ways that counted.

He stared at the plane, waiting for any sound other than a gunshot. Hoping against hope that Anna would appear with the twins and walk out into safety, that he hadn't just let the woman he loved risk her life.

Praying God hadn't allowed him to live only to take away everything he had that was worth living for.

Anna ducked into the darkened interior, determined to focus only on her rage at Dana. The sight that greeted her shook her.

Cal lay sprawled across two side-by-side, blue-patterned seats, blood covering his entire right shoulder, his eyes closed. She couldn't see if he was breathing.

Another man, one of Dana's two goons, lay opposite him, his neck turned at an awkward angle.

Obviously dead.

The other man must be in the cockpit.

Dana stood at the rear of the plane in front of a long couch, her hands grasping the shoulders of the children standing in front of her. In her right hand was a gun, its muzzle resting obscenely down Rafe's slim chest, jostled by the small sobs of fear he couldn't control.

"Rafe, honey. It's okay," she said, smiling reassuringly at him. He didn't respond.

Dana pulled him back against her thigh, even though he made no attempt to move.

"Welcome to my humble abode, Anna."

She didn't answer. Instead, she met her daughter's too troubled eyes and winked, then looked around. The plane resembled the inside of a huge jet, with five rows of double seats on either side of the aisle, which, unfortunately, hid their view of the men outside.

"Let them go," she said quietly, meeting Dana's gaze. For the first time she saw the madness glowing in her friend's eyes. Why hadn't she seen it before? Why hadn't she sensed what Dana was capable of?

Dana laughed. "Sure. Let's make a deal. I'll give you back your family as soon as you give me back mine."

"What are you talking about?" The gun pressed against the small of her back reassured her that she may have one ace up her sleeve. Dana knew her fear of guns and wouldn't expect her to be armed. That may be why she hadn't searched her. Question was, would she be able to use it if she had to?

"What are you talking about?" Dana mimicked her. "As if you don't know! Your *boyfriend,* the *love of your life,* killed my whole family!"

Anna darted a look at her children. Rafe seemed to be in shock. He stared off to the right without blinking, and the soundless sobs continued to shake him. Rebecca's alert gaze stayed on her as if waiting for directions.

"Dana, this is between you and me, not these children. Please, at least let them sit down. Rafe looks like he's going to collapse."

Oblivious to the threat of the gun, she rushed to her son and dropped to her knees. Taking his cold face in her hands, she turned him to her.

Anna needed to get her children out.

Pulling Rafe forward had left the gun hanging down at Dana's side. Holding him by the shoulders, she quickly turned him and lunged for the gun in Dana's left hand, clearing the way for her children to run down the aisle.

"Run!" she screamed, hoping they'd obey, and knowing the men would hear.

She'd caught Dana off guard, but she recovered quickly. Not even bothering to turn around, she focused on keeping the gun and Dana's arm pointed up.

The gun went off.

* * *

At Anna's scream, everyone flew into motion. Men swarmed the plane from all sides, guns drawn.

The gunshot echoed in the silence of the forest, the blast sending everyone but Rico's team to ground.

Rebecca appeared in the doorway, terror etched over her features. She twisted around, her back to them.

Rico ran hard, ahead of everyone rushing the plane. He saw Rebecca pulling Rafe. Just as he reached her, the cockpit door opened and a man grabbed Rafe. Rico grabbed Rebecca and yanked her out with his left arm, his right hand holding the gun steady on the man with his son.

The man holding a gun to his son's head.

"I'll kill him! Back off!"

He twisted so Rebecca would be less of a target.

"Give," Runt said from behind him, and as much as it killed him, he ignored Rebecca's distressed sound and let her go.

With her weight gone, he held the gun in both hands and focused on the big man holding Rafe, whose gaze flicked back and forth between Rico and the back of the plane. Rico heard struggling and knew Anna was inside fighting for her life.

His peripheral vision caught Lucky crouched under the plane, near the cockpit.

Another gunshot. Glass sprayed out one of the windows to his right.

"Enough!" Dana screamed.

Anna pushed her hair out of her eyes and sucked in breaths, leaning to her left against a seat. A knee to her stomach had weakened her just enough for Dana to pull away.

She turned to the front of the plane, and her rapidly beating heart dropped. Rafe lay against a man's chest like a rag doll, unaware of the gun pointed at his head or the arm around his middle.

Dana breathed erratically, making furious sounds. "I may just kill you for that. I wasn't going to, you know. I was going to let you live and suffer, since Rico Carella isn't here—you're the next best thing.''

She casually gestured with the gun to the man holding her son. ''Victorio, what's going on out there?''

''There are military guys all over this place.''

Dana cursed and mumbled to herself. ''One of those damn agents must have lived.''

''Agents?'' Anna asked, realizing Rico was right when he said Dana had killed them.

Dana laughed, a totally different laugh.

''You didn't even know. You're so stupid, Anna. Didn't you know you've been watched for months? Years? By me and them! Unfortunately, a friend of mine set off some alarms while getting me more information on Rico. That's why the agents showed up. Too bad, too. I liked him.''

''Too bad? What was too bad?''

Dana looked at her, her beautiful blue-green eyes empty. ''His having to die. But he was stupid and of no use any longer.''

How many people had Dana killed in her quest for revenge?

''Who brought you here?'' she asked suddenly.

Anna hesitated then went for the truth. ''Pete Joncaluso was behind you when you left with the twins. He thought he'd follow you to the hospital and was confused when you came this way so he tailed you.''

Dana sighed. ''Stupid town cop catches me. By the way, how is dear Lina?''

Chills raced down her spine at Dana's too sweet question and malicious thrill in her eyes.

''Lina's going to be fine,'' she answered slowly.

''I know that! I didn't try to kill her. She may be Rico's mother and spawned that devil, but she's had to suffer for that already!''

She was evil. There was no other explanation for the twisted behavior. ''What did you do to her? How did you cause her to have a heart attack?''

Dana grinned, a shadow of the grin she used to flash when she was about to tell Anna something secret. "The cake."

Anna thought back, remembering when she'd gotten back downstairs with the posterboard, Lina had been sprawled on the kitchen floor. A plate with half-eaten cake had been on the table. "You put something in the cake?"

"Yup," Dana said. "You never even suspected. It was perfect!"

"But why aren't the twins sick?"

"I didn't let them eat it! I told Lina I'd put some alcohol in it for taste, so she didn't let them have any. She gave them a few cookies instead."

Anna's thoughts spun. The unreality of this whole nightmare kept threatening to overwhelm her.

"Oh, Anna, really! Relax already. It only made her look like she was having a heart attack. She'll be fine in a couple of days."

Dana's breezy dismissal of Lina's pain blew her mind.

Keep her talking, Anna thought. "If you wanted everyone out of the way, then why didn't you wait until I could eat the cake, too?"

Dana shrugged. "I thought about it, but all I needed was a distraction. Plus, I thought you might figure it out too soon if you ate with Lina. You'd have told the police when the ambulance showed up. You know, if you didn't eat as quickly or got distracted by the twins, you might not have collapsed."

Anna forced herself to play along. "That's true. That would have really messed things up. If it wasn't for Pete, you would have gotten here without anyone knowing."

Dana's lip curled. "That cop ruined everything!"

"But, Dana, why haven't you taken off already? By the time Pete got backup here, you could have been gone."

Dana looked at her and nodded, her eyes wide. "I know! But that damn Victorio!" She gestured with the gun towards the dead man. "Something's wrong with the engine. Every time it starts up, the instrument panel in the cockpit goes haywire. He'd been on the phone with his other pilot and was about to go outside to fix the problem when that stupid blond stud over there walked up.''

"What did you kill him for?''

"Oh, please, Anna. I'm getting so tired of having to explain everything to you. Can't you see he's official? His gun and vest confirmed it. Too bad, too. He's awfully sexy looking." She sighed. "And I probably wouldn't have killed him if he hadn't broken Victorio's neck."

Silence fell between them. For Anna, the violence made her stomach roll and a cold sweat to cover her skin. Dana looked to be basking in it.

"What the hell are you doing this for?" Anna asked with a tired, beaten tone. She let her hair fall forward as she looked around. She needed to think. She needed to do something. She had to get Rafe out of that man's clutches.

"I'm talking about my family, An-na," she drew out her name in mocking syllables. "I'm talking about every living person I loved dying because of Rico Carella."

"Listen. I don't know what you're talking about and, frankly, I don't give a damn. Rico's dead, Dana. He's been dead for years and he's been out of my life for longer than that."

"I know all about your precious Rico. I had to listen to you whine about him enough. It used to make me sick to my stomach!" She paused, and Anna glanced at her. Dana stood with her right elbow on her hip, the gun held up in her right hand the way a waitress held a tray. Her lips pursed, she cocked her head and her disconnected gaze met Anna's. "I was going to kill them, you know. A few times you'd leave me alone with them and I thought about how easy it would be to kill them. Make it look like an accident."

She inwardly shuddered at the danger she'd unknowingly put her babies in. Movement to Anna's right caught her eye, but she didn't look. Someone was by the doorway.

Dana straightened and put the gun in her left hand. "But

then I found out that Rico may be alive. So I waited. And dug around. And waited, just in case. But no-o-o-o. It was a horrible lie. He really is dead.''

''Why did you want him alive?'' Anna asked, looking at the now-quiet Antonio and seeing his gaze focused out the open doorway. She looked, too, but from her opposite angle saw Kid, his gun trained on her. Hoping he was focused on her face, she moved her eyes and head slightly to the left, trying to indicate Dana's position.

Maybe if Dana died, Antonio would give up and let Rafe go.

''I wanted him to know I was taking his children. I wanted him to worry about them. *Mourn* for them. I'd wait a few years then come back to kill him. But I wanted him to *suffer* first, just as I've suffered!''

Her fevered spiel ended on a yell.

Although Mike told her to remain calm and not provoke Dana, she couldn't prevent her sarcasm. ''Dana, you're making no sense. Rico didn't even believe the twins were his. He thought I was sleeping around on him! He wouldn't have suffered, because he wouldn't have believed you! This whole crazy plan of yours was for nothing!''

Dana's eyes widened, and she looked confused. Then she swung out and caught Anna in the side of her jaw with the gun.

Thankful she'd started to duck or Dana probably would have broken it, Anna held her throbbing jaw in her left hand and blinked back tears.

''You know nothing! Nothing!'' Dana yelled.

Anna's swerving had caused her to move deeper in between the row of seats.

What could she do? She needed to help Rico get the advantage. If she pulled the gun in her waistband, it would only complicate things and probably get Rafe killed. She stared across the aisle and saw the bullethole through the window shade.

The window shade.

Inspiration struck. She made a show of being dizzy from the blow and stumbled back against the side of the plane, her back against the shade. Unable to feel the edge of the shade with the cushioning of the vest, she dropped her head and hair forward and let her raised left arm provide further coverage. With her right hand behind her, she raised the window shade a few inches. A quick glance to Antonio showed he'd missed her move.

Dana, pacing the small space in front of the long bench along the back of the plane and shouting about getting the plane going, also missed the maneuver. With a prayer she stepped groggily back to where she'd been standing before. Dana kept spouting off about revenge and lies.

Anna looked to the door.

Kid was gone.

"Anna just took a nasty blow to the face," Kid said into the mike. Rico stood far enough back to keep the guy in the plane calm, but close enough to put a bullet in him.

"Status?" he asked.

"No visual," Kid replied.

"Runt?"

"She's fine."

Putting aside concern for Rebecca, he focused on the plane and the shouted words from Dana.

Dana wanted the kids for revenge. And for a new family.

"Heads up," Lucky's voice filled his ear. "Kid, I've got visual. Anna raised a shade just enough. Don't know how long we got."

Kid was running in a crouch before Lucky finished speaking. From his vantage point, Rico could see the two men on the other side of the plane, Kid with his rifle up to his shoulder.

"I'm going to keep this guy's attention on me," he said into the mike, before moving it away from his mouth.

"Hey!" he shouted. "Why don't we talk about this?"

The guy looked at him, then into the recesses of the plane, his squinty eyes and crewcut making him look like an overblown cartoon character.

"I've got visual," Kid whispered. "Going for it."

Dana screamed in pain.

Even though she'd instigated it, Anna was stunned by Dana's scream and the blood that appeared on her left shoulder. She dropped the gun on the floor and grabbed her arm, falling back against the bench.

Anna looked at Antonio, who immediately started down the aisle toward them. She rushed into the aisle and lunged to the floor for the gun. Dana was oblivious, clutching her arm and wailing.

Rolling into a sitting position, her back against the bench, she raised the gun at the man charging for her. He held Rafe under his right arm like a football, above the seat level, and his left arm extended with the gun pointed straight at her.

Cal's leg flew up in the air. Antonio's arm flew up, and the blow knocked him off balance. He dropped Rafe and twisted to face Cal who'd struggled to stand.

Anna crawled forward, grabbed Rafe and dragged him back. Tucking his limp but breathing body behind the seats on her right, she knelt up against the back of the seat. Dana still rolled on the seat crying, so she focused on the grappling men, her arms propped and gun trained on them.

Rico burst through the door, taking control. Felling Antonio with a blow to the side of his neck, he grabbed the gun in blurring movements and caught Cal as he collapsed. Lucky, right behind him, relieved him of Cal and quickly helped him from the plane. Irish and Kid rushed in as Rico strode toward her. The two of them grabbed the almost-unconscious Antonio.

Anna blinked, realizing it was over. Sitting back, she put the gun on the floor and gathered Rafe onto her lap just as

Rico reached her. His hand curved around the back of her neck, and he pulled them close.

Dropping a hard kiss on her mouth, he said gruffly, "Don't ever put me through that again." He searched her eyes and the side of her jaw.

Then he turned his attention to Rafe. "Rafe, son, look at me. Come on, buddy." He lightly patted Rafe's cheeks. "Hey, it's all over. You're safe. Mommy and I are here."

Irish appeared again, looking down on them. "The ambulances are here. Do you want a stretcher?"

"No, I'll carry him," Rico said, then looked at her. She nodded and transferred her baby into his father's strong arms. He looked so small and defenseless. So traumatized.

Rico stood, cradling Rafe with utmost tenderness as he started down the aisle. Irish stood staring at Dana with revulsion, then reached down and pulled her to her feet.

"The Feds are here. They can cuff her. I don't even like touching her." He turned his back and raised his voice. "Rico, send in the guys waiting at the steps. They want Dana."

"Rico?" Dana's voice whispered, her wailing abruptly halted. "Rico?" As if in slow motion, Anna watched the next few moments in horror. Spurred by rage, Dana's right hand reached down and whipped out a gun from her ankle. Irish's gun came up the same time hers did.

Anna reached around and grabbed the gun from her waistband, thumbing off the safety the way Pete had shown her. Two gunshots rocked the airplane, and she saw Irish stumble back. Dana stood still, her gun pointed toward the front of the plane.

Pointed at Rico and Rafe.

Anna didn't hesitate as she screamed Rico's name.

She fired.

Chapter 14

On her knees yet again, Anna looked at Dana's fallen body. She crossed herself in quick motions, whispering the prayers she grew up with and tried so hard to live by.

Thou shall not kill.

She put trembling hands together in prayer only to find her palms cradling the gun. The black weapon looked so wrong in her hands. So violent. Yet, without it she might have lost Rico and Rafe.

Maybe guns weren't the promoters of violence.

People were. Twisted, sick people.

Maybe guns were at times, necessary weapons against them.

She laid the gun on the floor and, using the back of a seat, pulled herself up. Rico, without Rafe, rushed back down the aisle to her.

"Anna! Are you okay? Were you hit?"

"No, I'm fine…" Her voice trailed off as she looked down between the seats in front of her. Irish lay there gasping. Rico ripped open Irish's shirt, and right above his heart lay a hole in the vest. He pulled the vest from Irish's chest.

There was no blood.

"Damn, that hurts," Irish gasped. Relieved, Anna closed her eyes and felt herself sway.

"That's it," she heard Rico say, and she snapped her eyes open when he swung her up into his arms. "Irish, you okay?"

"Fine," she heard him say.

Heartsick, Anna closed her eyes and lay in Rico's arms, soaking up his strength, vaguely wondering if he would be reinjuring himself by carrying her. Behind her closed lids, she still saw Dana's body crumpled on the floor. Her friend. But not.

She wound her arms around Rico's neck, hugging him to her.

"I got you, baby. I got you," he said against her ear.

Anna opened her eyes and was astounded. Rico carried her farther and farther from the plane, revealing more and more people. People in police uniforms, plain clothes, fatigues. Many of them stood watching their progress across the field.

Looking up, she was stunned by the spectacular colors brushed along the sky and above the plane. Fuschias, violets, oranges and reds. How could it be so beautiful out here when something so ugly had just happened inside?

Closing her eyes again, she asked about the twins.

"I'm taking you to them. Kid took Rafe to the ambulances."

She twisted and looked in the direction Rico was walking and saw they were halfway up the incline. "Rico, put me down. I don't want you hurting yourself."

He halted but didn't let her go. He stared at her intensely with those fake-brown eyes. "Say it again."

"Say what?"

"My name."

She frowned at him. "Why?"

"Because that's only the second time you've called me by my name in years."

She huffed. "That's not true."

"Yes, it is," he said, and started walking again. "You screaming my name in the plane was the first time I heard you use my name since the last time I saw you."

"No way."

"Yes," he said simply, and looked down at her quickly. She could see the hurt she had so unintentionally inflicted.

"I didn't realize."

"I know you didn't. I hoped that when you finally did, it would mean you'd accepted me back into your life."

She opened her mouth to answer him when she heard Rebecca.

"Mommy!"

Rebecca came flying at them, and Rico lowered her to her feet. She knelt and caught her now sobbing daughter. Rico looked at her and smiled.

"We'll talk later. Let's take care of our children."

She nodded, and they went to find Rafe amidst all the confusion. She saw him curled in Runt's arms, drinking from a cup Runt held for him. Runt noticed them, lowered the cup and said something to Rafe.

Their son looked at them, his eyes wide, and began to cry.

Runt grinned.

Rico reached out and picked Rafe up, rocking him against his chest.

"Excuse the smile, Anna. I'm just so glad the little guy's reacting."

Anna's eyes filled with tears as she rubbed Rebecca's back. Her children weren't the only ones reacting. "Thank you for taking such good care of them for us, Runt."

He smiled and reached out to tug one of Rebecca's curls. "You have the bravest children I've ever met."

Rebecca's head popped up off her shoulder, and she looked at Runt. With a shuddering sigh, she examined him, her brow furrowed.

"Why's your name Runt?" she asked.

Surprised more that Rebecca's first question was about Runt

and not Dana or everything that had happened, Anna looked at the men. All around them, people had quieted.

Runt's booming laugh had a ripple effect. The stranglehold of tension in the forest broke, and everyone's relief trickled out in chuckles.

"I'm a twin, too," he told her, rubbing her back with a huge hand. "I'm smaller than my brother so they call me the runt."

Rebecca's eyes widened as if imagining this, and she gave a wobbly smile, a bit unsure of herself. Rafe, still nervous, curled his small arm around Rico's neck and pressed his cheek against his father's. Looking around at all the people, he pulled away and looked at Rico.

"Rico was my daddy's name," Rafe said, his gaze intent on Rico's face. "Does that mean you're him?"

Rico smiled through the tears in his eyes and nodded, "Yes, son, I am."

"Mommy said you went to heaven," Rebecca said, sounding only mildly confused by the revelation.

Rafe looked at his mother and after gauging her expression, he nodded and sighed. His body shuddered slightly with his breaths and he relaxed completely against Rico, "'Kay."

Rebecca leaned out of Anna's arms and patted Rico to get his attention. "Maybe you need some ice cream, Daddy?"

Deep chuckles camouflaged the emotions Rico's men couldn't hide, but Anna's tear-stained face and relieved smile said it all.

Hours later Anna and Rico stood at the end of Lina's hospital bed. Although she was still on monitors, the doctors felt her prognosis was very good. They said she was extremely lucky the drug hadn't triggered a real heart attack, and they wanted to monitor her for a few days to make sure her own stress didn't cause one.

"I cannot believe this day," Lina said, more under control than she had been when they first told her the day's events.

Both children, sound asleep, curled alongside their grandma, braced from falling off the sides by the bed rails. White, nubby blankets covered them up to their elbows. "To think I could have lost all of you today."

Anna looked at Rico, hearing the words her heart had dwelled on for hours. Dana could have taken everything from them. As it was, she'd taken her children's trust and sense of safety. Anna worried about the long-term effects on them, but the doctors who checked them over suggested a wonderful hospital therapy program.

"Instead, Dana lost her freedom for the rest of her life," Rico said grimly. His whole demeanor had started changing when they arrived in the emergency room with the twins. "I'm not sure that's punishment enough."

Maybe the whole situation had made her paranoid, but Anna could swear he was pulling away from her.

"Will she go to jail or a mental hospital?" his mother asked. Anna couldn't claim relief that Dana had survived her gunshot wounds, but she was glad she didn't have her death on her conscience.

"I don't know, Mama. She has serious psychiatric problems, but she's responsible for a lot of deaths. It will be up to a judge."

There was a brief knock on the door, and Irish stuck his head in.

"Excuse me, am I intrudin'?"

"No, please come in!" Lina exclaimed in a low voice, playing hostess from her hospital bed. "Let me guess. Irish?"

He grinned. "Ah, you're as perceptive as your son, Mrs. Carella. How are you feelin'?"

Lina laughed, then sobered. "I'll be back to new in a day or two. Thank you for helping my family." She blinked back a tear. "Are you okay?"

Irish waved the question away as if taking a bullet in the chest was as common as bumping your knee. He walked up to the bed and ran a finger lightly down Rafe's cheek. "Just a bruise. Nothin' to concern yerself with."

"What about California?" she asked.

Irish smiled at the use of Cal's whole nickname. "He's doing very well. They gave him somethin' to knock him out and keep 'im from leavin' and now his snores are fillin' the ICU. The bullet went right through him but missed all the important things."

Lina smiled, relieved. "I'm so glad."

He faced Anna. "Anna, there's a young lady downstairs lookin' for you. I would have brought her up, but I needed to ask you a few questions."

"Who is it?" Dread knotted her stomach. She wasn't up for any more nasty surprises. But who would know to look for her here?

"She says she's your cousin, Brooke."

Relief allowed her to smile. "How did she find me?"

"Well, apparently she called you 'fore Layton got the taps and call-forwardin' set. He tried questionin' her, and she demanded to know where you were. When he wouldn't, she drove to yer home, and they finally brought her here. From what I understand, Layton's ears are still burnin' from the blisterin' she gave 'em."

Anna laughed, she couldn't help it. She'd seen Brooke on trial in court. She turned even more formidable when it concerned her family.

"You can bring her up, Irish."

"Uh, I was goin' to. I jes wanted to know if the lass was single."

Rico's amused tone came from behind her. "Thinking of settling down?"

"Well, I'm gettin' a bit old runnin' around like this. Who knows what could happen?"

The lights in his eyes danced, and Anna knew Brooke didn't stand a chance.

"Don't count on settling down with Brooke," she warned. "No one's ever been able to catch her."

Irish narrowed his eyes at her. "They don't call me Irish for nothin' ye know." He looked down at the bed. "How are the wee ones?"

Anna looked at Rico as he answered. "They're doing as well as can be expected."

Irish's gaze took in Anna's swollen jaw, from which she'd just removed the ice pack before he walked in. "You are a brave lass, Anna. We were all very proud of you out there."

She flushed from the praise and felt tears welling up again. She felt like a wimp.

Irish grinned and started out the door. "By the way, does all that red hair of yer cousin's mean she's Irish?"

Anna shook her head and chuckled. "No, she's Scottish."

Now outside the room, with only his head sticking in, he made an approving noise. "Good strong stock, those Scottish."

He disappeared as quickly as a leprechaun.

"Did you do that on purpose?" Rico asked, amused.

"Do what?"

"Give him a challenge about not catching Brooke?"

"Well, not exactly. Brooke refuses to settle down, that much is true. But she needs someone who'll fight for her and give her a reason to."

Rico smiled, and Lina chuckled.

Seconds later Brooke burst in the door with Irish at her heels. Wearing a suit the color of sage and full of wrinkles, tendrils of hair falling around her face and her green eyes darkened with distress, she was as disheveled as Anna had ever seen her. Seeing the full bed, Brooke stopped, her gaze darting over all of them.

"First, is everyone all right?" she asked in a low voice.

"We're fine," Anna assured her as Brooke dropped her purse on a chair and swooped her up into a tight hug.

"I want the whole story, but Irish here says it's long. We'll keep it for later.'' She loosened the embrace to watch Anna carefully. "I just want to know what this has to do with Rico. I kept hearing his name, but they wouldn't give me details.''

Anna looked at him, and Brooke followed her gaze.

"You must be Gage,'' she said with one of her devastating smiles. "I've heard a lot about you.''

Anna waited for Rico to glaze over the way all males did when they met Brooke.

He didn't glaze, but he did smile back. "I've heard a lot about you, too. But my name's not Gage.''

"Oh, I'm sorry,'' she chuckled, only slightly embarrassed. Not much threw Brooke for a loop.

Rico looked at her, and she gave him a small nod.

He took a few steps closer to them and held out his hand. "My name's Rico.''

Brooke paled, and the arm encircling Anna's waist slackened and fell to her side. "No, you're not.''

He looked at Anna and pointed to an eye. "Do you think I can finally throw these things out?''

"Please do,'' Anna said with a smile.

He bent his head and, with two pinches, removed the contacts and threw them in a small trash can beside the bed. Then he looked at Brooke. The effect wasn't as stunning as it had been outside that afternoon, with the sunlight striking them to pure gold, but Brooke's eyes widened just the same.

She took a step closer to him.

"I don't understand,'' she said dazedly.

"I don't blame you,'' he said wryly. "I have a hard time with it myself.''

Brooke looked over at Anna with a frown. "This is your Rico?''

Anna stared at her cousin, remembering their conversation about him just days ago. Remembered saying how he'd never seemed more alive to her. Remembered Rico saying that her heart already knew the truth.

"Yes, that's my Rico.''

Brooke's eyes widened again, the daze gone. She faced Lina. "Oh, my! Lina!"

Lina's beatific smile said it all. Irish, the level of emotion in the room maybe too much for him, made his exit silently.

Brooke faced Rico again, blinking and taking in his every feature. Then she walked up to him and gave him a hug.

Pulling away, she looked up into his face. "Welcome home."

Anna, swallowing the lump in her throat, knew Brooke couldn't have said anything more appreciated. The words, even from a total stranger, gentled his expression.

"I'm going to have a lot of questions, but I'll save most of them for later," she said in her best trial lawyer tone. "Just tell me, is Irish single?"

Anna rolled her eyes as Rico burst into laughter and gave Brooke a squeeze.

With Runt carrying Rebecca and Rico cradling Rafe, the small army of adults left the hospital. All of the men and Brooke were going to follow them to the house. Rico had pointed out that he was staying at a bed and breakfast, so he had more than enough room for everyone.

Brooke suggested she stay in Lina's room downstairs and get up with the children in the morning so Anna and Rico could sleep late. The offer, Anna knew, was mainly because Brooke was so worried about her godchildren. She wanted to see them awake and okay for herself.

As far as she and Rico were concerned, Anna didn't know what to think. So much had happened. While she'd already decided to take another chance with him, the closer they got to home, the farther he had pulled away from her.

They made one long convoy back to Anna's cozy home and trouped inside her house. Brooke went upstairs ahead of them and pulled down the twins' bedcovers. They woke briefly, thrilled to see their aunt Brooke, but too tired to do anything besides make her promise to stay.

Back downstairs Anna found the men checking every nook and cranny of her house. Lucky saw her on the stairs as he checked the bottom of one of her lamps with a black wand.

Holding the lamp in midair, he gave her a sheepish smile and looked at Rico, who had stopped on the stair behind her.

"Looking for bugs?" Rico asked.

"Just a precaution. Mike wants to make sure no one tapped the house while they were here this afternoon. You know how these bureaucrats get. They want to keep tabs on everyone."

At first upset at the thought, but then relieved her house would definitely be her own, Anna nodded and walked into the kitchen.

The guys were into everything. Drawers, cabinets, light fixtures, heating vents in the walls. She should have been really upset.

But she wasn't.

"I should probably freak out," she mused aloud, and they all stopped to look at her with varying degrees of alarm. "You guys have been doing this longer than I. Can you actually get to a point where nothing bothers you because you've been up and down so much that your nerves give up and die?"

Kid nodded and answered her with dead seriousness. "Kind of. But you're just tired. Don't worry, it'll all come back to you."

"Probably when the twins escape the backyard again," Joncaluso teased from the den.

"Or when Rebecca brings home her first boyfriend," teased Irish from his perch on the kitchen chair, where he inspected the hanging light.

Anna smiled. "So you're all saying I'll be better after a good night's sleep."

They agreed and went back to work, occasionally sharing other amusing ways the twins would test her nerves.

"Rico, we'll be going over to the B&B and out of your hair in about ten minutes," Mike said, walking by them and onto the back porch.

Rico had sprawled into a kitchen chair, and she wondered how badly he'd strained still-healing bones and muscles. She might just use the doctor's suggestion on how to ease the pain.

"No problem. I've been using the first two bedrooms at the top of the stairs. If you need to log into anything, my office is up there with the computers, and it's got an extra bed. Most of the rooms have double beds and their own bathrooms, so you guys should be set." He reached up and rubbed the back of his neck, twisting and stretching. "You probably should order pizza and beer tonight, and tomorrow we'll stock up the fridge."

Mike nodded. "We'll be fine. I don't know how many of them have to leave tomorrow."

"I hope none do. I'd like to explain all this," he said, gesturing to his face.

Irish breezed past them to the foyer saying, "Jes' try and get rid of me."

"He just winked at me," Brooke said in her ear.

"I saw that," Anna answered wryly.

"You know, I could arrange a few days off to help you until Lina comes back. And once Mom finds out, you're not going to be able to keep her away."

A part of her wanted privacy for her and Rico, but they did need to concentrate on the twins. If the men were going to be around, anyway, Brooke and Aunt Clare could be a big help to her.

"Sounds great. Thanks," she said, giving Brooke a hug. "I could use the support. I'm considering having a nervous breakdown."

Brooke pulled away and arched a perfect auburn brow. "I can't imagine why."

It was another half hour before everyone left and she had Brooke installed in Lina's room with clean sheets and a T-shirt to sleep in.

Strangely, she wasn't exhausted. She'd passed that state

about two hours ago, and her second wind was a gale force now.

Slight creaks were the only sounds as the house settled in for the night. The light above the sink glowed with comfort, and even though the heavy threat of danger had disappeared for good, she made sure all the doors were bolted. She glanced out the gauzy curtain by the front door and saw Rico's house ablaze with lights. The guys were still up. Even after Dana's confession to the police that she'd hatched the plot and not Enzo, it was a relief to have the guys close just in case.

She smiled, thinking about what a family they all were in their own right and how nice it was to be included in the circle. She turned to the stairs and the light that tumbled so welcomingly down them.

Rico was up there.

She let that thought swirl around inside her. Relief, gratitude, need and butterflies.

Shaking her head, she smiled. After today she could handle anything.

She put her hand on the railing.

Rico stood in the shadows of the twins' bedroom. He couldn't stop staring at them. He'd lost all track of time and realized Anna's and Brooke's voices no longer floated up the stairs.

What would he have done if he'd lost them?

He couldn't get the thought out of his head and he couldn't shake the guilt.

He'd brought it here…the violence, the deaths. His children had almost died because of him.

"Are they sleeping okay?" Anna's low voice from the doorway startled him. He hadn't heard her approach.

He turned and nodded, holding his breath as he met her eyes. Every time he looked at her he expected to see anger and accusation. At first, when they'd found the plane, he'd thought they would get the twins out safely and get on with their lives. But now, after gunshots and death, how could he expect Anna to welcome him into their lives when he'd brought the very thing she feared most?

She walked past him and dropped a kiss on each forehead, straightening covers and smoothing back sleep-damp hair.

Then she held out a hand. "Come on."

Surprise made him hesitate before he took her hand. She led the way to her bedroom where several fat, white candles blazed.

"I didn't hear you," he said, looking around.

She grinned, but the exhaustion on her face took away from her lightheartedness. "I was very quiet. Now, take off your shirt."

He didn't answer. He couldn't. Uncertainty dimmed her smile, and she bit her lip.

"Unless you don't want to and that's okay—I mean, it's fine," she said haltingly.

His hand rose and cupped her swollen jaw, careful not to press the heated skin his thumb caressed. "I can't stand this. It's tearing me apart. Just tell me if you're going to ask me to leave. Maybe you're not planning to today or tomorrow. Maybe your generous heart wants to give me a week with the kids, but I can't deal with not knowing. It's killing me, Anna."

Her confusion apparent, she stared at him without answering.

"Anna…"

"Wait a minute," she said, her hand clasping his forearm. "I know I'm reacting slow, and I'm sorry. But you've lost me. Why on earth would you expect me to tell you to leave?"

"I'm responsible for what's happened. I brought it here."

"We discussed that! I know it wasn't intentional. God, Rico! Crazy things happen in this life. I'm just grateful you were here in time. What if she'd decided to take them earlier?"

His arm dropped, but she linked her fingers with his.

"You just told me today that you loved me. Were they only

words? They must have been if you are willing to walk away again!''

He closed his eyes against the sting of tears. ''I wouldn't have wanted to. I don't want to! But I know how you feel about violence. When I saw you holding that gun, shooting Dana, it made me sick. Not because you did, but because I know how you feel about it.''

She sighed. ''You're right, we need to talk about this, but not now. The day's been too long, and I'm not sure I can explain how I'm feeling about what I did.''

She took a step closer and laid her head against his chest. ''I will say this— I don't want you to leave. If you do, it's for your own reasons, not for my benefit or the children's.'' Without waiting for a response, she pulled away, led him to the bed and grabbed the bottom of his T-shirt. He was too tall for her to be able to push it past his shoulders, so he bent forward at the waist and let her tug it the rest of the way off. Then she studied him. He expected a remark about the disfiguring scars. ''Take the jeans off, too, and lie facedown on the bed.''

He would never be able to figure her out.

Seduction didn't seem to be what she had in mind. Not that he was sure his body could take it. The mind, heart and soul were willing, but the body was a wreck.

She left the room, and he stripped off his jeans. The comforter, blanket and sheet had all been pulled down and lay in a heap at the foot of the bed. Only the peach bottom sheet and two plump pillows remained.

He crawled onto the bed, feeling every muscle, and sprawled on his stomach, not even bothering with a pillow.

''Good. You listened,'' she said, walking back into the room behind him. ''Now, where does it hurt most?''

He chuckled, the sound half-muffled against the mattress. ''That would take me too long to figure out.''

''Is the pain in muscles or bones?'' She sounded like a lot of the nonsensical nurses he knew.

"The bones are healed. I think I strained a few of the muscles around them."

He could hear her pouring water in the bathroom then felt the bed tilt on his other side.

"Okay. I asked the doctor what would help you and this is what he suggested."

Wet heat blanketed his back and stole his breath.

"Too hot?" she asked anxiously.

"No. No, it's good. Real good." The heat seeped into him, dulling the twinges of pain. Immediately muscles loosened their hold and began to relax. "You asked the doctor?"

"Mmm-hmm," she murmured, moving once again. "I could see by the way you held yourself that you strained something. He said hot, wet towels for ten to fifteen minutes should loosen you up."

"I didn't *do* anything to get hurt," he mumbled.

"Yes, you did. Lucky told me you crawled on your stomach all the way down the incline to get into position and that you were the first one to reach the plane. Which miffed him, I think, because he said he should be in better shape than you. But you still beat him. And you fought off Victorio. You made it look easy, but your muscles didn't think so. Anyway, how are your legs?"

"Right one," he managed to say. Even his tongue felt loosened by the healing heat invading his body.

"I should have put a towel under you," she muttered. More indistinct sounds, and then her bare hands slid under his right leg. "By the time I'm done, you'll won't have a knotted muscle left in your body."

If she moved a few inches north, she'd find a muscle reacting to her touch, he thought. And if she kept touching him, the hot towels were going to be useless in stopping his body's reactions to her. Seemed when it came to her, his body was never too weak.

Her hands kept moving, and although he realized she put a towel under his leg, with his eyes closed he focused only on her cool fingers sliding across his skin. He pictured her hands, so small compared to his, with their long fingers and small, rounded nails. Nails that managed to scrape against his skin in a delicious way.

He took a deep breath—and she rolled up the leg of his underwear. The air shuddered out of him.

"I knew you weren't a boxer man and I couldn't picture briefs, either," she said teasingly. "I like this compromise."

He grunted and hid a smile. How was a man supposed to reply to a teasing witch bent on torture?

The mattress dipped again as she left. He willed his body to ease up. Within seconds another hot towel was draped from his knee to upper thigh.

He groaned.

He'd had treatments like this in the hospital, so maybe it was being in Anna's bedroom with her administering that made it more enjoyable.

"Want one on the other leg?" she asked.

He opened one eye to see her beautiful, concerned face. He was so relaxed, he didn't think about his words. "No they didn't knife that one."

Instead of looking distraught, her expression looked eerily cold. "I'm glad they're dead."

"Anna!"

"I'm sorry, but when I think of what they did to you, I'm glad they're not walking this earth. The kind of sadistic person who'd be capable of torturing someone shouldn't be allowed to mix with other people."

She pulled up a chair and picked up the bottle sitting on the nightstand. Pouring lotion out of it, she rubbed her hands together and picked up his left hand.

"Tell me if this hurts," she said. Starting at his palm, she kneaded gently, spreading out to his fingers.

"You don't have to do this," he managed, the words difficult to form. She was stealing the strength from his body.

She smiled gently. "I want to. I want to take care of you."

Man, this woman was incredible.

"I should be taking care of you, after the day you had today," he slurred.

"Can I have a rain check?"

"Baby, you can have thousands."

Anna straddled Rico's waist and worked the lotion into his still-warm back. Her fingers glided over his shoulders and back between the blades, her massage a combination of soft kneading and gentle caresses. She was so afraid of hurting him she didn't try to dig in to loosen the muscles.

Peeking at his face, she could see his lashes lying on his cheeks. He was motionless except for the slight flaring of nostrils that told her he was probably asleep.

Sitting back on his butt, she flexed tired fingers. His back looked so much better than his front she was willing to bet he'd been chained to a wall or chair during the torture.

She'd surprised him as much as herself when she'd said she was happy the men who did this were dead. She'd hated them for it before, but now she was just relieved they couldn't hurt anyone else.

Today had changed her.

Maybe not necessarily for the better, but she felt as if she was seeing things through different eyes. Rico always claimed she wore rose-colored glasses even though she'd grown up with violence.

She'd wanted to believe she was above it, better than others, in that she could handle situations without resorting to violence.

Today she'd learned the necessity of fighting, learned the necessity of having people like Rico and his men to protect people from the reprehensible violence of others.

Slipping off his back, she stood and decided to bunch up the bedcovers and sleep on the floor. He looked so incredibly comfortable, she wouldn't dream of waking him to move him over.

"Don't go," he mumbled.

"Hey, you. I thought you were sleeping," she said, kneeling down and brushing his hair off his face. Although, she admitted silently, she loved touching him. She just felt more comfortable with an excuse.

"I thought I was dreaming. Then I opened my eyes and you were here."

Her heart swelled with love for him.

"I'm here. I'll always be here."

He shifted his head to look her more fully in the eyes.

"Always?" he whispered.

"Always. How can I not be? I love you."

She would remember his expression for the rest of her life. He'd said the words would be a precious gift to him, and she could see how honest he'd been.

"Come here." He gave a tug and rolled to his side. Instead of wincing or groaning, he sighed.

"Wait a sec," she said, taking off the khaki shorts she'd worn to make the massage easier. Standing there in only her red cotton shirt and high-cut underwear, she felt not an ounce of self-consciousness.

"You may have made me boneless, but I'm still a man," he said, a wicked, heated glint in his eyes.

She smiled and curled up along his side, easing her bare leg between his.

"Say it again," he asked.

She tilted her head up. "I love you."

His expression stilled.

"What's wrong?"

"Do you realize that everything I have worth living for is because of you?" He ran a finger down her cheek, then saw the look in her eyes. "What did I say?"

"I don't want to ruin this by arguing," she said, sliding her fingers across his chest.

"We won't. As long as we know we love each other, we should be able to discuss anything."

She took a deep breath. "It's hard for me to get past the fact that you didn't come here for me."

She couldn't look at him, and as the silence ticked on, a suffocating hurt rose up in her chest.

He squeezed her and rested his cheek against her forehead. "You'll never believe this, but I was scared. I'd had enough time to think about the past and even accept my responsibility in our breakup. I'd gotten past the idea of you cheating, because I'd realized how young we were. And I knew I'd have to find a way to face you. I was terrified." His free hand stroked her back. "When I found out someone was searching in my files and I had to concentrate on finding Mama, which is another issue I have to bring up with Layton for not telling me about you, my plan was to make sure she was safe. Once the danger cleared, I was going to find you. Now, I don't know if this helps, but when Mike first searched around Miami for Mom, he searched for you, too."

She immediately looked up into his eyes, her hair rustling against the pillowcase. "He did?"

"I asked him to make sure you were at the same address. He couldn't find a forwarding one for you, but found Mom's."

She nodded slowly. "So, if I didn't have the twins, would you still be here with me?"

His eyes widened. "I should really be angry with you for asking that." He blew out a big breath. "Even if the twins weren't here and even if you were still so angry with me you wouldn't give me another chance, I'd still find a way to live around here. I know, deep in my heart, that we belong together."

With his heartfelt words, her reservations slipped away.

"I love you," she whispered.

He lowered his mouth to hers and brushed a kiss over her lips. "I love you too, Bella."

She smiled as his mouth lowered again.

Rico's exhaustion had melted away beneath the loving

touch of Anna's hands. Lying here with her half-naked in his arms was having a revitalizing effect.

"You need to sleep," he whispered, although he hadn't thought of that while gently kissing her for the past ten minutes. Her frustrated noises told him she wanted more than teasing, but he was too aware of her injured jaw.

"Sleep? Are you kidding?" The teasing smile and meaning behind it slid right to his groin.

He smiled back and pushed himself up onto his knees. Although twinges remained, the hot towels had loosened him enough to move without pain.

"Come here, you," he said, shifting her into the middle of the bed and rolling her onto her stomach. The move left him kneeling between her legs.

She smiled back at him over her shoulder, her hair tumbling around her shoulders, a pink flush gracing her cheeks.

She'd never looked more beautiful.

"I didn't turn in my rain check, you know," she teased.

"I know. But I'm feeling so much better I thought I'd ease some of your aches."

She laughed. "Was that an innuendo?"

"Maybe. You sure you're up to this?" he teased.

"Are you?" she asked, arching a brow with a meaningful glance down his body.

He laughed and although he tried to make it sound wicked, his enjoyment of her was too hard to hide. He leaned forward and pushed her shirt up, baring her back and white panties.

"Relax," he told her.

She did with a sigh, and he placed his hands on her tiny waist, his thumbs on either side of her spine. Pushing in and up, he massaged the muscles up her back to her neck, marveling at how big his hands looked against her. Without a word she pulled her shirt off and reached around to undo the clasp of her bra.

Her absolute ease and trust slammed into him, helping control the desire surging through his body. He leaned down and kissed the small of her back, working his way up with lips and tongue. Her little shivers and sighs told him she was enjoying it almost as much as he was.

At her neck he nipped her smooth shoulder with his teeth, and her eyelids lifted, revealing eyes dark and filled with desire.

"Let me roll over," she pleaded.

He realized this would not be a slow exploration. They'd missed each other for too long, and their bodies needed the other too much.

She turned under him, and her bare body slid against his. Twining her arms around his neck, she pulled him down against her.

They both sighed at the contact.

"You feel so good," he whispered, tangling his fingers into her hair, kissing along her uninjured jaw to her ear.

She raised her knees on either side of his hips with a little arch. "So do you."

"I'm trying to go slow here, and you're making it difficult."

Her saucy grin faded, and she let him see her desire. "I need you, Rico. You don't know how many times I dreamed of having you here."

"I don't want to hurt you," he whispered, touching her swollen jaw with care and trying one last time to be unselfish.

"I have a lot of other places to kiss," she said, nuzzling his neck and smoothing her hands up and down his back.

His response came in a low growl as he buried his face in her neck.

She arched against him, squirming to get closer. He tortured her with kisses and soft nips, his large hands cupping her aching breasts. She pulled his head down, loving the feel of his mouth on her, the hot, open kisses leaving trails of moisture on her skin.

"Rico, please," she implored.

He looked at her with an expression so full of love and desire her throat tightened.

"Tell me," he whispered, his hand sliding down her leg and wrapping around a knee. "What do you want?"

She didn't reply, couldn't. His fingertips tickled the back of her knee, making breathing difficult.

"Hmmm, Bella?" His mouth started following his hands, and before she knew it, his rough cheek was brushing against her shin as his mouth traced a path to the arch of her foot.

She reveled in sensation, giving herself up to the desire spiraling so tight within her. Vaguely registering him peeling her underwear off, she struggled to lift her heavy lids when his hands began their ascent from her feet. Molding to her shape, they traveled up so slowly she bit her lip to keep from urging him faster. He watched his hands, glancing at her every so often.

The desire in his face brightened his golden eyes and darkened the color of his cheeks. His mouth parted on his shallow breaths, and her body swelled in response.

She wanted him as much as he wanted her.

His hands reached her inner thighs and she caught her breath, gasping as he reached his destination. He stopped and looked at her, watching her like a hawk as one finger slid into her.

She arched and choked out a cry. Another finger joined the first, and she could feel her body welcoming him.

"Bella?" he questioned, and she forced herself to focus on him.

She held open her arms, and he withdrew his fingers, taking off his own underwear. He stood there, letting her look her fill. She reached out a hand, wanting so badly to feel the hard evidence of his desire, but he shook his hand.

"Not this time, love," he whispered, his voice deep and husky. "If you get your hands on me, this will be over before we start."

She answered his smile with one of her own as he came

down onto her. One arm slid underneath her hips, and as his chest touched hers, he slowly joined them.

Their gazes locked.

"Oh, my," she whispered. "I forgot."

He smiled. The most beautiful, loving smile. "So did I."

He moved slightly, allowing her to adjust to him, scattering light kisses on her face. It quickly became a teasing movement, and she arched up, wrapping her legs around him, feeling him tremble. That was all the encouragement he needed, and he took control, thrusting into her with a force that took her breath. Within moments they both cried out and held on to each other, finally one after so long.

Rico brushed the tear from her cheek, the two of them lying on their sides and catching their breath.

"Please tell me this is a tear of happiness."

She opened an eye to see apprehension knitting his brows, a sheen of sweat covering his face. "You know it is."

He exhaled in relief, and she smiled. "I love you, you know."

He stared at her, so serious. "Thank God."

She pulled his head to her for a soft kiss. After a couple of minutes he pulled away.

"Don't move," he said, swinging out of the bed and walking naked across the room.

All those scars and still he was the most handsome man she'd ever seen, naked or not. He reached into one of the bags sitting on a chair in the corner of her room.

"Close your eyes," he said with a smile.

She giggled. Why she didn't know, but the laugh felt completely natural as she closed her eyes. She heard him walk back to her.

"Open," he said.

He was kneeling by her bed in the candlelight from her nightstand. In his hand was a diamond ring.

She gasped from shock and the sheer beauty of it. It twinkled at her, balanced so delicately between his two fingers.

"I love you more than anything in this world. Will you marry me, Anna, and make me complete?"

She laughed and cried at the same time. "Yes!" she said as she pushed herself into a sitting position.

He slid the ring onto her shaking finger. It fit perfectly.

"I bought this for you the night I came home before re-enlisting, right before I took Mama to dinner."

Her head jerked up to look at him. "You've had the ring this long?"

He nodded. "At first I didn't know what to do with it, but I carried it everywhere with me. When I came to terms with what had happened, I vowed I was going to put it on your finger one day."

"I love you so much," she whispered, her tears starting again although her wide smile remained.

"Thank you," he whispered, and pulled her into his arms.

Epilogue

The sun beat down on everyone gathered in Anna's back-yard, although a lake breeze relieved them of the Indian summer's heat. Four days after the kidnapping, and anyone walking in would see a party of mostly men and two happy, screeching children playing tag.

"Anna?" Aunt Clare called her name, pulling her attention from her ring. She found herself looking at it constantly, especially when Rico was out of sight.

Reminding herself it wasn't a dream.

"Sorry, Aunt Clare," Anna said with a grin. Her aunt just smiled and shook her head.

"Brooke's been trying to get your attention."

Anna turned to see Brooke at one of the picnic tables, surrounded by the unshakable Irish, Lucky and Cal. She walked off the deck, dodging Rafe, who squealed past her with Runt in pursuit.

Rico hadn't been kidding about Runt's love of children. The big man spent most of his time entertaining the twins, and they adored him.

"Anna, did you know why Mike and Rico don't have nick-names like the rest of these guys?"

"No, come to think of it, I didn't realize it," she answered, looking for Mike. He had disappeared a few hours earlier to pick up his wife at the Spokane airport.

Brooke smiled, her hair glowing vivid red in the sunlight. "Mike's real name is Michaelangelo, so they figured Mike was enough of a nickname!"

Lucky chimed in with, "And every time we called Rico by his full name we felt like we were calling him America."

Anna laughed along with them and then glanced at the healthy-looking Cal. "Can I get you anything?"

"No, I'm fine," he assured her, his arm in a sling and his free hand holding a beer.

The men spent most of their time at Anna's house, which Rico loved. Anna did, too. Between the men, her cousin, Aunt Clare and Lina, the children were surrounded by loving adults who talked about the kidnapping whenever they had a question. So far Rebecca had suffered a nightmare and was never too far from her grandmother, and Rafe constantly checked on Cal. He had more difficulty remembering details than Rebecca did, but the doctors said it could still be shock and he'd remember when ready.

Lina sat under the table umbrella on the porch, arguing with Aunt Clare about helping. Aunt Clare, of course, won again, giving Lina more cheese to slice instead of allowing her to do dishes.

The back door opened, and Rico stepped onto the porch with a present in his arms.

"There you are!" Anna said, running to him for a kiss and ignoring the groans of the men. They always made a show of groaning, laughing and other sound effects whenever they kissed, and she tuned them out. She wouldn't stop kissing Rico for anything. "You said you'd be right back!"

"Sorry, took me a bit longer to find the one I wanted," he grinned, and handed her the present.

She smiled and decided against telling him he didn't have to get her anything. It hadn't made a difference every other day when he'd bought her something small or picked her flowers.

Lina said he was wooing his fiancée.

She unwrapped the box with the help of the twins and gasped.

A video recorder.

"I don't want to miss one more thing," he said, pulling her into his arms for another kiss.

Everyone joined them on the porch to ooh and ahh over the gift. Just then the back door opened again, and Mike stepped out, an enormous smile on his face. He stopped, his hand still on the door handle but his body blocking anyone's access.

"About time!" Irish yelled, his hand playing with a blushing Brooke's hair. "Where's that bonny wife and child of yers?"

If possible, Mike's grin spread wider. "They're inside with my gift for Rico."

All the guys quieted their teasing, and Rico looked at them. Anna picked up on their sudden seriousness, but couldn't get nervous because of Mike's grin. Whatever his surprise, it was a good one.

"Rico, you gave up so much for me when you made me go that night." He looked down and cleared his throat before finishing. "Since then you've asked only one thing of me, and I've finally succeeded."

He opened the door and a beautiful girl stepped out, her long curling black hair in a ponytail and her face free of makeup. In jean shorts and a black cotton top, she looked anywhere from fifteen to twenty-five years old.

Anna looked up at Rico. Pale, his eyes wide as if seeing a ghost, he whispered, "Carmen?"

Carmen's gaze darted through the group of people on the deck, chin high, lips pressed tight and expression unsure. Finally she caught sight of the man who'd called her name, but her expression looked more confused.

She glanced back at Mike, who nodded and smiled.

She took a step closer, then her heavily lashed brown eyes widened. "Rico?"

He nodded again, and she burst into tears, unleashing a torrent of Spanish and throwing herself into his arms like a child seeking comfort. Anna's throat tightened at the relief on Rico's face and the tears in Mike's eyes.

Carmen reached out a hand to Anna, gripping it tightly, although she still burrowed deep in Rico's arms. She asked him something, and he answered in English, the two of them staring at Anna.

"*Sí*, Carmen, this is my angel."

* * * * *

INTIMATE MOMENTS™

presents a riveting new continuity series:

FIRSTBORN SONS

Bound by the legacy of their fathers, these Firstborn Sons are about to discover the stuff true heroes—and true love—are made of!

The adventure continues in August 2001 with:

BORN OF PASSION by Carla Cassidy

When top gun pilot Kyle Ramsey embarked on a mission in Montebello, he shared a passionate reunion with a mysterious beauty who was harboring a precious secret. Could this rootless Firstborn Son finally find a home in the arms of the woman he loved?

July: **BORN A HERO**
by **Paula Detmer Riggs** (IM #1088)
August: **BORN OF PASSION**
by **Carla Cassidy** (IM #1094)
September: **BORN TO PROTECT**
by **Virginia Kantra** (IM #1100)
October: **BORN BRAVE**
by **Ruth Wind** (IM #1106)
November: **BORN IN SECRET**
by **Kylie Brant** (IM #1112)
December: **BORN ROYAL**
by **Alexandra Sellers** (IM #1118)

Available only from
Silhouette Intimate Moments
at your favorite retail outlet.

Where love comes alive™